POLISHED OFF

**Center Point
Large Print**

**This Large Print Book carries the
Seal of Approval of N.A.V.H.**

POLISHED OFF

Barbara Colley

CENTER POINT PUBLISHING
THORNDIKE, MAINE

This Center Point Large Print edition
is published in the year 2004 by arrangement with
Kensington Publishing Corp.

Copyright © 2004 by Barbara Colley.

The text of this Large Print edition is unabridged. In other
aspects, this book may vary from the original edition. Printed in
Thailand. Set in 16-point Times New Roman type.

ISBN 1-58547-480-0

Library of Congress Cataloging-in-Publication Data

Colley, Barbara.
   Polished off / Barbara Colley.--Center Point large print ed.
     p. cm.
   ISBN 1-58547-480-0 (lib. bdg. : alk. paper)
    1. Women cleaning personnel--Fiction. 2. Birthfathers--Crimes against--Fiction.
  3. New Orleans (La.)--Fiction. 4. Middle aged women--Fiction. 5. House cleaning--Fiction.
  6. Large type books. I. Title.

PS3603.O44P65 2004
813'.6--dc22

                                   2004004460

For my grandchildren.
Gaboo loves you.

ACKNOWLEDGMENTS

My sincere thanks and appreciation to all who gave me inspiration, advice, and encouragement while I was writing this book: Marie Goodwin, Rexanne Becnel, Jessica Ferguson, Lou Reese, Happy Dodson, and Geraldine Galentre.

As always, thanks to Evan Marshall and John Scognamiglio. Without them, Charlotte wouldn't exist.

Chapter One

Charlotte LaRue removed the large bowl of rice from the microwave. Everything was ready . . . well, almost everything. Now if only Madeline would show up.

No sooner had the thought entered Charlotte's head than the sound of the front door opening and closing reached her ears. Seconds later, her sister breezed into the kitchen.

"Here you go." She handed Charlotte a loaf of French bread. "I figured one loaf would be enough, and it's fresh. Still warm," she added.

"One should be enough," Charlotte murmured. "Thanks, Maddie. You're a lifesaver. I still can't believe I forgot to buy bread."

Madeline shrugged. "No big deal." She walked over to the stove. "Umm, that's gumbo, isn't it?" She peered into the huge pot and sniffed. "Chicken and andouille?"

Charlotte nodded as she slid the long loaf of French bread out of its paper wrapper. "Not exactly traditional Easter Sunday fare, but I didn't get a chance to shop for a ham. Or bread," she added with a grin. "And since I already had all the ingredients for gumbo . . ." She shrugged. "Got it started before church this morning. Besides, it seems to me, if I remember right, chicken and andouille is your favorite."

Madeline laughed. "And it seems to me, if I remember right, that's because it was the only kind of gumbo you ever made. Really strange," she added,

9

"considering we live in a city known for its seafood."

"Only kind I could ever *afford* to make," Charlotte shot back. Placing the bread on a cookie sheet, she began slicing it into pieces, careful to slice only about two-thirds the way down. "The ingredients for the seafood kind—even in New Orleans—were too expensive on my limited budget." She quickly inserted a pat of butter in between each slice, then slid the bread into the oven to melt the butter.

What she could have pointed out but didn't was that the reason she'd had to be so thrifty was partially her sister's fault. Years ago, after Madeline's first divorce, she'd become so depressed that she'd been unable to function on a day-to-day basis. She and her two young children had moved in with Charlotte, and for months, Charlotte and her maid service had been the sole provider for all of them as well as for herself and her own son.

"Whatever," Madeline quipped.

Charlotte glanced out the window into the backyard, where the rest of the family and their friends had gathered to watch three-year-old Davy, the son of one of her employees, hunt for Easter eggs. "Correction. Make that the only kind I can *still* afford," she added with a grin. "Our family is growing by leaps and bounds."

Madeline followed her gaze. "Bite your tongue. Only my Judith and Daniel, and your Hank, qualify as family." She waved her hand toward the window. "Those others don't qualify—not yet, thank God. They're just—just what? What do you call grown girlfriends and boyfriends anyway?"

"I believe the term now is 'significant others,'" Charlotte answered.

Madeline rolled her eyes. "Oh, pu-lease, give me a break. Yuck!" She shuddered. "Anyway, whatever they are, it looks like they all showed up today—all except for that Billy character that Judith's been seeing."

"She could do worse," Charlotte pointed out. *A whole lot worse,* she thought. But Charlotte didn't dare say so. Madeline didn't know about Judith's affair with Will Richeaux, thank goodness, and Charlotte wasn't about to be the one to tell her, especially now that Judith had come to her senses and ditched him. But if Madeline had known, Charlotte was sure she would have changed her tune about Judith's relationship with Billy Wilson in a heartbeat. Even now, months later, the thought of how Will Richeaux had duped Judith still made Charlotte see red.

"Do worse?" Madeline repeated, then made a face. "I don't know how. This Billy character isn't even a detective like Judith. He's just a plain old street cop. I tell you, Charlotte, I shudder every time I think that she could end up marrying another cop. One cop in the family is plenty, thank you very much."

Though she was sorely tempted, again Charlotte didn't dare comment. The last thing she wanted was to get into an altercation with her sister, especially today. Along with Christmas, she considered Easter to be one of the most important holidays they celebrated. Besides, arguing with Madeline was like arguing with a brick wall.

Madeline turned away from the window and walked

over to the oven to check on the bread. "By the way," she said, "just why isn't this Billy character here today?"

"Judith said he had to work," Charlotte answered.

Madeline grunted. "Just as well," she retorted. She faced Charlotte. "Maybe Judith will come to her senses. One can always hope. Besides, she can do a lot better than someone like him." Without missing a beat, Madeline launched into yet another complaint. "And then there's that son of mine. Why on earth is Daniel still fooling around with—"

"Now, Maddie—"

"Don't 'now, Maddie' me! Ever since he started hanging around with that woman who works for you, I never see him anymore, not without her and that brat of hers tagging along."

"Madeline, shame on you. Little Davy is a precious little boy. And 'that woman' has a name. Nadia—"

"Yeah," Madeline interrupted. "And that's another thing: both this Billy character and this Nadia have the same last name. Makes me wonder if there's some kind of weird conspiracy going on. Now wouldn't that be just my luck?" She glared at Charlotte. "Well? Are they? Are they kin to each other?"

Charlotte sighed. "No, according to Nadia they are not related. Just because they have the same last name—"

"Yeah, yeah." She waved a dismissing hand. "Okay already."

"One more thing, Maddie. Nadia Wilson is one of the finest young women I've had the privilege to come in contact with." Charlotte grabbed an oven mitt. "And hardworking to boot," she added. "Now here—" Charlotte removed the warmed bread out of the oven, and gingerly placed it into an oblong bread basket that she'd lined with a clean hand towel. She folded the edges of the hand towel over the bread, then handed the basket to her sister. "Take this to the table for me, and please try to be nice. If not for Daniel's sake, for my sake."

"Well, at least your Hank had the decency to pick a woman who didn't already have a kid. I'm not ready to play grandma—not by a long shot. And when I do become one, I'd rather the little rug-rat was my own flesh and blood."

The sudden urge to slap the living daylights out of her spoiled, selfish sister was so strong that Charlotte grabbed hold of the cabinet. "What a mean, hateful thing to say. You should be ashamed."

"Ashamed! For what? For telling the truth? If you ask me, telling the truth is a lot better than being a hypocrite about it."

"Nobody asked you," Charlotte retorted through gritted teeth. "And if being charitable and kind are hypocritical, then I'd rather be a hypocrite any day than a selfish witch."

The stunned look on her sister's face would have been comical if Charlotte hadn't been so angry. So much for avoiding an altercation, she thought irritably, but then her sister had always known exactly which of her buttons to push.

In an effort to calm herself, Charlotte breathed deeply and counted to ten. Releasing her grip on the cabinet, she turned to her sister. "Maddie, all I'm saying is—"

"I think you've said enough." Madeline glared at her for several seconds. Then she rolled her eyes upward and shrugged. "Maybe we both have," she muttered.

Charlotte figured it was as close to an apology as she would get. She sighed. "For once you're right," she finally relented in an effort to keep the peace. "I'm afraid we'll just have to agree to disagree. Truce?"

Albeit grudgingly, Madeline nodded. "Truce."

"Good. Now if you'll put that bread on the table, and"—Charlotte motioned toward the refrigerator— "get the stuffed eggs out of there while I put the ice in the glasses for the tea, I think everything will be ready."

Madeline headed for the refrigerator, then frowned. "Why haven't I seen these before?" She pointed at the snapshots that were held in place with magnets on the refrigerator door. "They're from your birthday party, aren't they?"

"Yeah. I keep meaning to put them in an album," Charlotte answered. "And you haven't seen them because I just got around to getting copies made from Hank's negatives."

Madeline stared at the snapshots. "Well, it took you long enough. Your birthday was months ago. Guess the wait was worth it, though. These are really nice, especially this one of you and Judith." Madeline shook her head. "It's just too weird: she's *my* daughter, but, I swear, the older she gets, the more she looks like you."

Will wonders never cease? Charlotte thought, too surprised by Madeline's admission to do more than just stand there and stare at her. Over the years, people had said as much. And while it was true that she and Judith both had the same dark blond hair, the same petite body build, and even the same sky blue eyes, the whole issue had always been a sore point with Madeline. Secretly, Charlotte had been pleased and flattered by the comparison, but because Madeline had been so touchy about it, Charlotte had learned to hide her feelings.

A few minutes later, Charlotte called everyone inside, and once they had all gathered around the table, she nodded at her son. "Hank, would you please say the blessing?"

"Sure," he answered.

The second that Hank ended the blessing with "Amen," Daniel cleared his throat loudly and held up a hand to get everyone's attention. "Hey, everybody, hold up a minute." He stood. "We have an announcement to make." Reaching down, he scooped little Davy up into his arms, then held out a hand to Nadia as she pushed out of her chair to stand beside him.

It was more than evident to Charlotte that "we" included all three of them. And from the sober look on her nephew's face, she knew that something big was brewing besides the pot of gumbo still simmering on the stove.

In Daniel's day-to-day life as a highly respected attorney, he was always serious and focused, but when he was around family, it was rare that he was ever serious about much of anything. He'd always been the clown in the family, and Charlotte had her own home-grown philosophy about that. She figured that his clowning around was his way of compensating for being so totally rejected by his father at such a young age after his parents' divorce.

When Daniel pulled Nadia closer, a smile tugged at Charlotte's lips. They made such an attractive couple. Nadia's dark hair and exotic looks were a contrast yet a perfect complement to Daniel's dark blond hair and fair complexion. They were both tall, but while Nadia was model-slender and feminine, Daniel personified rugged masculinity.

After all these months, was he finally going to do it? Charlotte's insides suddenly felt jittery with excitement. Had Daniel finally asked Nadia to marry him?

Charlotte's gaze slid downward, seeking the ring finger of Nadia's left hand. No help there, though. Nadia's hand was hidden inside the pocket of her skirt.

When Daniel cleared his throat again, it suddenly dawned on Charlotte just how nervous he was. But why on earth would he be so nervous if he was just announcing their engagement? Unless . . .

At the exact moment that Charlotte realized what her nephew's big announcement was really all about, Daniel said, "Just thought I'd better let you know that as of day before yesterday, Nadia has become the newest addition to our family. She's now Mrs. Daniel Monroe. And, furthermore, just as soon as I can finalize the adoption, Davy will become my son."

Charlotte heard her sister's horrified gasp of disbelief, but, thankfully, the cheering and clapping of the rest of the group smothered Madeline's less than enthusiastic reaction.

Suddenly, Judith stood. Slapping her hands on her hips, she faced her brother. "How dare you!"

The whole room abruptly grew quiet, as if, along with everyone there, it was holding its breath.

"How dare you sneak off and get married without me being there," Judith told him sternly. Then she grinned, and tears sprang in her eyes. "But even if you are a dirty rotten sneak, I still love you and can't think of anyone I'd rather have for a sister-in-law than Nadia."

"Thanks, sis. And you'll be happy to know that just as soon as we can arrange it, we plan to have a big blowout reception to celebrate with the family and our friends—probably around the first of April."

Judith shook her finger at him. "Still not as good as being there for the wedding, but I guess it will have to do." With a big grin, she hurried around the table and hugged Daniel first, then Nadia. "Congratulations, you guys." With a teasing smile and a wink directed at Davy, Judith reached up and gently pinched his cheek. "And I can't think of anyone I'd rather have for a nephew, either," she added.

Still beaming with genuine happiness for her brother, Judith turned to Charlotte. "Hey, Aunt Charley, now I can have a favorite nephew, too."

Everyone roared with laughter—everyone but Madeline, Charlotte noted. Daniel and Judith were Charlotte's only nephew and niece, and for as long as any of them could remember, it had been the family joke that Charlotte always referred to both as her *favorite* nephew and *favorite* niece.

Hank, his friend Carol Jones, and Charlotte quickly

joined Judith and offered hugs of congratulations. The only person conspicuously absent from the group huddled around the beaming couple and little boy was Madeline, who remained seated at the table.

Though Charlotte could understand her sister being disappointed that Daniel had eloped without telling her, that was no excuse for her being so rude and hurtful. She eased away from the group and walked over to her sister.

"Don't do this, Maddie," she murmured. "I know you're disappointed that none of us were invited to the wedding ceremony—I am, too—but I'm sure they had their reasons. Please don't make a scene. Don't ruin this happy moment for them."

Charlotte might as well have been whistling in the wind for all of the attention that her sister paid to her pleas. Without a word to anyone, Madeline pushed out of her chair and stomped out of the room. Seconds later, they heard the front door slam, and within moments they heard the roar of a car engine and the squeal of tires.

Nadia stared up at Daniel. "I told you she would be upset. I'm so sorry, honey." She buried her crimson face against his shoulder, but not before Charlotte saw the tears spilling down her cheeks.

After Madeline's abrupt departure, the food could have been dust as far as those who were left at the table were concerned. Little Davy's excited chatter was the only thing that kept the meal from being eaten in complete silence.

As soon as the meal was over and the table cleared,

everyone said subdued good-byes, then left—everyone but Judith.

"Why, Aunt Charley?" she demanded as she followed Charlotte back to the kitchen. "Why does my mother have to be like that? Nothing's ever good enough for her, and nothing any of us does ever pleases her."

Charlotte had begun loading the dishwasher but paused. "I know it seems that way, hon, but—"

Judith threw up her right hand, palm out, and shook her head. "No buts, Auntie. It doesn't just *seem* that way. It *is* that way, and no use you making excuses for her."

As much as it pained Charlotte to admit it, Judith was right. But an admission of the truth out loud would be even more painful for Judith, so Charlotte lied. "To be honest, hon, I don't know why she acts that way."

Long after Judith had left, Charlotte remained at the open front door and stared at the empty driveway with unseeing eyes as pangs of guilt about Madeline battered her conscience.

It had all started with the death of their parents. Charlotte had been only twenty to Madeline's fifteen when their parents had been involved in a fatal accident. She'd been much too young to take on the responsibilities of caring for a teenage sister as well as her own infant son. Indeed, she'd been too overwhelmed to do anything but get through each day as best she could, and she'd overcompensated by indulging her sister and giving in to her every demand.

Charlotte stepped back inside the house. It had taken

her years to finally come to terms with the guilt she felt about Madeline, years to finally realize that as a grown woman, Madeline was ultimately responsible for her own spoiled, selfish actions.

But old habits were hard to break, and even now Charlotte couldn't decide whether she should phone Madeline and try to placate her or simply leave her sister alone and mind her own business.

"Well, what do you think I should do, Sweety?" She directed her question to her little parakeet whose cage hung on a stand by the front window. "Should I call her or not?"

For an answer, the little bird gave a squawk and pranced back and forth on his perch.

"Humph. Should have known better than to ask you. Probably wouldn't do any good to call her anyway." Charlotte closed and locked the door. "More than likely she wouldn't listen. And that's a shame—a crying shame. Anyone with half a pea-brain could see that Daniel, Nadia, and Davy are a perfect match."

Still debating whether to call her sister, Charlotte walked over to the sofa and sat down. Suddenly, she stiffened and went stone still.

What about Ricco Martinez, the man Nadia had lived with, the father of her son? It had been a year since Ricco, without a word to anyone, had simply disappeared one day. What if, after all this time, he suddenly decided to show up? What then?

Chapter Two

Charlotte normally avoided scheduling herself to clean for clients on Thursdays, reserving that day so that she could run errands and catch up on the book-keeping for her maid service. Thursday was also the day that she took care of her own housecleaning chores. By the time Thursday rolled around though, she was more than ready for it, but for other reasons. She was exhausted. Marian Hebert, the client she worked for on Mondays, Wednesdays, and Fridays, had suddenly decided that in addition to Charlotte's regular chores, all the baseboards in her house needed scrubbing and all of the closets needed cleaning out.

Bitsy Duhe, her client on Tuesdays, also had had additional chores for Charlotte. Bitsy had decided that every window in her house needed cleaning, which meant taking down all of the drapes, then putting them back up once she was done.

Charlotte figured it was spring fever. But who could blame them? Springtime in New Orleans was so brief, and the cool nights and humidity-free daytime temperatures such a rarity, that everyone who lived in and around the Crescent City made the most of the pleasant weather.

Under normal circumstances, Charlotte could have coped with the hard work. She'd had to work hard all of her life. But she hadn't felt well at all, not since Sunday. All week long she'd kept telling herself that if she could just make it until Thursday, she could rest up, and then she might be able to make it through Friday, her last scheduled workday for the week.

It had been several months since Charlotte had discovered that she was a borderline diabetic, and most of the time she kept the disease under control with her diet and a tiny pill she took each morning. But, for whatever reason, her blood-sugar level had gone from one extreme to the other over the past three days.

"Probably just stress," she murmured as she gathered her dirty clothes from the hamper in the bathroom. She'd read that stress wasn't good for a diabetic, and being at odds with her sister had always stressed her out.

If nothing else, Madeline could be mule-headed stubborn when she chose to be. None of the phone calls that Charlotte had made to her sister during the week had been answered or returned. All she'd gotten was her sister's answering machine. She'd even tried calling Madeline at the accounting firm where she was employed, but she'd been told that Ms. Monroe was in a meeting and couldn't be disturbed.

At first Charlotte had figured that Madeline was still pouting about Daniel's marriage announcement and simply didn't want to talk about it. But it had been over three days now without a word from her, and Charlotte was beginning to really get aggravated . . . and angry.

Knowing her sister as she did, Charlotte figured that Madeline had somehow gotten it into her head that Charlotte was at fault for Daniel's relationship with Nadia. And maybe, in a teeny-tiny way, she was.

It had been almost a year since Nadia had come to her

in tears because Ricco, her live-in boyfriend and the father of her son, had been arrested as part of the gang that had been stealing cemetery artifacts. Nadia had needed legal expertise that she could ill afford, and Ricco's court-appointed attorney had been next to useless. Charlotte had solicited Daniel's help on Nadia's behalf, so, in essence, she *had* brought the two of them together.

But that was all she had done. Once Daniel had secured Ricco's release from jail, without a word to anyone, Ricco had abruptly disappeared. What had developed between Nadia and Daniel afterward had been totally their own doing.

In the laundry room, once Charlotte had measured out the laundry detergent, she dumped it into the washing machine, then turned the machine on. Most of the time she waited until the machine completely filled with water, and she let it agitate a minute or so before adding the clothes. But today she had no patience for waiting on anything. As soon as she had separated the dirty clothes into whites and colors, she stuffed in the first load.

Charlotte figured that just because she'd brought Daniel and Nadia together initially didn't mean that their marriage was her fault. After all, they were two grown people perfectly capable of making their own choices in life. Madeline was just being ridiculous about the whole thing, and, in Charlotte's opinion, her sister would live to regret her attitude.

Charlotte figured that the best thing she could do about the situation with her sister was to ignore it and get her mind on other things. The good Lord only knew that she had enough "other things" to think about. But knowing the best thing to do in a situation and actually doing it was easier said than done.

Maybe a nice brisk walk right after breakfast would help, she decided. It had been days since she'd been able to take her afternoon walks, and, according to all the brochures she'd read, regular exercise was really important for people who had diabetes.

Charlotte yawned as she closed the lid of the washing machine. What she'd really like to do was crawl back into bed and sleep another couple of hours. Even just thinking about a walk made her tired.

As she emerged from the laundry room, the phone rang, giving her a start. When she glanced at her wrist-watch, she grimaced. Charlotte's maid service consisted of three full-time employees and one part-time employee. When the phone rang between seven and eight in the morning, it usually meant problems with one of them.

With dread weighing down each footstep, she trudged into the living room to answer the call. The last thing she needed or wanted was to have to deal with business problems today.

She picked up the receiver. "Good morning, Maid-for-a-Day. Charlotte speaking."

"Charlotte, this is Nadia."

Charlotte frowned with worry, her own problems suddenly forgotten. "What's wrong, hon? You don't sound so good."

"I don't feel so good, either. I'm afraid I have that

nasty stomach virus that's been going around. I've been throwing up since early this morning."

"Oh, you poor thing. How can I help?"

"I hate doing this to you—I really do—but today is my day to work for Patsy Dufour. There's just no way I—"

"Don't even think about it, hon. I'll get someone else to—"

Nadia interrupted with a groan. "Uh oh, I think I'm gonna be sick again. Sorry. Gotta go."

Charlotte depressed the switch hook, and after a moment she released it and tapped out the number for Janet Davis, her part-time employee.

Please be able to work today . . . please. But all she got was Janet's answering machine. With a sigh of disappointment, she hung up the phone without leaving a message.

Janet was the only backup help she had on Thursdays. Her other two full-time employees had regular clients of their own scheduled for that day. If Janet wasn't available, Charlotte either had to work the job herself or cancel it.

Lost in thought, for several moments Charlotte stared at Sweety Boy, who cocked his head and stared right back at her.

For one of the few times since she'd formed her own maid service, Charlotte seriously considered canceling the job. Maybe Hank was right, after all. For over a year her son had been trying to persuade her to retire and let him take care of her for a change, and since her sixtieth birthday, he'd become more insistent.

As a renowned surgeon who was much in demand, her son could certainly afford to take care of her. But while the possibility of retiring was nice to think about, she had never truly considered doing such a thing. For one thing, she'd always taken care of herself without anyone's help, thank you very much. But maybe it was time to give his offer some serious consideration. Maybe she *should* think about retiring.

"No!" she whispered and firmly shook her head. *You're just tired and you don't feel good. Besides, you'd go stark raving mad without anything to do.*

"Just do it," she grumbled. "So much for a day off, huh, Boy?" she told the little parakeet as she grabbed her Rolodex and thumbed through it until she found Patsy Dufour's phone number.

Four rings later, Charlotte felt like screaming with frustration when Patsy's answering machine kicked in. "Just great!" she muttered. Didn't anyone ever answer their phones any more? "She's probably either in the shower or outside in the garden," she told herself, waiting for the beep to sound so she could leave a message.

After the beep, she said, "Patsy, this is Charlotte LaRue with Maid-for-a-Day. Your regular maid, Nadia, is sick, so I'll be taking her place. I'm afraid I'm running a bit late, though, and I wanted to let you know that I will be there as soon as possible."

Charlotte hated being late almost as much as she detested gossip, but she especially hated being late for work. Besides a sloppy cleaning job, the other thing that clients frowned on the most was the maid not showing up at the appointed time.

Within thirty minutes of her call to Patsy, Charlotte had eaten a bowl of cereal and quickly dressed. The last thing she did before leaving was check Sweety Boy's food and water supply.

"See you later, Boy," she told the little bird, once she'd determined that he had enough to last until she returned. "Be good, now." Locking the door behind her, she headed for the van.

After a quick inventory of the supplies that she kept in the van, she found that she needed to replenish several of the cleaners she normally used from the stock she kept in the storeroom.

When Charlotte had first began cleaning homes as a profession, Hank had been a toddler. As a single mother, she'd been on a shoestring budget. It hadn't taken her long to realize that buying cleaning products in bulk from a supply house was a lot less expensive than buying stuff off the grocery-store shelves.

The only problem with buying in bulk, though, was storage. And since some of the supplies were hazardous, she'd been uncomfortable about the idea of keeping them inside the house, especially with a small child around who seemed to get into anything and everything in spite of all the precautions she'd taken.

The solution had been to build a storeroom on to the back of the carport that was attached to her half of the Victorian double she owned.

As Charlotte refilled containers, she tried to recall if there was anything else she needed. Early on, she'd learned that each of her clients had her own idiosyncrasies about what she wanted done and how she wanted it done. It had been a couple of years since she had personally worked for Patsy, but if she remembered right, Patsy was one of the most particular clients that she'd had to deal with. And just one of Patsy's peculiarities was that she insisted on each of the ten ceiling fans she had in her home being dusted every week.

Charlotte eyed a brush hanging on a peg. The odd U-shaped brush stuck out at a ninety-degree angle to the handle, and the yard-long handle was telescopic and could be extended to almost twice its length. It had been designed to dust ceiling-fan blades. But even with the handle fully extended, she would still need a ladder to do a thorough job.

Charlotte shivered at the thought of climbing to the top of the ladder. Some of the ceilings in Patsy's century-old home were as high as twelve feet, and Charlotte never had liked heights. Like it or not, though, to Charlotte, a thorough job included not only dusting the fan blades, but wiping them down with a scented cleaner as well. That way, when the fans were turned back on, the motion of the blades would spread the scent and leave the room smelling fresh and clean.

Propped against the wall near the brush was an aluminum ladder. Charlotte was pretty sure that Patsy kept a small stepladder in one of the ground-floor closets in her house, but if she remembered right, Patsy's ladder wasn't very tall. Maybe she should bring her own ladder as well as the brush, just in case.

But would her ladder be tall enough? She estimated that the ladder was six-feet high, then she added her own height of five-feet-three plus another two feet for an upstretched arm. Shrugging, Charlotte picked up the bottles she'd refilled. Patsy's fans, she recalled, hung from extensions that varied in length from six inches to a couple of feet from the ceiling. If she really stretched, she might be able to reach them without having to climb to the very top of the ladder . . . if she really stretched.

After she'd loaded the brush and the refilled bottles of cleaner into the van, she went back for the ladder. Though it was made of aluminum and wasn't that heavy, it was cumbersome, especially in the small, crowded confines of the storage room. With a firm grip on it and being careful not to knock anything over or off the shelves, she slowly backed out the door. She'd just cleared the storeroom door with the ladder when—

"Hey, let me help you with that."

At the unexpected sound of the deep male voice, Charlotte let out a startled squeal, then whirled around. The end of the ladder just missed Louis Thibodeaux's head by inches.

Jerking his head back in the nick of time, he yelled, "Hey, watch it!"

"Well!" she snapped back at him. "What do you expect? You scared the living daylights out of me."

Charlotte could still feel her heart pumping overtime from fright. Lately the newspaper had been full of stories about people living in Uptown and the Garden District being accosted and robbed right in their own driveways or garages.

"I swear, Louis, the least you could do is let a body know when you're around."

Louis threw up his hands in defense. "I thought for sure you knew I was standing here."

"Well, I didn't!" she argued.

Louis Thibodeaux was Judith's ex-partner. He had officially retired from the New Orleans Police Department back in December and had needed a temporary place to stay until the work at his camp on Lake Maurepas was completed, so Charlotte had rented out the other half of her double to him.

"Here," he said, grabbing hold of the ladder. "I'll load that for you."

Along with Louis's other irritating faults, Charlotte had learned that he could also be a bit overbearing at times. Unsure whether it was the tone he'd used or whether it was just her own perverse mood, it suddenly became terribly important that she prove to him that she could load the ladder without any help. Especially without his help.

Charlotte tightened her grip on the ladder. "I can do it myself. I always have," she grumbled as she pulled on it. "Besides which, once I get to where I'm going, I'll have to unload it by myself, so what's the difference?"

Louis pulled right back. "Don't be so stubborn, Charlotte. I know you're perfectly capable of doing anything you want to do. *By yourself,*" he added with mocking emphasis. "That's not the point."

For long seconds they stood, almost toe to toe with the ladder between them, both unwilling to relinquish their hold on it to the other.

Finally Charlotte had had enough. "Oh, all right!" she snapped, shoving the ladder at him at exactly the same moment that he'd decided to release his hold on it. The ladder fell, and as it clattered and bounced against the concrete floor, both jumped backward to avoid getting their feet smashed.

All Charlotte could do was stand there red-faced with frustration and embarrassment as she stared down at the dumb ladder. Then, she heard it—that irritating sound that meant that Louis was trying his best to keep from laughing out loud. And, as aggravated as she was, she couldn't hold back the smile that trembled at the corners of her own lips.

Louis cleared his throat. "Now can I load it for you?" Without waiting for an answer, he picked up the ladder. "I swear, you're too stubborn for your own good," he muttered as he stalked off to the back of the van. A minute or so later, he called out, "By the way, the reason I was looking for you in the first place was because I've got something I need to talk to you about."

About what? Charlotte wondered, as she headed for the driver's side of the van.

Louis slammed the rear van door shut, then walked around to where Charlotte was standing. "I hear congratulations are in order."

Charlotte frowned. "Congratulations?"

"Yeah, I ran into Judith the other day, and she told me about her brother getting married to that employee of yours who has the little boy."

"Nadia's her name, and thanks." Ever conscious of the time, Charlotte glanced at her watch. "Was that what you needed to talk to me about?"

"No. I—"

"Then, I don't mean to be rude, but can we talk later? I'm already late as it is. Of course, if it's urgent," she added. "Or really important . . ."

"I thought you didn't work on Thursdays."

"Depends on your definition of work," she retorted defensively.

"Aw, come on, Charlotte, you know what I mean."

Charlotte sighed. "Yes—yes, I do. Sorry. Guess I'm a bit touchy this morning. One of my maids called in sick at the last minute, and since I couldn't get a replacement, I have to take her place. Like I said, I'm already late, so I really do need to leave now."

"Sure, no problem." Louis opened the door for her. "What I need to talk about can wait. How about I cook dinner for you?"

"Ah—dinner?" Though she was taken aback by his abrupt change of subject, she climbed into the van.

Talking was one thing, but dinner?

The idea of a man cooking for her had taken some getting used to, not that Louis had cooked for her that many times. But ever since he'd kissed her on her birthday back in October, their relationship had been a bit strained and had taken a subtle change of direction.

That he hadn't kissed her since that night nor had he even acted like he might want to do so had contributed to the uneasiness she felt when around him. The whole situation bothered her and confused her so much so that she no longer knew how to act when she was around him.

She knew she was being a coward, but, unlike her niece's generation, which was forward and open about such matters, she simply couldn't get past her upbringing to work up the courage to approach the subject or discuss the issue with him. The women of her generation had been raised to believe that the man should be the aggressor and that only trashy women made the first move. Of course, that was all hogwash, and if she was honest with herself she'd admit that the real reason she couldn't just come right out and confront him was because she still wasn't sure how she felt about him.

At times she truly liked Louis—liked him a lot. And she respected him. But there were other times when his chauvinistic attitude and know-it-all ways irritated her no end.

Louis shut the driver's door. Then he tapped on the window. "Well?" he mouthed. "How about it?"

Charlotte rolled down the window. "Ah—I . . ." *Now be gracious, Charlotte. Mind your manners.* "Sure." She forced a smile. "Why not? That's very nice of you," she hastened to add.

Louis nodded. "Good. Supper will be ready around six." He pointed to the seat belt. "Don't forget to buckle up."

Charlotte's home was located on Milan Street, just outside the Garden District. The family mansion that Patsy Dufour had inherited was located on Prytania Street and was reputed to be one of the oldest homes in the Garden District, if not the oldest.

Traffic was light on Prytania, and the drive to Patsy's house took less than ten minutes, not near enough time for Charlotte to sort out her confused feelings about Louis or his dinner invitation. To do that might take a lifetime, and Charlotte figured that with the advent of her sixtieth birthday back in October, more than half of her lifetime was already over—unless some scientist somewhere discovered a way to stop the aging process right away, which wasn't likely.

Patsy Dufour's raised cottage-style home had seen many modifications during its hundred and sixty years of existence. The one-story house was raised above ground on brick piers, forming what was called a basement by the locals who lived in the below-sea-level city of New Orleans. Each new addition to the home had changed it over the years; a whole wing of rooms had been added along one side as well as galleries.

The house had been in Patsy's family for generations, and it, along with the furnishings and the grounds surrounding the house, were her pride and joy.

Years ago, when Patsy had first inherited the old house, it had been designated as a national historic landmark by the Department of the Interior. Ever since, Patsy had become a connoisseur of historical correctness as well as an avid gardener, and for most of Patsy's adult life she'd totally devoted herself to the upkeep and historical integrity of the house and its grounds.

Located on one of the largest lots in the Garden District, the Dufour home was surrounded by a white picket fence. On the inside of the fence there was a thick wall of various tropical plants, so thick that the house was almost hidden from the prying eyes of the many tourist tours that roamed the Garden District.

The first thing that Charlotte noted when she approached the house were the trucks parked along the curb. At least once a year Patsy did a major landscaping project, and, judging from the equipment and various plants in the truck beds, she was at it again.

Patsy was extremely paranoid about security, but to Charlotte's surprise, the main entrance gate was unlocked.

Once Charlotte had unloaded her supply carrier, she locked the van and climbed the steps leading up to the front gallery. At the door, she rang the doorbell and waited. She rang it again. When Patsy still didn't answer, she left her supply carrier by the door and headed around to the side of the house to where stepping-stones formed a path to the back of the property.

The backyard was a beehive of activity. Men armed with shovels were scooping up the black dirt and loading it into wheelbarrows as fast as a noisy backhoe could dig it out of the ground. Even with all the noise and bustle, Charlotte spotted Patsy almost immediately. And in her arms was Missy, the little Pekingese that was Patsy's constant companion.

Dressed in spotlessly clean lime green Capri pants and a matching short-sleeved sweater, Patsy was standing on the edge of the huge hole that was being dug out by the backhoe.

A divorcée in her early forties, Patsy lived alone except for Missy. Charlotte had always heard that pet owners sometimes resembled their pets, but she'd never really thought much about it until she'd met Patsy Dufour and Missy. She'd decided that in Patsy's case, it was true.

Though not an ugly woman, Patsy wasn't exactly attractive, either. Like Missy, she was compact, with a heavy front and lighter hindquarters. The one real asset that Patsy possessed was her thick, dark hair. She wore it in a classic pageboy style, and it was streaked with a healthy sheen of auburn highlights.

The moment that Patsy spotted Charlotte, she flashed her a huge smile, then signaled to the man operating the backhoe to cut off the machine. Once the noisy machine shut down, Patsy walked briskly toward Charlotte.

Just like Patsy, thought Charlotte. *Overseeing every little detail.*

"Hey there," Patsy greeted her. "What on earth are you doing here?"

Charlotte gave her a quick smile. "I guess that means you didn't get my phone message. I'm taking Nadia's place today. She's ill with a nasty stomach virus."

"Oh, that's too bad—poor thing—and, no, I'm afraid I didn't get the message." She motioned toward the men. "But I've been so busy this morning that I haven't checked for any messages. Here, let me show you." Without waiting for a response, she promptly took Charlotte by the arm and pulled her toward the hole being dug.

"Just look at it. After almost a year of planning, my dream is coming true. I'm finally going to get my pond. Of course it won't be as large as I had originally hoped for, but the design and landscaping will make up for what it lacks in size.

"Just as well," she continued. "My next project will need lots of room." The excitement in Patsy's voice grew. "I've been studying the Rosedown gardens and would just love to duplicate some of what's been done there—on a much smaller scale, of course," she added. "But what I'd really love is to get my hands on some of those heritage plants growing there. And what I wouldn't give to have copies of Martha Turnbull's diaries. . . ." Her voice trailed away.

Smaller scale indeed, Charlotte thought, vaguely recalling an article she'd read in the *Times-Picayune* about the attempt to renovate the gardens of the St. Francisville plantation. What she remembered most about the article was the scope of the project. The original gardens were begun in the 1830s by Rosedown founder Martha Turnbull, and there were no less than twenty-eight acres of gardens that would take years to restore to their original splendor.

After a moment, Patsy shrugged. "Oh, well. For now I'll just have to make do with my pond. At least I'll finally have a place to showcase my collection."

For as long as Charlotte had known Patsy, the younger woman had been obsessed with acquiring artifacts, Italian marble statues that were patinated with age, and urns of various shapes and sizes, all mostly antique.

"By this time tomorrow," Patsy continued, "the pond should be finished and the men can start placing everything. I can hardly wait," she added, excitement crackling in her voice.

Though Charlotte didn't quite understand Patsy's

obsession with a bunch of old statues and urns, nor did she understand her excitement over a hole being dug in her backyard, one that would no doubt attract even more mosquitos than normal, she found herself smiling at the younger woman's enthusiasm.

"I'm sure it will be just lovely when it's finished," she told Patsy. "Now, if you'll let me in the front door, I'll get to work."

Like most of the homes that belonged to Charlotte's clients, Patsy's was never really messy or terribly dirty. Besides dusting and cleaning the ceiling fans, Charlotte's work consisted mostly of dusting furniture, polishing it, vacuuming up the dog hair, changing the bed linens, and cleaning the kitchen and the bathrooms.

By two that afternoon, Charlotte had finished everything except for making up Patsy's huge four-poster bed. She'd even been able to dust and clean the ceiling fans without much trouble. Just as she'd thought, Patsy still had a ladder stored in the pantry closet. Since it was taller than she'd remembered and more sturdy than the aluminum one she'd brought with her, the height of the ceiling fans hadn't really been a problem after all.

Charlotte had just smoothed out the comforter on top of the bed when her cell phone buzzed. Almost the second that she switched on the phone, and without waiting for even so much as a hello, Madeline launched into a tirade.

"You've got to do something about Nadia, Charlotte!"

"Guess this means you're speaking to me again."

Madeline ignored Charlotte's jeer. "She's nothing but

white trash, Charlotte, and the girl has the manners of a goat."

"Shame on you! Nadia is not—"

But Madeline didn't give Charlotte a chance to finish. "Do you know what she's done?" she wailed. Without waiting for an answer, she raved on. "She's canceled on me. The very nerve! And to think that I'd decided to give her a chance—for Daniel's sake. Here I'd arranged this lovely high tea at the Windsor Hotel for this afternoon and invited my boss and some of my friends to meet her. And now she's gone and canceled—just like that—an hour before our reservation, saying she's ill. I tell you, breeding shows through every time. I knew from the—"

"Madeline! Nadia *is* ill. She's—"

"Yeah, right. Sure she is. She's just still in a snit because I wasn't bowled over by their stupid announcement on Sunday, and it's her little way of getting back at me."

"That's absolutely not true," Charlotte argued. "In the first place, she's not like that. She doesn't play those kinds of games. And in the second place, she has a stomach virus."

"Yeah, and I'm the queen of Mardi Gras. Can't you see it? Not only has she pulled a fast one on my son, but she's got you hoodwinked, too!"

"Madeline, stop it!" Charlotte shouted, no longer able to keep a rein on her rising temper.

"Don't you dare 'Madeline' me," her sister shouted right back. "I should have known better than to call you—should have known that you'd take *her* side against your own sister. You've never supported any-thing I did. Why—"

Charlotte's temper snapped. When Madeline was in the throes of one of her hissy fits, there was no talking to her, no reasoning with her at all. Charlotte jerked the phone away from her ear and with one click discon-nected the call. With her hand shaking almost uncon-trollably, she turned the phone off.

For several long seconds, all she could do was stare at the floor while she tried to calm down. But not even breathing deeply and counting to ten helped this time.

"Spoiled," she muttered. "And selfish to the bone."

With her insides still churning, she marched into the kitchen and snatched up her supply carrier. Only later, after she was already driving up Prytania, did it occur to her that she should have told Patsy she had finished cleaning and was leaving.

Just as well, she thought. In the mood she was in, she didn't trust herself to even speak to another human being. Besides, Patsy was too caught up in her newest project to care one way or the other.

The short drive home didn't help to improve Char-lotte's mood a whole lot. She kept replaying the shouting match she'd had with her sister and fuming. Charlotte knew that it was more than just this particular incident with Maddie. It didn't help that she was tired and didn't feel well, but she was also feeling the effects of years of having to put up with her sister's selfishness and pettiness. Today it was like a dark curtain had been yanked away to reveal the blinding sunlight—and the revelation was devastating.

All this time, all these years, she'd been burying her head in the sand as far as Madeline was concerned. She'd purposely ignored just how selfish and shallow her sister could be in order to avoid dealing with it. How many times had she made excuses for her? How many times had she bailed her out of financial difficulties? All the while, she'd chosen to ignore Madeline's hurtful and destructive ways, even though she'd had to step in and take over the raising of Judith and Daniel. The question was, why? Why had she put up with Madeline's behavior?

Charlotte steered the van down Milan as she grappled with the answer. That she loved her sister was the obvious answer. And she did love her. Yet, the answer was more complex than simply loving her. Other than herself and her own memories, Maddie was Charlotte's only connection to her parents. So was the old saying true? Was any port in the storm better than no port at all? Maybe once it might have been true, but now . . .

It wasn't until Charlotte pulled into her driveway that she noticed Louis sitting on the front porch swing. She figured he was waiting for her. Still, it was such a beautiful day, he could be sitting there just enjoying the spring weather.

"Nah," she muttered. And if he was waiting for her, that meant he had something to discuss, something that couldn't wait until later at dinner.

"Please, not now," she grumbled as she parked the van and shut off the engine. For a moment she was tempted to simply go inside through the kitchen door.

With a sigh, she climbed down from the van and trudged toward the front porch. If nothing else, Louis could be persistent; it was just one of the traits that had made him such a good police detective. Knowing Louis, if she didn't come in through the front, he'd just bang on the door until she answered it.

Chapter Three

"What's wrong?" he asked as she climbed the steps. "You look like you could chew nails."

"I'd rather not talk about it right now, if you don't mind."

"Well, I do mind, but I know better than to push when you're like this."

Charlotte rolled her eyes. "Was there something that you wanted in particular?"

Louis nodded. "Actually, I'm going to have to cancel our dinner tonight. Something's come up, but I wanted to talk to you before I leave."

Charlotte couldn't honestly say that she was disappointed about the dinner. Given the mood she was in, she wouldn't have been fit company for anyone. She waved a hand at him. "So? Talk."

Though he gave her an odd look, he motioned toward the side of the double that he'd been renting from her. "I know I was supposed to move out at the end of the month, but I'd like to rent the place a while longer." He rushed on to explain. "I've had a job offer from Lagniappe Security Company, and now that my son and his family are back in my life, I've decided against moving to the lake house. It's too far away from everything."

And too far away from everyone. Charlotte silently filled in the blanks. After years of being estranged, Louis and his son had finally reconciled, and "everyone" now included not only Louis's son, but his son's wife and his son's little daughter as well.

"But it might take some time," Louis continued. "You know, to sell the lake property and find something affordable in the city. In fact, that's where I have to go this evening. I've got a couple interested in seeing the lake property, so I was wondering if it would be okay with you if I could continue to rent the double a while longer?"

Charlotte wanted to ask him just how much longer he would need but held her tongue. From the beginning his stay was supposed to have been temporary. She'd only agreed to rent to him as a favor to her niece, and she'd rented the double to him cheaper than she would have rented it to a stranger. So what guarantee did she have that he really would look for another place to live? Louis was no dummy. Property in New Orleans could be expensive, and he could be a real penny-pincher.

No guarantees, she decided. None but his word. And even if he did stay for a while, she had to admit that it had been a comfort knowing that someone reliable and trustworthy was right next door, especially after her last tenant.

Any other time, she might have confronted him and pinned him down to a timetable, but at the moment, all she wanted was to be left alone. Later she would deal with Louis, she decided. But not now. Now, somehow, some way, she needed to decide what she was going to do about Madeline.

"Well?" Louis asked. "Is that okay with you? Is it okay if I stay a while longer?"

Charlotte shrugged. "Sure. I guess. Until you can find something," she added for good measure. "Now, if you'll excuse me—" She walked to her front door and unlocked it. "I'm tired." Without waiting for a response from him, she went inside and closed the door behind her.

But once inside, with no one but Sweety Boy for a distraction, she found herself restless and confused . . . and obsessing about Madeline. For long minutes she paced between the kitchen and the living room, only stopping occasionally to stare at the telephone.

"Should I call her or not, Sweety?"

For an answer, the little bird fluttered his wings and did his own pacing, back and forth on his perch inside the cage.

"Just as I thought," she muttered. "No help at all." Charlotte flopped down on the sofa, but after a moment she jumped up again and marched over to the phone. She'd always hated contention of any kind, but it especially bothered her when it concerned her own family. To Charlotte, her family meant everything, and, like it or not, Madeline was her sister, the only sibling she had.

Charlotte reached for the receiver, but the second she touched it, she felt her temper rise all over again. Jerking her hand away, she did an about-face and stomped into the kitchen. If she called Madeline now, they would end up in another shouting match for sure. Later, she decided. She'd call her later, after she'd calmed down.

But later proved to be sooner than she'd expected. Charlotte had just poured herself a glass of iced tea when the phone rang. For a moment she was tempted to let her answering machine catch it, but only for a moment. Not everyone who called always left a message. Call it superstition or whatever, she always figured that the one phone call she didn't answer would be the call she should have answered. Besides, it could be business.

With her glass of tea in hand, she trudged back into the living room and picked up the receiver.

"Don't you dare hang up on me again."

Madeline.

"What do you want, Maddie?"

"I—I want to—to apologize."

Charlotte blinked several times and wondered if she should get her hearing checked. She could count on the fingers of one hand the times that Madeline had ever apologized about anything.

"I'm sorry, Charlotte. I had no right to take out my frustrations on you. And I was wrong."

Charlotte set the glass of tea on a coaster and sat down at the desk. Maybe there was hope for Madeline after all.

"You know I *want* to do what's right," Madeline continued. "It's just that . . . I—oh, Charlotte, I've made such a mess of things. Judith has barely spoken to me at all since Sunday, and Daniel won't take my calls. And I didn't mean what I said about you," she rushed on. "You know, about not supporting me? You've done more for me than anyone has a right to expect. It's just that . . . oh, dear Lord, how can I say this? I wanted more for Daniel—more than a woman who already had a kid. I think we can both agree that Daniel is a good catch for any woman, and I just can't get past the notion that all that woman saw was a meal ticket and a father for her bastard son."

Charlotte winced at her sister's graphic description of Nadia and Davy.

"Well, don't you have anything to say?"

Charlotte had a lot to say. *Do right, and you'll feel right. Judge not lest ye be judged. Do unto others as you would have them do unto you.* Just to name a few things. But none of that was what Madeline wanted to hear or would even listen to at the moment. So what could she say?

"You know I love you, Maddie. All I've ever wanted was what was best for you and Daniel and Judith." She took a deep breath and prayed that she was saying the right things. "Daniel is a fine man. But he's a man now, not a boy," she emphasized. "He's intelligent, educated, and well respected in his profession, and I think you need to trust him—trust that he knows his own heart and mind. And I also think you need to be careful how you judge people. We all do," she added. "Both of us know from personal experience that things are not always what they seem on the surface. And neither of us can afford to throw stones at someone else because we both have things in our own past that we'd just as soon

46

no one else knew about or held against us."

As Charlotte waited for a response, the silence grew on the other end of the line. Still, she waited, all the while telling herself to be patient. Then she heard it—that faint telltale sniffle.

Long moments later, Madeline finally cleared her throat. "You're right," she said, tears in her voice. "I know you're right. So why is it so hard for me to do what's right?"

Because you're selfish and spoiled. But giving voice to those thoughts would only cause more contention. Charlotte squeezed her eyes closed and again prayed for patience. Then she said, "That's something you have to figure out on your own, Maddie. But, for what it's worth, I think you've made a good beginning. To admit we're wrong is the first step . . . and it's sometimes the hardest step."

After Charlotte hung up from talking with Madeline, she called Nadia. Daniel answered the phone.

"Hey, hon. This is Aunt Charlotte. I was just calling to check on Nadia. Is she feeling better?"

"Not a whole lot," he answered, "but at least she's stopped throwing up."

"Can I do anything to help?"

"Naw, Auntie. We'll be fine. But thanks for asking."

On Friday morning, Charlotte couldn't believe how much better she felt as she locked her front door and headed for the van. Climbing inside the van, she found herself humming the old song, "What a Difference a Day Makes."

And it was true, she thought. Just as the song title implied, one day could make all the difference in the world. And so could something as simple as an apology.

While she was waiting for several cars to pass before backing into the street, her thoughts turned introspective. Though Charlotte truly didn't believe that one person's happiness and well-being should depend on another person, she was a realist. Being at odds with her only sister had been a miserable experience and had really had an effect on her. It wasn't the first time it had happened, and it wouldn't be the last, she was sure. And in theory, yes, happiness had to come from within, but theory didn't always take into account that people were only human, and humans needed to live in harmony with those they loved.

The street was clear of traffic, and as Charlotte backed onto Milan, her gaze strayed to the driveway on the other side of her house and her thoughts turned to Louis Thibodeaux. Louis's blue Taurus was gone, she noted. So where was he at this time in the morning? she wondered as she drove past her house. She didn't remember hearing him leave earlier, but he could have left while she was in the shower.

None of your business. "And what do you care, anyway?" she muttered as she ignored the tiny voice in her head that answered back, insisting that she did care, probably more than she should.

The drive to her Friday client's home usually took about ten minutes, depending on traffic. Though there was a steady flow of traffic today, it moved along without any delays for a change.

Almost a year had passed since Charlotte had begun working for Marian Hebert on Mondays, Wednesdays, and Fridays. In that year she'd seen Marian undergo some dramatic changes.

A widow in her late thirties, Marian was well on her way to overcoming an alcohol addiction and getting a firm hold on raising her two sons. But the journey to sobriety hadn't been an easy one. It had taken a murder and a life-threatening experience to jolt Marian out of the quagmire of self-pity and guilt that she'd buried herself in.

Charlotte shivered, recalling the particular incident all too well. In retrospect the whole thing seemed like a bad dream, but unlike a nightmare, the memory of which usually faded with time, even now, five months later, Charlotte could still recall each terrifying minute. She and Marian had both done well to escape with their very lives, and Charlotte wasn't sure she would ever forget the horror of it all.

As Charlotte parked the van alongside the curb in the front of Marian's home, she couldn't help noticing the difference between Marian's home and Patsy's home. Both were architecturally the same raised-cottage type, but that was where all similarities ended.

Though Marian's house was old, too, it wasn't nearly as old as Patsy's, and whereas Patsy was a stickler for historical accuracy, with only a few concessions for modern conveniences, Marian had no such compunctions. Patsy's home was a historical showplace. Marian's home was . . . well . . . it was a home.

Before his death, Marian and her husband had remodeled their home to include two large rooms across the back, one a modern kitchen-family room combination, and the other a home office. The bottom level had been turned into a master suite and a huge game room for their two sons.

Sons. Children. Maybe that was the real difference. Patsy had no children, no one to think of but herself and her little dog, Missy.

From the back of her van, Charlotte gathered the supplies she would need and filled her supply carrier. She was thinking that she'd make a second trip for her vacuum cleaner when it suddenly dawned on her that her vacuum cleaner wasn't in the van. So where on earth was it?

When she suddenly remembered, she smacked her forehead with the heel of her hand. "Just great!" she muttered. "Just wonderful!" Of course. It was right where she'd left it. It was still at Patsy Dufour's house.

Charlotte preferred to use her own equipment when cleaning. There had been too many times she'd had the experience of pulling out a client's vacuum only to find that it was either broken or there were no vacuum bags to replace the full one inside the machine.

"Thanks for nothing, Maddie," she grumbled as she added a bottle of window cleaner to the supply carrier. "That's what I get for letting my temper get the best of me and not thinking straight."

All she could do for now was hope that Marian's vacuum was in working order, she finally decided. Charlotte pulled out the notepad and pen she always kept in her apron pocket and jotted down a reminder note. *Call Patsy Dufour about vacuum cleaner and arrange a time to pick it up.* Slipping the notepad and pen back inside her pocket, she grabbed the supply carrier, slammed the van door shut, and locked it.

Once through the front gate, she climbed the steps to the porch. Just as she raised her hand to knock, the door swung open. Like a whirlwind, Aaron Hebert rushed past her.

"Hi, Ms. LaRue. I'm late. Gotta go. Bye, Ms. LaRue."

"Hi and bye, Aaron," she called after him. "Have a good day." Charlotte smiled as she watched the eight-year-old boy lope down the sidewalk. With his blond hair and blue eyes, Aaron reminded her a lot of her nephew, Daniel, when he had been Aaron's age. Though not as mischievous as Daniel had been, Aaron was just as full of life, and loved to talk about anything and everything.

"Aaron Hebert, you come back and shut that door! Oops!" Marian Hebert's face flushed with embarrassment. "Hi, Charlotte. Sorry. I didn't realize you were standing there."

Charlotte laughed. "No problem."

It was around two that afternoon when Charlotte stopped off at Patsy Dufour's to pick up her vacuum. When Patsy didn't answer the doorbell, Charlotte figured she would find her in the backyard.

Just as she rounded the back corner of the house, she came to an abrupt halt. Once again, the old song she'd hummed earlier came to mind. The large, ugly hole in

Patsy's backyard had been transformed overnight into a lovely pond, complete with a fountain in the middle. The mounds of dirt on either side of the hole had been leveled and carpeted with squares of lush green grass. Tropical plants and shrubbery had been added around the edges of the pond, and, almost like magic, the whole area had been turned into a serene, lush garden.

"Hey, watch it! Be careful with that." Patsy's loud command jerked Charlotte's attention toward the patio.

"That" turned out to be a huge statue. So why did it look familiar? Charlotte wondered as she narrowed her eyes in concentration. She'd seen that statue before . . . somewhere. But where?

"Of course," she murmured. If memory served her right, it was a copy of a famous Henry Moore sculpture, one called *Madonna and Child.* And a smaller, poor copy at that, she thought as she watched the two burly workers struggle to move it to the opposite side of the pond. As the workers positioned the statue near the edge of the pond, the sight of it opened a floodgate of memories for Charlotte, memories mostly of her father.

Though her father had made his living as a mechanic, he'd been a gentle man, an artist at heart. He'd loved all art forms, but his favorite had been sculptures. And he'd passed on that love to his oldest daughter.

Above all, Charlotte's parents had wanted her to get a college education. And she'd wanted that, too . . . until she'd met her son's father. Even after Hank Senior had been killed in Vietnam and Hank Junior had been born, her folks had still insisted that she continue her college education. It had been during her second semester that her father had urged her to take an art course, one that concentrated on modern sculptors, and she'd chosen Henry Moore and his works for her term paper.

A signal from Patsy caught Charlotte's eye, and Charlotte shook her head to dispel the painful memories. Patsy waved and held up her forefinger, indicating she'd be done in a minute. It was then that Charlotte realized that the statue was in place and that the men were in the process of moving a huge urn from beneath the portico.

The urn was almost as tall as the men moving it. The foot and lip of the vessel appeared to be about the same size, probably about two to three feet in diameter. But the girth of the urn had to be a good four or five feet in circumference. Unlike the many ornate ones she'd seen that decorated the famous aboveground cemeteries in and about New Orleans, the design of Patsy's urn was smooth and simplistic to the extreme. And though its simplicity was its beauty, it was also a major problem for the workers.

Getting a good hold on it was almost impossible. Both men were drenched in sweat from their efforts, and by the sounds of the grunts coming from them, Charlotte decided that the thing had to weigh an enormous amount.

The workers almost had it out from beneath the overhang of the porch. But the going was slow, and Charlotte began to wonder if they would be able to make it all the way to the pond.

"A whole person could fit inside that thing," she murmured, watching the men struggle.

"Be careful with that," Patsy demanded. "It's old and—"

The words had no sooner left Patsy's mouth when one of the men lost his grip and dropped his side. The movement caused the other worker's hold to slip, and the urn hit the flagstone patio with a resounding thud.

Patsy shrieked in horror. "Now look!" she cried. "Just look what you've done to my beautiful urn. You've cracked it."

Shading her eyes against the afternoon sun, Charlotte stepped closer. Sure enough, there was definitely a large half-moon–shaped crack on one side just above the foot of the base.

For long minutes, Patsy, the two workers, and Charlotte simply stared at the crack. Finally the larger of the two men spoke up. "It can be fixed, ma'am," he said nervously. "I—I know a man down in da Quarter who does dat kind of ting. He can fix it so you never know it wuz ever cracked."

Patsy shifted her gaze to glare at the worker. After several moments, she finally emitted a large sigh and nodded. "Yes—yes, of course it can," she retorted, straightening her back and lifting her chin. "But until then—" She motioned toward the porch with a jerky movement of her arm. "Let's move it back for the time being. But pu-lease—move it ve-ry carefully," she added, dragging out her words as if instructing a couple of two-year-olds instead of grown men.

Both workers looked so relieved it was comical. The larger of the two nodded at the smaller one. "On three," he said gruffly. Both men squared their feet on either side of the urn and each grabbed hold. "One . . . two . . . three—"

The moment the men picked up the urn and moved it, the cracked portion broke loose.

"Wait!" Patsy shouted. "Stop!"

But the men had already shuffled a couple of steps sideways and the damage was done.

"Oh, for pity's sake," Patsy cried, staring at the bottom portion that had fallen free. "Now look what you've done!"

But Charlotte went stone still. "Oh, no," she murmured, her eyes on the gaping hole in the bottom of the urn. The urn hadn't been empty, and almost immediately she recognized what had fallen out of the hole.

Bones.

Large bones that looked suspiciously like a hand and fingers. Charlotte shivered. But were they really human bones?

A deep dread spread within her. No matter how much she would have preferred them to be the bones of some poor animal who had crawled in the urn and died, she had a horrible feeling that they were exactly what they appeared to be.

"Charlotte? What's wrong?" Patsy glanced over at Charlotte.

At the moment Charlotte couldn't utter a sound, nor could she take her eyes off the bones. All she could do was point at the bones.

With a puzzled frown, Patsy followed Charlotte's gaze back to the hole, then stepped closer to the urn. As she bent to inspect the hole more closely, her eyes widened in horror. With an earsplitting scream, she threw up her hands to either side of her head and quickly backed away.

Chapter Four

Totally unnerved by Patsy's screams and unable to pull her gaze from the bones, Charlotte couldn't move at first. Only when she realized that no one else was moving either and Patsy had yet to stop screaming did she decide that someone had to do something.

Charlotte rushed over to Patsy. "It's okay." She pulled Patsy even farther away from the gruesome sight and placed herself squarely between Patsy and the urn. Keeping a firm hold on Patsy, she barked out instructions over her shoulder for the men. "Hey, one of you go call the police."

Both men were pale and seemed to be as mesmerized by the sight of the bones as Charlotte had been. Neither of them moved, nor did they show any indication that they had heard her. And no wonder, Charlotte thought, what with Patsy still screaming like a banshee.

Charlotte turned to Patsy, grabbed her by the shoulders, and shook as hard as she could. "Stop it! Stop that screaming right now, or I—I'll slap the fool out of you."

Patsy stopped screaming, but the moaning sounds she began making were almost as bad.

With a moan of her own, Charlotte turned back to the men. "Hey, you!" she yelled. "Snap out of it! Get a grip! I need some help here!"

As if coming out of a trance, the larger of the two men

blinked, shook his head, and finally looked her way.

"Go into the kitchen and call the police," Charlotte told him crossly. "And you"— she motioned at the other man—"don't touch anything else. Just leave it."

Getting Patsy into the house proved to be more of a problem than Charlotte expected. Sobbing and close to hysterics, Patsy didn't seem to hear anything Charlotte said to her, and all of Charlotte's attempts to calm her were useless.

But finally Charlotte had had enough. She signaled to the remaining worker. "I need some help here. I'd like to get her inside before the police come." When he just stared at her and didn't move, Charlotte felt like screaming herself. "Now!" she shouted. "I need help now!"

With the reluctant worker on one side of Patsy and Charlotte on the other side of her, they were able to force her to go inside the house. Once inside, they again had to force her to sit on the sofa.

"Thanks," Charlotte told the worker. "And just one more favor, please. Would you go out front and wait for the police? And when they get here, show them around back to the urn."

After the worker left, Charlotte hurried to the kitchen for a glass of water. If she could just get Patsy to drink something, maybe the poor woman would stop that horrible moaning and crying.

When Charlotte returned, Patsy had stopped the moaning only to take up babbling. She was staring straight ahead as she rocked back and forth on the sofa.

"Should have known better," she kept muttering. "If

something seems too good to be true, it usually is." She began shaking her head from side to side. "Too good to be true . . . too good to be true . . . no wonder that thing was so cheap . . . no wonder he sold it to me. But why? Why me? Why me?"

Half of what Patsy said didn't make a lick of sense to Charlotte, but after a bit of coaxing, she was able to get Patsy to drink some of the water. The moment she stopped drinking, though, she started babbling again, and Charlotte began to really get worried.

Charlotte had just about decided that she needed to call an ambulance and get Patsy some medical help when the sound of distant sirens reached her ears.

"Thanks goodness," she whispered.

Whether Patsy had simply gotten it all out of her system or just plain worn herself out, Charlotte wasn't sure. By the time the police arrived, she had stopped moaning and babbling and was staring into space with a vacant look that was almost as frightening to see as the bones had been.

Charlotte still didn't feel comfortable leaving her alone. Keeping a wary eye on Patsy, she stood at a window that overlooked the backyard and watched as one of the policemen questioned the workers while another officer knelt down near the urn. Something about the officer near the urn seemed vaguely familiar, but at the moment, Charlotte couldn't recall where or when she'd seen him before.

When he finally stood up again, he pulled a radio from his belt, said a few words, then joined the other officer and the two workers. The two officers talked a moment, then the one who had seemed familiar stepped away from the small group and headed toward the house.

By the time that he knocked at the back door, Charlotte was already there to open it. The moment she was face to face with the man, she recalled just why he'd seemed so familiar.

Charlotte's mouth went dry as dust and she swallowed hard. Maybe he wouldn't remember the last time they had met. She'd certainly like to forget it.

But one look at his expression told her no such luck. He remembered all right. He narrowed his eyes suspiciously. "Ms. LaRue, isn't it?"

Charlotte felt her cheeks grow warm, but she nodded. Things could be worse, she figured. At least this time he wasn't pointing a gun at her like he had been the first time they'd met. "Officer Joe . . ." Her voice trailed away when she couldn't recall his last name.

"Joe Blake, ma'am. And I need to ask you some questions—you and Ms. Dufour."

Charlotte moved back and motioned for him to come inside. "She's in there." Charlotte pointed toward the doorway leading to the small sitting room where she'd left Patsy. The officer stepped inside and Charlotte closed the door.

"I've called the crime lab unit and the detectives," he told her. "But I just need to clarify a couple of things before they get here."

"Does that mean that the bones are human?"

"I'm afraid it looks that way, ma'am."

"Can you tell if they're male or female?"

"That's something the crime-scene guys will have to determine."

Charlotte wasn't sure just why she'd asked that particular question, and, in fact, she wasn't sure of much of anything except that she really wanted to go home. She glanced toward the doorway to the room where she'd left Patsy. Surely now that the police were here, they would make sure that Patsy had the proper medical attention if she needed it.

She took a deep breath. *All he can say is no.* "Ah, Officer Blake, now that you're here, may I leave?"

He shook his head. "I think you know better."

Her mouth twisted in annoyance. Yes, she had known better, but it had been worth a try anyway.

"Now . . ." As if gathering up all the patience he could muster, he took a deep breath and sighed. "Why don't you tell me what you know."

Charlotte thought about it for a moment, then slowly shook her head. "Not much, I'm afraid. I got here just in time to see the men moving the urn. They lost their grip; it fell and cracked. Then, when they moved it"—she made a vague motion with her hand and shrugged— "the cracked part fell off."

"How long has Ms. Dufour had the urn?"

"I really don't know," she answered. "You see, Ms. Dufour uses my maid service, but one of my employees usually cleans for her."

"Usually?"

"She was ill yesterday, so I cleaned in her place. I'm just here today because I accidentally left my vacuum

60

cleaner here yesterday."

He stared at her for a moment, then nodded. "You said Ms. Dufour is in there." He pointed toward the door leading to where she'd left Patsy. Charlotte nodded and led him into the other room. Patsy had moved from the sofa to the same window that Charlotte had been standing at previously. When they entered the room, Patsy turned away from the window and gave a cursory glance at the officer before turning her attention to Charlotte.

"Patsy, this is Officer Blake," Charlotte told her.

The officer inclined his head. "Ms. Dufour, ma'am, I need to ask you a couple of questions." When Patsy slid her gaze his way, he continued. "How long have you had that urn?"

"About six months, I believe," she told him, her voice whispery soft and just a bit hesitant. "I believe it was back in September when I bought it."

"Where did it come from before you got it?"

"I-I really don't know. I bought it at a clearance sale down in the warehouse district. It came out of a warehouse on Tchoupitoulas. The new owner was getting rid of the contents so he could renovate the old building and turn it into condos instead."

A warehouse on Tchoupitoulas? Charlotte frowned as something niggled in the back of her mind.

"Did you arrange for the delivery, or did the owner have it delivered?"

"The owner had it delivered," Patsy whispered. "I paid him extra—a delivery charge."

But Charlotte was only half-listening, her mind still

61

on the warehouse. Why did anything to do with a ware-house on Tchoupitoulas sound familiar? It wasn't as if she ever went down to that part of the city . . . except years ago when the World's Fair was held in New Orleans. No, not that, she decided. It had to be something more recent. Maybe some kind of controversy about something. But what?

After a moment she gave a mental shrug when she couldn't recall any details and dismissed the familarity of the phrase "warehouse on Tchoupitoulas" as nothing important. It was probably just something she'd read in the newspaper or heard about on the news.

"Ma'am, the crime lab unit and the detectives should be here soon. Until then, if you remember anything significant, you might want to write it down so you can tell them."

"Like what?" Patsy asked.

"Well, for one, do you have any idea as to who those bones might belong to?"

Patsy's mouth worked like a fish, but when no sound came out, she covered her face with her hands and shook her head. "No," she finally moaned. "Why on earth would I know who they belonged to?"

"Now, now, ma'am," the officer soothed. "Don't get upset. I'm not accusing you of anything or saying that you do know. But the urn does belong to you, and if you've had it for six months, there's a possibility that without your knowledge, a body could have been placed inside while it was on your property. And, another thing: I'm sure the detectives will want to know the name of the person who sold it to you."

Patsy looked as if she was going to protest again when the sound of a loud rap on the back door interrupted.

"That's probably the detectives now," the officer told them.

He left the room, and a few minutes later another man appeared in the doorway.

Charlotte immediately recognized the man who entered the room. Out of all the detectives in the Sixth District, it was just her luck that the one who got this particular case would be Will Richeaux.

Louis had once called the detective a "snotty hotshot." At the time, Charlotte hadn't understood Louis's animosity toward the man. On the outside, Detective Will Richeaux was clean-cut and well-groomed, even handsome with his dark hair and piercing blue eyes. But how true the old saying, "Never judge a book by its cover," was. In Charlotte's opinion, he was a sleazy snake of a man who was both a liar and a cheat.

Will Richeaux had been Judith's partner for a while just before Louis retired. But the partnership had quickly escalated into more. Never mind that he was a married man with a child. Claiming that he was in the process of getting a divorce, he'd gone after Judith anyway. It was the oldest line in the world, and when Charlotte had found out about the affair, she'd told Judith so. Ultimately, thank goodness, Judith had come to her senses and finally realized that he'd just been stringing her along.

The detective stared hard at Charlotte for several seconds. His eyes were cold, but there was nothing about his expression that revealed what he was thinking.

He finally inclined his head at Charlotte. "Ms. LaRue."

Then his glance slid to Patsy. His eyes narrowed, and his lips thinned. "Ms. Dufour." He said her name in a sneering tone that made Charlotte frown. Still staring at Patsy, he said, "I'll need to ask you both some questions."

When he stepped farther into the room, Patsy abruptly stood. If possible, her already pale face paled even more. "You," she whispered, her eyes wide as she stared at the detective. "You're a cop?"

Charlotte's frown deepened. Patsy was acting like she'd just encountered the devil incarnate. What on earth was going on? She could understand Patsy being nervous about being questioned by the police. The whole thing made her nervous, too. But why fear? What would Patsy have to fear from Will Richeaux? And why had Will reacted so strangely to Patsy?

"Do you two know each other?" Charlotte asked Patsy.

"We've met before," the detective retorted before Patsy had the chance to answer. "Another incident." He glared at Patsy as if daring her to contradict him.

"I-I want a different detective," Patsy blurted out. "You—I—"

"Sit down, Ms. Dufour," he ordered. "This is my case, and the sooner we get on with it, the better everyone will feel." He continued to glare at Patsy until she finally gave in. Then he turned to Charlotte. "Ms. LaRue, step into the kitchen," he said, "I'd like to question you first."

The whole thing left a bad taste in Charlotte's mouth. Something was going on between Patsy and Will Richeaux, and that something, whatever it was, had Patsy scared half out of her wits.

"Ms. LaRue?"

Charlotte finally nodded. "Okay," she replied warily, her eyes still on Patsy. "But I don't know what I can tell you that I haven't already told the other officer."

"I'll be the judge of that," he shot back.

It was hard to miss the sarcasm underlying his reply, and though Charlotte felt like telling him to take a flying leap, she held her tongue. The sooner she answered his questions, the sooner she could go home.

With one last look at Patsy, Charlotte reluctantly moved into the kitchen. Will Richeaux stopped just inside the doorway, but Charlotte continued on to the other side of the island that was near the sink area in order to put some distance between the two of them.

"Okay, Ms. LaRue, why don't you tell me why you're here."

Charlotte didn't like Will Richeaux, and, unlike Patsy, she had no intention of allowing him to scare or intimidate her.

"I own a cleaning service," she told him. "And Ms. Dufour employs my cleaning service two days a week on Tuesdays and Thursdays."

"But today is Friday."

Charlotte ground her teeth. With barely veiled annoyance she grudgingly explained that because Nadia was ill, she accidentally had filled in for her. She was there today only because she had left the vacuum cleaner behind on Thursday.

"So *you* don't work here on a regular basis."

"No."

"And this Nadia, does she have a last name and an address?"

Charlotte glared at him. She was tempted to tell him that, no, Nadia was hatched from an egg, but instead she rattled off Nadia's name and address.

He jotted down what she told him in a small notebook. Then he asked, "Just how well do you know Ms. Dufour?"

"Ms. Dufour is a client."

When Charlotte offered nothing more, he simply stared at her with eyes that could chip ice. "O-kaay," he finally drawled after several moments more. "So"—he tilted his head forward—"why don't you tell me your version of what happened out there today."

All Charlotte wanted was to go home. As quickly and succinctly as she could, she repeated what she'd told the other officer earlier. Although at intervals Will Richeaux jotted down some of what she told him, for the most part, he simply listened and gave her what could only be described as intimidating looks.

When she'd finished, he glanced over the few notes he'd taken, then raised his gaze. "I guess that should do it for the time being. Now if you'll give me a number where I can reach you in case I have more questions, you can leave."

Charlotte told him her home phone number and her cell phone number.

"I guess that's all," he told her, then added, "for now."

"I can leave?"

He nodded and without another word headed for the back door.

Even though all Charlotte wanted was to leave right then and there, she decided to check on Patsy and let her know she was leaving. She found Patsy digging through a drawer of a small desk in the corner.

"Ah—Patsy? Excuse me, I was told I could leave. Are you going to be okay?"

Patsy paused a moment to glance over her shoulder. "I'll be fine," she said. "I'm trying to find the receipt for that urn. I need the exact date I bought it." She turned back to the desk. "I know it's in here . . . somewhere."

Charlotte hesitated a moment more. Patsy seemed okay now, seemed more like herself. But, still, Charlotte was reluctant to leave. Yet . . . if she seemed okay and said she was okay, then she must be okay. *Don't get involved!* With a shake of her head, Charlotte forced herself to leave the room and went in search of the vacuum cleaner she'd come for in the first place.

The vacuum was exactly where she'd left it the day before, still sitting in the corner of the dining room next to the kitchen. With the vacuum firmly in hand, Charlotte was finally ready to leave when she heard Will Richeaux come inside again through the kitchen door. She stepped to the entrance of the kitchen.

"I'm leaving now," she said. But as she turned to leave, the back storm door slammed and another man entered the kitchen. He was carrying a small plastic bag and was dressed in regular clothes, so she figured that he had to be another detective. More than likely, he was Will Richeaux's partner.

"What'cha got, Tom?" she heard Will Richeaux ask.

"We lucked out," the detective named Tom said and handed over the bag to Will. "It's a billfold. Found it inside the urn."

"Please tell me there's an I.D. still readable in that billfold."

Tom grinned. "Thanks to good old laminate, the driver's license is still readable."

"And?"

"License belongs to one Ricco Martinez," the detective said.

"Hmm . . . well . . ."

But Charlotte didn't hear the rest of what Will said to his partner. At the sound of Ricco's name, she went stone still and her heart began pumping overtime. Nadia's abusive ex-boyfriend.

If the billfold had belonged to Ricco, did that mean that the identity of the skeleton in the urn was Ricco?

Chapter Five

O nce Charlotte got over the initial shock of hearing that the bones might possibly belong to Ricco, all she could think about was leaving, getting out of there and going home.

Feeling as if she were in a fog, she forced herself to move. Clutching the vacuum with both hands, she turned and stumbled down the hallway toward the front door.

But seated in the driver's seat of the van, instead of

going home, she simply sat staring at nothing while her mind struggled to sort out what she'd just seen and overheard.

It had been almost a year since Ricco Martinez had been arrested as a member of one of the gangs that had been caught stealing cemetery artifacts. Because of Daniel's help, Ricco had been released from jail, but then Ricco had immediately disappeared. And no one had seen or heard from him since.

Could the skeleton really be Ricco's? If it was, then that would certainly explain why no one had seen or heard from him. But if the skeleton was Ricco's, then how on earth had he ended up in the urn to begin with? And who had put him there?

"Ma'am, are you okay?"

The sudden intrusion of the deep male voice gave Charlotte a start. Her heart thumping against her rib cage, she jerked her head around to the window. Standing just a couple of feet away was Joe Blake, the police officer who had first questioned her.

"I—I'm f-fine," she stuttered. "I—" But words escaped her.

"Are you sure, ma'am? You look kinda pale."

Charlotte forced a quick smile. "Just tired." She reached down and switched on the ignition. The last thing she wanted was another conversation with the police. "Just need to get home," she told him.

Though he didn't look convinced, he nodded. "Take it easy, Ms. LaRue."

Charlotte barely remembered the short drive home

because of the myriad of questions swirling through her head. What if the skeleton did turn out to be Ricco's? What about Nadia and Daniel . . . and Davy? What was going to happen when they found out?

"Poor little guy," she murmured, her thoughts mostly on Davy. Even if Daniel did adopt him, one of these days Davy would want to know about what had happened to his real father. How awful it would be to find out that your father had been murdered and stuffed into an urn like so much garbage.

Charlotte shuddered. What kind of person would do such a thing to another human being? And why?

If you lie down with dogs, expect to get fleas. The minute the old saying popped into her head, she muttered, "Yeah, yeah, and birds of a feather and all of that stuff." But as much as she would have liked to dismiss the adages as having no relevance to reality, there was no dismissing the truth in them. Ricco had chosen to associate with criminals, the kind of people who were liars, thieves, and possibly even murderers, and for his association, he'd ended up dead.

So what now? she wondered. Should she tell Nadia and Daniel or not? *Mind your own business.*

What if she told them and then it turned out that the skeleton wasn't Ricco after all? *Mind your own business.*

But what if she didn't tell them and the skeleton was Ricco's? *Mind your own business.*

"Okay, okay," she answered the nagging voice in her head. Two of the things that Charlotte disliked with a passion were gossips and busybodies. Whether work-related or personal, she'd always adhered to the policy of minding her own business, and she expected others to do the same. She figured that taking care of her own problems was enough to handle without borrowing other people's problems or prying into others' lives.

Just as she turned into her driveway, it suddenly hit her that whether the skeleton was Ricco's or someone else's, Nadia would be one of the first people the police would want to question, not only because of her relationship with Ricco but also because she worked for Patsy. And the police would find out about Nadia and Ricco's relationship. Of that she had no doubt, especially since Will Richeaux had asked for Nadia's name and address. And if the skeleton did turn out to be Ricco's, then . . .

A cold knot formed in her stomach. Nadia wasn't just an employee any longer. She was family. Whether Charlotte wanted to get involved or not, now she had no choice. This *was* her business. Family business. Panic welled in her throat. *Call Daniel. Call him now!*

Charlotte snatched her cell phone out of her purse, then realized that she didn't know Daniel's phone number by heart. Shoving the phone back into her purse, she slammed out of the van and ran up the steps. At the door her hand shook so badly that it took several attempts before she was finally able to fit the key into the lock.

Inside, she threw her purse onto the sofa and made a beeline for the telephone. She glanced up at the cuckoo clock. Daniel should still be at the office, she decided as she fumbled through the Rolodex until she was able to locate his work number.

As if sensing her panic, Sweety Boy squawked, and, wings flapping, he paced back and forth along his perch inside the birdcage.

Her foot tapping impatiently, Charlotte ignored the little bird as she waited for the receptionist at Daniel's law firm to put her through to his office.

"Hey, Aunt Charley!" Daniel said the minute he came on the line. "What's up?"

"I need to see you right away," she told him.

"What's wrong, Auntie?"

"Not over the phone," she replied. "I need to talk to you face to face."

"Aunt Charley, has something happened? Nadia or Davy? Judith or Mom?"

"No—nothing like that, hon."

"Can it wait until—"

"No! It can't wait. I need to see you now," she insisted.

"Hey, Auntie, try and calm down. I'm on my way. Okay?"

"Okay."

It seemed like an eternity before Charlotte finally heard the sound of a car pulling into her driveway. She rushed over to the window and peeked out, just to make sure.

"Oh no," she groaned. "Not now!" What to do . . . what to do? Any other time she would have welcomed a visit from her sister, especially after their recent altercation being resolved. But not today and not now. And especially not with Daniel on his way over.

So how could she get rid of her? Charlotte glanced around the room as if it held the answer. Then inspiration struck. She grabbed her purse and keys and headed for the door. She opened the door just in time to see Madeline climbing the steps to the porch.

Charlotte pasted a surprised look on her face. "Oh— Maddie! Hi, there."

Madeline paused on the top step, her eyes straying to Charlotte's purse. "You on your way out?"

Charlotte nodded and tried to look disappointed. "Afraid so. An appointment—I have an appointment." It wasn't totally a lie, she consoled herself. She did have an appointment of sorts with Daniel.

Liar liar, pants on fire. Charlotte ignored the accusing voice in her head. "Sorry, Maddie. If I had known you were coming . . ." She shrugged and deliberately left the sentence unfinished.

"It's okay," Madeline said. "I couldn't have stayed long anyway. I just dropped by to give you this." She held a small sack. "It's a peace offering."

Words stuck in Charlotte's throat as she accepted the sack, and shame for deceiving her sister filled her.

"I know you're not supposed to have a lot of sugar," Madeline continued, "but I also know how much you love pralines. So I stopped off at Jax Brewery and got some fresh ones. Maybe if you just eat half of one every other day or so, it won't hurt."

"Thanks, Maddie," Charlotte whispered. "I'm sure that half of one every day or so won't hurt, but you didn't have to do that."

Madeline smiled. "Oh yes I did. If nothing else, it

makes *me* feel better. And besides, I snitched one on the way over here, and, boy, was it ever yummy."

Charlotte laughed, and, feeling like the biggest hypocrite and liar that ever lived, she turned and locked the front door.

Madeline only hesitated a moment more before she took the hint. "Well . . . guess I'd better go now and let you get on your way."

"Thanks again, Maddie," Charlotte called out after her as Madeline headed for her car.

Madeline opened the car door, smiled back at Charlotte, and gave a little wave. Then she climbed into her car, leaving Charlotte still standing on the porch to battle with her conscience.

The second her sister's car disappeared down the street, Charlotte unlocked the front door and went back inside.

Maybe a praline would make her feel better, she thought, eyeing the sack.

It would serve you right if you choked on one. With a groan and clutching the sack, Charlotte marched into the kitchen and deliberately placed the sack on the counter. Only minutes had passed before the sound of a car door slamming reached her ears.

Please let this be Daniel, she prayed, hurrying back to the living room. Peeking out the window, she sighed with relief as she watched Daniel approach the steps to the porch.

"Talk about a close call," Charlotte murmured. A little too close for comfort. Thank goodness that Milan was a one-way street, she thought as she headed for the door.

Otherwise, Daniel and Madeline would have passed each other.

But Charlotte's relief was short-lived as the memory of the reason for Daniel's visit settled around her like a cloak of doom. Even though she was expecting Daniel to knock or ring the doorbell, she still jumped when he rapped on the door.

Taking a deep breath and whispering a quick prayer that she was doing the right thing, Charlotte opened the door.

"Come in, Daniel."

He brushed past her, then turned to face her, his expression tight with worry and concern. "What's going on, Aunt Charley?"

Charlotte closed the door and motioned toward the sofa. "Let's sit down."

Daniel's lips thinned with impatience, but he did as she asked. Once they were seated, Charlotte began. "As you may or may not know, I worked in Nadia's place for Patsy Dufour yesterday."

Daniel nodded. Charlotte went on to explain about leaving her vacuum and about going back to Patsy's house to pick it up earlier that day. She also told him about the pond and the men moving the statues and the urn. "The urn was heavy, though," she said. "Too heavy. The men dropped it, and it cracked. And when they moved it again, the cracked portion fell—"

"Aunt Charley," Daniel interrupted, holding up his hand, "I don't mean to be rude, but what does any of this have to do with me, and why all the urgency?"

"Be patient, Daniel. Please. You'll understand in

just a minute. Okay?"

Once he nodded, she continued. "There were bones inside that urn. Human bones."

"What?"

Charlotte held up a hand. "Just let me finish. We called the police, and when they showed up, they confirmed it. They questioned all of us—the two workers, Patsy Dufour, and me. When the detective finally said I could leave, the other detective came in with a billfold they'd found in the urn. Daniel, honey"—Charlotte reached over and squeezed his arm—"that billfold belonged to Ricco Martinez."

Daniel blanched. "Martinez?" he whispered.

"They—the crime-scene team—found Ricco's driver's license inside the billfold."

For what felt like an eternity, Daniel simply stared at her with a stunned look of disbelief. When he finally found his voice, it was a harsh whisper. "Are—are they sure?"

Charlotte slowly shook her head. "I don't think they're absolutely sure. I figure they'll have to do some further testing—forensic stuff or something like that to be certain. But you see now why I needed to tell you, don't you? One way or another they'll want to question Nadia . . . and probably you, too," she added, "since you're the one who arranged for him to get out of jail."

Daniel shoved his fingers through his hair, then abruptly stood and began pacing. After a moment, he sat back down. Turning toward Charlotte, he took her hands in his own. "Okay, Auntie, as best as you can remember, I need to know everything. I need to know exactly what the police did and said. Who were the detectives—their names—and what kind of questions did they ask? Think you can remember all of that for me?"

Charlotte nodded, and with a reassuring squeeze, Daniel released her hands.

"The detective who questioned me was Judith's ex-partner, Will Richeaux," she told him. She waited a heartbeat to see if Daniel had any kind of reaction to his sister's ex-partner's name. But Daniel's only reaction was a frown.

"Guess I didn't realize they weren't partners anymore," he commented.

When he said nothing more about it, a wave of relief rippled through Charlotte. Thank goodness he didn't know about the affair his sister had had with Will Richeaux. On top of everything else, she didn't want to be the one to have to explain about that, too. As far as she knew, she was the only member of the family who had known about the disastrous affair. Of course, Louis had known about it, but he didn't count.

Charlotte cleared her throat. "The other detective's name was Tom," she continued, "but I never heard his last name. Anyway, Detective Richeaux was the one who asked all the questions. He questioned me first," she explained, then she went on to tell Daniel exactly what Will had asked her and Patsy. When she got to the part where Patsy had mentioned that she'd bought the urn at an old warehouse, Charlotte's voice trailed off.

What was it about that warehouse? Out of the clear blue, she suddenly remembered. "That's why!" she exclaimed. "That's why it sounded so familiar."

Daniel's brow furrowed with confusion. "Why what sounded so familiar?"

"The address—the address of the warehouse where Patsy bought the urn. It's the same one—no, wait." She slowly shook her head. "That can't be right. Remember back when you got Ricco out of jail? Not long after that, a bunch of stuff—statues and things—were discovered in the back room of an old warehouse. The warehouse had been sold, and when the new owners started their renovations, they found some of the stolen cemetery artifacts there."

Daniel still had a blank look on his face.

"It was in the paper for days."

When he finally nodded, she continued. "Well, supposedly the police confiscated all of it. For evidence," she added. "But if they confiscated it all, then how could Patsy have bought the urn there?" Another thought occurred to her. "Patsy said 'he,'" she murmured. *No wonder he sold it to me.* So who was 'he'? Charlotte wondered.

Daniel shifted and turned so that he faced her. "Look, Aunt Charley, I vaguely remember reading about that stuff being found, but right now I think there are more urgent problems to consider. I'm more concerned about Nadia and what all of this is going to do to her . . . and to Davy," he added in a whisper. "Poor little guy."

Daniel's voice was hoarse with emotion, and Charlotte strongly suspected that he was remembering his own loss so many years ago. Though Daniel and Judith's father hadn't died, he might as well have. When he'd divorced their mother, it was as if he'd divorced his children, too, leaving them to forever wonder what they had done so wrong that their own father would have nothing to do with them.

"Davy still remembers his father, you know," Daniel continued. "Still talks about him and even dreams about him sometimes."

Charlotte's throat tightened with sympathy. "Oh, honey, you're right. I'm so very sorry."

"No, it's okay," Daniel assured her. "But tell me, Auntie . . ." He paused. "How do you explain to a three-year-old that his father is dead?"

"Not very easily, I'm afraid," she murmured. Like Daniel, Charlotte also knew about loss, knew what it felt like to lose someone you love. Unlike Daniel, her loss had been permanent. She'd been eighteen when Hank's father had died. Then, only two years later, her own parents had been killed in a horrible accident. But Charlotte had been old enough to understand about death. Davy . . . Davy was just a child, a very young child.

Daniel stared past Charlotte for several moments. "No, not easy at all." After a moment he drew in a deep breath. "Right now, though, I need to break the news to Nadia—prepare her for when the police show up. And they will show up," he added. "You can bet on it. If, in fact, those bones do belong to Ricco, there's a good chance that Nadia could end up being their number one suspect. We might have some time, though, depending on how long it takes them to confirm the identity. But not much."

"Daniel, I'm sure they will want to question Nadia, but what about those people he ran around with, the other thieves who were arrested with him? Seems to me that they'd be a lot more suspect than an upstanding citizen like Nadia?" Charlotte hesitated, her mind mulling over the events. "Of course, there's another possibility as well. Maybe, just maybe, the skeleton isn't Ricco," she suggested. "It's possible it *could* be someone else."

After a moment, he gave a one-shouldered shrug, and, though he still looked skeptical, he said, "I suppose anything's possible. But you and I both know that's a long shot. What other reason would his billfold be in the urn?"

Charlotte thought about it for a minute. "There *could* be other reasons," she said. "Who knows? Maybe it was stolen or he just lost it. Maybe the person in the urn is a pickpocket. Or maybe the person in the urn simply found it on the street somewhere—maybe a homeless person."

"Maybe," Daniel said. "But I doubt it. Regardless, I still have to warn Nadia."

Charlotte narrowed her eyes. "Why do you think she would be a suspect in the first place? I know they lived together and all, but—"

"I don't think it," he said. "But the police will, once they check their files and start digging into Ricco and Nadia's backgrounds. Ricco Martinez was an abusive bastard—sorry, Auntie, but that's exactly what he was. Nadia and Davy both have the mental and physical scars to prove it. And there are hospital records— emergency-room reports. One time he broke her arm.

Another time he split her lip. Of course, she told the hospital she'd fallen, but if the police dig deep enough . . ." He shrugged.

Charlotte was shocked at what Daniel was telling her. But at the same time, a deep anger took root within. She never had liked Ricco Martinez, and now she knew why. Maybe all along she'd sensed what kind of man he was.

She frowned. "There's something I don't understand. If Ricco was abusive to her, why was she so anxious to get him released from jail? Looks like she would have been glad that he was in jail. And if I remember right, she told me—"

"Oh, I know all about what she told you, Auntie— about Davy missing his father, crying for him. It was all a bunch of bull to get you to help her. Ricco had used his one phone call from jail to call her. He'd told her that if she didn't find a way to get him out, she and Davy would live to regret it. He claimed he had connections to certain people who would make sure they regretted it." He shook his head. "Can you imagine? A father threatening his own little boy like that. What a sleazebag."

The anger within Charlotte grew. "Humph! Worse than a sleazebag, if you ask me," she answered. Threatening anyone was bad enough, but threatening an innocent child was reprehensible.

Daniel abruptly stood. "I need to get home now."

Charlotte stood, too.

"One thing, though," Daniel said. "I hate to ask you, but would you mind going with me to tell Nadia about all of this? She respects you, and I think she'd be glad you were there—you know, for moral support and all. I would really appreciate it."

Charlotte nodded. "Of course, hon. Just give me a minute and I'll follow you in my van. That way you won't have to worry about bringing me back home."

New Orleans is divided into distinctive sections by the natives. There's the CBD, which is the Central Business District, the French Quarter, the Garden District, the Irish Channel, New Orleans East, Uptown, Downtown, and more, depending on who is talking.

Daniel's home, like Charlotte's, was located in Uptown, but his home was in the Broadmoor area of Uptown. The drive from Charlotte's to Daniel's could take anywhere between five to ten minutes. Travel time depended on the route taken and the time of day. It also depended on the amount of traffic congestion along the stretch of South Claiborne where repairs were being done to the city's century-old water lines running beneath what most people in the rest of the country would call the median. New Orleanians referred to the strip of land that separated a street's lanes of traffic as simply "the neutral ground."

Six P.M. traffic was light. As Charlotte sat waiting behind Daniel at the traffic light at St. Charles Avenue, her stomach growled, and she was wishing that she'd grabbed a quick sandwich before they'd left. But not even the thought of food distracted her for long. Like a nagging toothache, she kept going over the conversation she'd had with Daniel—more specifically, the part about Nadia being a suspect.

"Not fair," she murmured. "Just plain not fair." Of all the people she knew, Nadia was the least likely to be a suspect for anything, much less murder. But considering the fact that she'd been abused by Ricco . . .

Charlotte shook her head. "No way," she whispered. Even though Ricco had abused Nadia, Charlotte still couldn't imagine Nadia killing him. It just wasn't logical. Unless she was defending Davy. . . .

But if, by some stretch of the imagination, Charlotte could believe Nadia had somehow managed to kill Ricco, there was still the fact that he had been stuffed into the urn. Since Nadia wasn't much bigger than Charlotte, it would have been physically impossible.

Not if she'd turned the urn on its side. In her mind's eye, Charlotte pictured the two large men in Patsy's yard struggling to even move the heavy urn. "No way," Charlotte whispered again. There was simply no way Nadia could have handled that heavy urn by herself.

A horn suddenly blared behind her, and Charlotte jumped. The traffic light had turned green. "Okay, okay," she muttered. "Just keep your shirt on." She eased the van across St. Charles Avenue.

The killer had to have been a man, she decided as she bumped across the streetcar tracks that ran down the middle of St. Charles. And a big man at that. A man a least the size of Daniel. . . .

Daniel.

Chapter Six

U ntil that very moment, the possibility of Daniel being considered a suspect had not even entered Charlotte's mind. But it should have, considering his intimate involvement with Nadia. Not for one second did Charlotte think that Daniel would have done such a horrible thing. She didn't. And he wouldn't. Not her Daniel, who was funny and smart, yet sweet and kind. Not in a million years. Besides, as an attorney, he was an officer of the court. That fact, along with his impeccable moral and spiritual convictions, was more than enough reason for Charlotte to reject the possibility of Daniel being a murderer.

But the police might think differently. Charlotte grimaced, and a hard knot of fear grew in her stomach. There was no "might" about it. If Nadia was their number one suspect, then Daniel would definitely be their number two suspect. Maybe even their number one, especially once they learned about his and Nadia's relationship during the past six months and their recent marriage.

Charlotte's hands trembled as she parked the van in the tight space between two vehicles alongside the curb in front of Daniel's house.

Stop it! Stop it right now. You're letting your imagination get the better of you. "Or else reading too many mystery novels," she whispered to herself. Everyone was suspect in a mystery novel.

For as long as she could remember, she'd always had

an active imagination. But having an active imagination could be both a blessing and curse, and Charlotte
sometimes envied those who could go along life's
merry way, taking things strictly at face value. Right
now, having an active imagination was definitely a
curse, she decided.

Maybe she should start reading romance novels
instead. Most of those were upbeat and, well, romantic.
And they always had a happy ending. Maybe she would
try one by that local author everyone was always talking
about, the one who lived in Daniel's neighborhood. But
what was her name? Rexanne something. Maybe
Becnel? Yep, that was it. Rexanne Becnel.

"Aunt Charley?"

Daniel's voice outside the window of the van gave her
a start. She jerked her head to the left just as he opened
her door.

"Is something wrong?" He leaned down to peer in at
her, his hand on the edge of the door.

"Ah—no, hon. Just wool-gathering. Something I
seem to be doing a lot of lately." She removed the keys
from the ignition, collected her purse, and climbed out
of the van. Daniel slammed the door shut. After she
locked it, she followed him around the front of the van
into the yard.

They were halfway to the steps leading up to the
porch when Charlotte reached out and took him by the
arm. "Daniel—hold up a sec." He stopped. "On the
way here I was thinking. Have you considered that
Nadia might not be the only suspect in all of this?
What I mean to say is—and not that *I* would ever

85

think such a thing—but the police might consider you a suspect as well."

Daniel smiled indulgently. "Oh, Auntie, you're something else." He gave her a quick hug. "And, yes, of course I've considered that possibility. You forget I'm a lawyer. And as a lawyer, I've defended a lot of clients who were suspects, so I do know a bit about such things."

"Oh, hon, of course you do." Her cheeks grew hot. "I didn't mean to imply otherwise. It's just that I—I—"

You what, silly woman?

Daniel chuckled. "It's okay, Auntie. No reason to be embarrassed, and no explanation necessary." He suddenly sobered. "I'm not worried about me, though. I'm more worried about Nadia and Davy. I have to tell you, Aunt Charley, I'm not looking forward to this, and I'm really glad you're here."

Though not nearly as large or as ostentatious as the historical houses found in the Garden District, Daniel's home was impressive in its own way. The two-story Mediterranean-style house with its salmon-colored stucco and its red-tiled roof had been built in the 1920s and was an elegant example of Spanish architecture.

The house had come on the market when interest rates were down and at a time when Daniel had decided he'd had enough of apartment living. In the two years since he'd bought the house, real estate values had skyrocketed, and his purchase had proved to be an extremely wise investment.

Charlotte followed Daniel to the steps leading up to

the porch. They were halfway up the steps when they heard a commotion from inside at the door. Then, even though the little boy's voice was a bit muffled, they heard him yelling, "Mommy, Daddy Danol! Daddy Danol here!"

Within seconds, the front door abruptly swung open. Like a miniature tornado, the little boy raced onto the porch. When he saw Charlotte he skidded to a sudden halt. Then he spied Daniel just behind her and made a beeline for him.

Daniel scooped Davy up into his arms. "Hey, there, buddy!"

The little boy giggled with delight. "I wait for you," he chortled. "Just like Mommy said."

"You did? That's great!"

"Davy! Come back—" Nadia appeared at the doorway. Her hands were on her hips and her face was a picture of frustration. She froze in the doorway at the sight of Charlotte. "Oh—Hi, Charlotte." She stepped onto the porch. "This is a nice surprise. I didn't realize we had company."

Charlotte smiled and stepped closer. "Not company, hon." She opened her arms and pulled Nadia into a hug. "We're family now," she said as she released her.

Nadia returned Charlotte's smile, but her smile quickly faded into a frown, and, with eyes narrowed, she turned her attention back to Davy. "You—you little scamp." She shook her finger at him. "How many times have I told you not to open that front door without me being there? What am I going to do with you?"

Davy ignored her by burying his face against Daniel's

shoulder. With a wink for Charlotte, Daniel tilted his head down and whispered loudly next to Davy's ear, "Uh oh, buddy, sounds like you're in trouble." When the little boy just burrowed his face deeper into Daniel's shoulder, Daniel chuckled. Then he stepped closer to Nadia, leaned over and kissed her. "Guess I'd better get that security chain put up after all, huh?"

"I put it up myself this morning," she told him. "For all the good it did," she added. "I made the mistake of telling him it was time for you to come home, and for the past half hour, he's been watching out the window for you. I only left the room for a minute, but that's all it took. The little devil pulled a chair up to the door and unlatched it."

Davy turned his head and glared at his mother. "I not devil. Devil's monster."

"Of course you're not, darling." She reached up and patted his back. "Mommy was just being silly." With an oh-well sigh, she faced Charlotte. "The place is a mess, but come on in." She motioned for Charlotte to precede her. "I'm still unpacking, but with both of us working, then me being sick . . ." She followed Charlotte inside. "I just can't seem to get it all done."

"Feeling better?" Charlotte asked.

Nadia nodded. "Better than yesterday."

Daniel followed them inside and closed the door.

The living room was large, with a high ceiling and two oversized windows that framed a fireplace on one wall. There were several packing boxes stacked in a corner and a small pile of children's books on the floor near one of the windows, but otherwise the room was orderly and spotless.

"You've made quite a few changes since the last time I was here," Charlotte told Daniel, her gaze lighting on the sofa. "That's a beautiful sofa. Much nicer than that other one you had. Must be new."

Daniel nodded. "Yes ma'am, it is. We couldn't decide whether to use the old one Nadia had or that old one I had, so we figured the best thing was to get rid of both of the old ones and buy a new one."

"Well, I love it. You both made an excellent choice."

"Thanks," Nadia said. "It's really comfortable." She motioned toward the sofa. "Have a seat. Try it out. And I'll get you something to drink. Coffee? Iced tea?"

Charlotte hesitated, unsure of just how Daniel wanted to handle telling her the news about Ricco.

As if he'd read her mind, Daniel shifted Davy in his arms and said, "Why don't we wait a few minutes on the drinks, honey. I'm afraid I have some bad news."

Charlotte held out her arms. "Why don't I take Davy into the kitchen?"

Nadia stared first at Daniel, then at Charlotte. "What's going on?"

"In a minute," Daniel told her. "I'll explain in a minute." To Charlotte he said, "Maybe that would be best for the moment, Auntie." He lowered Davy to the floor, then knelt down to the little boy's level. Gently cupping Davy's chin, he said, "But Davy's a big boy, aren't you, buddy?" When Davy grinned, Daniel released his hold on the little boy.

Davy nodded enthusiastically. "I big boy," he repeated.

"And big boys walk, don't they?"

Again Davy nodded.

"So, big fella, why don't you show Aunt Charley where the kitchen is? And maybe she can find you a cookie—" He glanced up at Nadia. "If that's okay with your mom."

"It's okay," she said. "He's already had his supper."

"Well, then." Charlotte held out her hand to Davy. "Let's you and me go find those cookies."

Davy grabbed her hand. "I show you, Aunt Chardy." He tugged on Charlotte's hand, and with a sympathetic but encouraging look for Daniel, she followed Davy out of the room.

"What's going on?" Charlotte heard Nadia ask as she led Davy down the hallway. But Davy was chattering away, and there was no way she could hear the rest of the conversation.

Charlotte tried to give Daniel and Nadia time, but once Davy got his cookie, it was hard to distract him for very long. The little boy adored Daniel, and since his precious "Daddy Danol" was home, he wanted to be with him.

When Charlotte and Davy returned to the living room, Daniel was seated on the sofa next to Nadia with his arm around her shoulders. Nadia was pale and staring straight forward with unseeing eyes.

Davy went straight to Daniel and crawled up into his lap. Only then did Nadia seem to realize that the little boy and Charlotte had returned from the kitchen. With a lost look, her gaze shifted back and forth between Charlotte and Daniel. "They're going to think I did it, aren't they?" she whispered in a strained voice.

"Right now all they want to do is question you," Charlotte told her firmly.

"B-but th-they'll think I did it!" her voice rose.

"Nadia, honey, don't—" Daniel reached out, but Nadia shrugged away his hand and abruptly stood.

"Why?" she cried. Wringing her hands, she began pacing between the door and the sofa. "All I ever wanted was a little happiness for me and my son. And now this!" She suddenly stopped and whirled to face Charlotte. "Oh, Charlotte, what if they arrest me? What if they take Davy away from me?"

Charlotte quickly closed the distance between them. "Nadia, stop it," she told her and took a firm hold of both her upper arms. Slowly and forcefully for emphasis, she said, "All they want is to question you. Don't borrow trouble, hon. Panicking will only make things worse. And *nobody* is going to take Davy from you," she added.

"You're right," Nadia murmured. "I know you're right, but—" Tears filled her eyes and spilled onto her cheeks.

Charlotte drew her into her arms and held her while she shook with silent sobs.

"Why Mommy cryin'?" Davy's wide eyes were focused on his mother, and his lower lip began to quiver.

"Mommy's just sad," Daniel told him. "Grown-ups get sad sometimes and need a hug."

"I hug Mommy."

"In a minute, buddy. In a minute we'll both hug Mommy."

Charlotte patted Nadia on the back. "Try and calm down now, hon," she murmured. "For Davy's sake if nothing else. It's okay. Everything will be okay."

But even as Charlotte spoke the soothing, reassuring words, she couldn't shake the ominous feeling that settled in her stomach like a chunk of lead.

When Charlotte left a few minutes later, Nadia seemed more in control of her emotions. Yet, as Daniel, Davy, and Nadia waved good-bye from the porch and Charlotte drove away, the uneasy feeling she'd had returned.

What if they arrest me? What if they take Davy away from me? Nadia's plaintive words stayed in her mind. Contrary to the assurances she'd given the young woman, and no matter how much she tried to convince herself that Nadia's fears were unfounded, the ominous feeling of doom just simply wouldn't go away.

Chapter Seven

Charlotte slept fitfully that night and awakened much earlier than normal on Saturday morning. Though she tried to blame her restlessness on the spicy tacos she'd picked up when she'd left Daniel's and on the fact that she'd eaten much later than usual, she knew the real reason was her worry about Daniel and Nadia.

Wondering if anything would be written up in the newspaper yet about the discovery of the skeleton, she took only enough time to go to the bathroom before grabbing her robe and heading for the kitchen. After she'd switched on the coffeepot, she made a beeline for the front porch to get the newspaper.

Though it should have been daylight outside, the sky was so overcast with dark clouds that it seemed as if it were still nighttime. The air was sticky-warm, and there was a smell of impending rain.

Charlotte spotted the newspaper on the bottom step. Just as she bent down to pick it up, the Doberman across the street growled and began barking and jumping on the fence.

"Aggravating mutt, isn't he?"

With a yelp of surprise, Charlotte whirled around to see Louis standing in the doorway of his half of the double. He was wearing a thick terry robe, and, from the looks of his bare, hairy legs, that was all he was wearing.

"I hope you know you just scared the daylights out of me. Again," she added, thinking of the ladder incident.

"Well, I didn't do it on purpose. And why so jumpy lately? Didn't you hear the door opening?"

She waved vaguely toward the house across the street. "How could I, with Prince over there making such a racket? Besides, you've oiled everything and anything around here that even thought about squeaking." And it was true. One of the first things he'd done after he'd moved in was to oil all of the noisy hinges on the doors.

"Hey!" He raised his hands in surrender. "I'm sorry, okay?" He stepped out onto the porch. "I heard you moving around, and I was coming over to ask if I could borrow some coffee. Oh, and, by the way, that robe really looks good on you."

Charlotte's cheeks grew warm, and she stepped back onto the porch. The only noise she'd made that he could have possibly heard was when she'd flushed the toilet. Maybe she should think about adding more insulation in the wall that connected the two halves of the double.

As for the leopard-print satin robe, she still wasn't really comfortable wearing it, mostly, she suspected, because it had been Louis's present to her for her six-tieth birthday party. Each time she thought about Louis shopping for her in Victoria's Secret she wanted to squirm with embarrassment.

"I meant to pick some coffee up yesterday," he continued. "But—" He shrugged. "I never got around to it. All I need is enough for a pot."

Charlotte walked to the door. "Come on in, and I'll get you some."

The moment that Louis walked into the living room, Sweety Boy squawked in protest beneath the cover over his cage.

"What is it with that bird of yours?" Louis said, glaring at the cage as he passed it. "Every time I come in, he sets up a ruckus."

Charlotte just shook her head. "I honestly don't know, unless you somehow remind him of his previous owner."

"Oh, that's just peachy. Didn't you tell me that his previous owner had left him to starve to death and skipped out on paying you back rent he owed?"

"Well . . . yeah, but if it makes you feel any better,

Sweety acts that way when Madeline comes over, too."

Louis grimaced. "Oh, right, that makes me feel a lot better," he muttered, sarcasm dripping with each word as he followed her through to the kitchen.

As Charlotte spooned out coffee into a Ziploc bag, she noticed Louis eyeing the freshly brewed coffee on the cabinet. She zipped the bag, handed it to Louis, and once she'd put away the coffee, she poured two cups from the pot.

"Here." She handed him one of the cups. "You might as well go ahead and have some."

Louis accepted the cup without a protest and immediately took a sip, then smacked his lips. "Mmm, thanks. Just what I needed," he said, propping himself against the cabinet. "Now, don't get testy, but I couldn't help noticing that you got in kind of late last night. Everything okay?"

Charlotte took her own coffee and sat down at the table. Normally she would have taken exception to his keeping tabs on her, but for a change, and considering the circumstances, she found it somewhat comforting. Besides, Louis might be able to help.

"No, everything is not okay," she answered. "Not exactly." After only a moment of hesitation, she launched right in and told him about the discovery of the skeleton in the urn, and finished up by sharing her fears about Nadia and Daniel being suspects.

For long moments, Louis didn't respond, but she could tell he was mulling it all over in his head. Never one to mince words, he finally said, "You're right to worry." He shoved away from the cabinet and seated himself across the table from her. "If, in fact, those bones do belong to Martinez, Nadia and Daniel will be suspects." He frowned. "You said that Will Richeaux is one of the investigating detectives?"

Charlotte nodded.

"Great," he muttered sarcastically. "Not good, not good at all."

Charlotte already half-suspected the answer, but she asked, "Why?" anyway.

Louis shot her a derisive look. "Aw, come on, Charlotte. You and I both know why, especially considering that Judith is Daniel's sister."

"But what about those others, those people Ricco ran around with? They weren't exactly upright citizens. Wouldn't they be suspect first? Besides, I thought cops stuck together. Loyalty and brotherhood, and all of that stuff. Surely Will Richeaux wouldn't— Not just because—" But she knew he could and he would, if given the opportunity. Any man who would cheat and lie would certainly be capable of revenge.

"Aw, come on, Charlotte. Judith didn't exactly keep it a secret why she put in for a new partner, and Willy boy got himself into hot water because of it. Not only with the captain, but word got back to his wife. Now she's threatening divorce, or so I hear. Threatening to take him to the cleaners. Even hired herself a big-time fancy lawyer. And guess who Mr. Hotshot blames?"

Charlotte groaned. It was even worse than she had thought. She shook her head. "I knew about the affair, but Judith never breathed a word about any of that other stuff. Not to me, anyhow."

"She wouldn't. Too embarrassed. But one thing I can tell you. Willy boy isn't playing games here. Judith had better watch her back. You'd better warn her what's going down. And do it right away. She needs to know. For her sake as well as Daniel's," he added.

After Louis left, Charlotte skimmed the headlines of the newspaper while she sipped on a second cup of coffee. Not sure whether to be glad or disappointed, she didn't find anything about the urn or the bones.

In the living room, as she uncovered Sweety Boy's cage, Louis's words played through her mind. *You'd better warn her what's going down. And do it right away. She needs to know.*

She glanced at the cuckoo clock, then eyed the phone. Only seven o'clock. No way could she call Judith at seven on a Saturday morning.

So what now? She eyed the phone again. *Take a walk. Clear your head. And think.*

Throwing on a pair of sweatpants, a T-shirt, and tennis shoes, she headed out the front door. She was halfway around the block when the sky grew even darker than before, and she felt the first drops of rain. Charlotte picked up her pace, but before she reached her house, the bottom fell out and she got soaked through and through.

A hot shower, dry clothes, and a warm bowl of oatmeal helped. By the time she'd finished breakfast it was eight, and she figured that surely Judith would be awake now.

Judith answered the phone call on the second ring,

and Charlotte grimaced at the sound of her niece's sleepy, "Hello."

"Judith, hon, I hope I'm not calling too early."

"No problem, Auntie." But Charlotte could hear her yawn through the phone line. "I should have already been up, but I was out pretty late last night, following up on a lead for a case I'm working on."

"Have—have you talked to your brother?"

"Not in a couple of days. Why? Is there something wrong? Do I need to talk to him?"

"Yes. Yes, you do," Charlotte told her, then she went on to explain about the urn and the possibility of the skeleton being Ricco. "Daniel seems to think that Nadia will be the number one suspect. I'm just afraid that he might be a suspect, too. Louis thinks so, too," she added. "In fact, Louis is the one who said I should call you right away, especially when he heard that Will Richeaux is the detective investigating the case."

The silence on the other end of the phone line was deafening. Then Charlotte heard a whispered curse. "This is bad," Judith said. "Really bad," she said even louder. "And Daniel's right. Nadia will be a suspect. Probably their main suspect."

"And Daniel?"

Judith swore again. "That's a real possibility, too. Maybe more so than Nadia." She paused, then forcefully said, "But not if I can help it."

"So you're going to check into it?"

"You bet, Auntie. Just as soon as I can throw some clothes on, I'll head over to the precinct and see what I can find out.

"Judith—"

"Look, Auntie, I'll have to get back to you."

"You will call me and let me know what's going on, won't you?"

"I'll call."

"Promise?"

"Yes ma'am. I promise."

"Oh, and one more thing," Charlotte added quickly. "Louis says to tell you that where Will Richeaux is concerned, you'd better watch your back."

Charlotte tried to stay busy. Besides cleaning her own house, there was a week's worth of laundry waiting to be washed, and she really needed to make a trip to the grocery store. If the rain ever let up. She didn't especially like grocery shopping even in good weather, but she simply refused to go in bad weather.

In spite of all of the work she had to do and even though she kept busy, the morning still seemed to drag by slower than a Mardi Gras parade.

The phone rang only twice during the entire morning, and each time it rang, she hurried to answer it, hoping that Judith had some kind of news.

One call was a telemarketer, trying to sell her vinyl siding for her house, and the other call was a potential client. She politely but firmly told the telemarketer that she didn't need siding, and after talking a moment with the potential client and learning that the lady lived in the French Quarter, she had to tell her that she was already booked up.

Taking on a new client meant she'd have to hire yet

another employee, and that was something she wasn't prepared to do, not at the present. Besides, extending her services into the French Quarter didn't appeal to her in the least. She had all the work she needed right there in the Garden District.

By two that afternoon, the waiting was beginning to really get on Charlotte's nerves big-time, and just as she'd about decided to brave the rain and run to the grocery store, the phone rang.

"Maid-for-a-Day. Charlotte speaking."

"Aunt Charley, have you heard from Nadia?"

The caller was Daniel, but something in his voice wasn't quite right. "Why, no," she answered. "I haven't seen or heard from her since last night. Is there something wrong, hon?"

"She's gone then. Dammit, she's gone."

"Maybe she just ran to the store."

"No! You don't understand. She said she wasn't feeling well, so I took Davy to the zoo so she could rest. I thought the rain would let up, but it didn't. Anyway, when we got back, she was gone. And so is her suitcase and some of her clothes."

"Oh, Daniel . . ." Charlotte was at a loss for words.

"What am I going to do?"

"Daniel, are you absolutely sure—about the suitcase and the clothes, I mean?"

"Wait a second, Auntie. Someone's at the door. I'll have to call you back."

"Daniel!" But it was already too late. He'd hung up the phone.

As Charlotte slowly replaced the receiver, she told

herself that Daniel was overreacting. Maybe, even now, he was opening the door, and Nadia was explaining how she'd either forgotten her house keys or lost them. But as much as she tried to keep a positive attitude, the nagging feeling she'd had all night and all day bloomed into deadly fear. The only viable reason Nadia would have to run would be if she was guilty.

Chapter Eight

As Charlotte paced the floor, no matter how hard she tried to picture Nadia as a murderer, she simply could not accept that the Nadia she knew could do such a thing. There had to be another reason why she had run—if in fact she really had run.

Waiting for Daniel to call was agonizing. An hour was all that Charlotte could stand. When exactly an hour had passed, she marched to the phone and tapped out Daniel's phone number. Five rings later, just when she was about to hang up, the call was answered.

The only word the man said was, "Hello." But something about his voice sounded familiar.

"Is this the Daniel Monroe residence?" she demanded.

"Who wants to know?" the man demanded right back.

There was something in his tone that grated on her already stretched nerves, and some sixth sense cautioned against giving out too much information. "I'd like to speak to Daniel, please."

"Like I said, lady, who's calling?"

"Who is this?"

"I'm a detective with the New Orleans Police Department. Now, who are you?"

Will Richeaux.

No wonder the voice sounded familiar. "This is Daniel's aunt. Now, may I speak to him?"

"Ms. LaRue?"

"Yes."

"Ms. LaRue, this is Will Richeaux. I'm sorry, but I'm afraid I have some bad news. I'm arresting your nephew for the murder of Ricco Martinez."

Charlotte felt her knees grow weak, and she sank onto the sofa. "That's absurd!" she cried.

" 'Fraid not, ma'am. And another thing. I understand that your nephew's wife is missing at the moment, or so your nephew claims. Have you seen her?"

As if she would tell him if she had. "N-no, I haven't. Not since last night."

"Well, if you do, you need to let me know right away. Or if you hear from her, you need to persuade her to contact the police. For her own good," he added with emphasis. "And another thing, unless someone in the family can be responsible for the kid, I'll be forced to call child welfare to come get him."

"Don't do that!" Charlotte protested. "I'll come. I'll be right over. It won't take me ten minutes." Without giving him a chance to say no, Charlotte hung up the phone.

Grabbing her purse, she rushed out the door.

As soon as she was in the van and headed up Milan, she fumbled in the purse for her cell phone. Her hands were shaking so badly that she could barely punch in the numbers of Judith's cell phone number and still drive. Judith finally answered on the fourth ring.

"Judith, where are you?"

"Aunt Charley, what's wrong?"

"Nadia's missing, and Will Richeaux just arrested your brother. He said if someone didn't come get Davy, he was calling child welfare. I'm on my way over to Daniel's house right now."

"Whoa, Auntie. Take it easy," Judith told her. "Where is Nadia?"

"I don't know," she answered, then she explained about the call from Daniel.

"Is Richeaux still at Daniel's?"

"Yes, he is—or at least he was just a minute ago."

"I'll meet you there." Judith disconnected the call.

Charlotte had to park half a block away due to the two squad cars and some other vehicles parked along the curb in front of Daniel's house. Much to her relief, she recognized Judith's tan Toyota, and she caught sight of her on the porch just before Judith disappeared inside the house.

As Charlotte approached the steps to the porch, she saw that there was a policeman standing guard near the front door. But even from the bottom of the steps, she could hear muffled voices arguing inside the house.

Charlotte was halfway up the steps when the policeman blocked the entrance to the porch.

"Sorry, ma'am. You can't go in."

Over the noise, Charlotte said, "My name is Charlotte LaRue and Detective Richeaux is expecting me."

"I'll need some I.D., ma'am."

With a sigh of impatience, Charlotte yanked her bill-fold out of her purse and showed him her driver's license. He glanced at it, then nodded and stepped aside, allowing her access to the porch.

When Charlotte stepped inside the living room, the first person she saw was Daniel. He was seated on the sofa, and tucked in next to him was Davy, his eyes wide and red-rimmed, his lower lip quivering.

Standing just behind Daniel was a uniformed policeman and another man that Charlotte recognized as the detective who had showed up with Will Richeaux at Patsy's house.

At first no one paid any attention to Charlotte. They were too focused on the argument going on between Judith and Will Richeaux.

"This is stupid, Will!" Judith shouted. "And you know it!"

"Back off, Judith," he shouted back. "This is my case, so just butt out."

"Like hell I will!" she retorted.

"I'm warning you—"

"And I'm warning you!"

"Judith!" Daniel interrupted. "It's okay," he told her. "My firm will eat this idiot's lunch before they're done with him."

Will Richeaux spun around and glared at Daniel. "You!" he yelled, pointing his finger at Daniel. "Shut your mouth now!"

But Daniel ignored him. "Hey, man, all this shouting and arguing is upsetting my son."

Will Richeaux took a step toward Daniel, and Charlotte cleared her throat loudly. "Ah—excuse me."

As if on cue, all four of the adults in the room turned their heads toward her.

"You come for the kid?" Will Richeaux demanded.

Charlotte nodded. "Yes—yes I did, and it looks like I'm none too soon." She stepped farther into the room. "Shame on you." She shook her finger at Will Richeaux. "Shame on all of you." She glared at each of the others in turn. "Can't you see that poor child is already frightened enough without all the screaming and shouting."

Not waiting for a response or for permission, she marched over to Daniel and lifted Davy into her arms. "Hey, Davy," she cooed, adjusting him so that he was riding on her hip. "How about going home with Aunt Charley for a little while, huh?" For an answer, Davy wrapped his arms around her neck and tucked his head against her shoulder.

"Daddy Danol come, too?" he pleaded.

Charlotte kissed his cheek. "Not just right now, sweetheart, but he'll come later." Ignoring Will Richeaux's glare, she turned to Daniel. "Are you okay, hon?"

A defeated shrug was the only answer she got. "You hang in there, honey. Now—which room is Davy's? I'll need to get some of his things. And a key—I'll need a key to the house."

Without waiting for Daniel's reply, she turned and faced Will Richeaux. Though her insides were quivering with fear, her voice reflected her indignant fury. "You should be ashamed," she scolded. "How would you like it if someone submitted your child to such a scene? This child does not need to be exposed to any more than he already has been, and you can darn well wait until I leave to finish your business here. Now"— she turned back to Daniel—"does Davy need a car seat?"

"No, ma'am," he answered. "He's passed the forty-pound mark."

Charlotte nodded. She suspected as much from the weight of the little boy, but it was best to make sure. "And his room?"

"First one on the left at the top of the stairs. And there's a spare key hanging on a hook near the phone in the kitchen."

Again she nodded. "Okay, Davy," she told the little boy as she slid him down to the floor and took him firmly by the hand. "Show Aunt Charley your room."

With Davy's help, Charlotte found a small suitcase and was able to gather a few clothes, his toothbrush, and a few of his favorite toys.

When she and Davy returned to the living room, Daniel and Judith were seated side by side on the sofa, and Will Richeaux was staring out the front window.

Charlotte knelt down beside Davy. "Go give Daddy Daniel a big hug now."

"Me first," Judith told the little boy and held out her arms. Once Davy had hugged her, she lifted him and sat him in Daniel's lap, then stood and stepped over to Charlotte.

"Why don't you let me be the one to call Mom, Auntie? Once I explain the situation, then I'm sure she will help out with Davy."

Though Charlotte nodded, she had her doubts about getting any kind of help from her sister, and the look on Judith's face mirrored her doubts.

Davy sat as still as a frightened mouse and barely said a word all the way to Charlotte's house. He'd been to her home on several occasions, and once she parked the van, she was vastly relieved when he went with her inside without protest.

The moment they entered the living room, Sweety Boy began squawking and prancing back and forth on the perch in his cage.

"You remember my little bird, don't you, Davy?"

The little boy nodded.

"Do you remember his name?"

Davy stared thoughtfully at the bird for several moments before replying. "Weety Boy. Name, Weety Boy."

Charlotte chuckled. "Well . . . that's almost right. Close enough. Tell you what. If you're a really good boy, I just might let you pet him. Would you like that?"

Even as Davy nodded that he would, tears filled his eyes and he looked up at Charlotte. "Where's Mommy? I want Mommy."

Charlotte felt like crying herself. "Oh, honey, of course you do." She knelt down beside the little boy and pulled him into her arms. "There, there, don't cry now. I'm sure your mommy will be home soon." But she wasn't sure, not sure at all, and the lie left a bitter taste in her mouth.

Chapter Nine

A t the sound of the phone, Charlotte jerked upright on the sofa. Afraid that the noise would awaken Davy and praying that the call was from Judith, she grabbed for the receiver and mumbled, "Hello."

"Aunt Charley?"

"Yes, hon, I'm here."

"Were you asleep?"

Charlotte yawned. "Hm, guess I was. Must have nodded off." Squinting, she peered up at the cuckoo clock on the wall behind the sofa. Almost nine.

As if Judith had read her mind, she said, "Sorry to take so long in getting back to you, Auntie, but I just got home."

"No, that's okay. I figured you were busy."

"So how's Davy doing?"

"I guess he's okay. After we got home, he watched some cartoons on TV; then I fed him and gave him a bath. He finally went to sleep a little after eight or so. Poor little guy."

"And how are you holding up?"

"Well, to be honest, I'm exhausted. It's been a long time since I took care of a three-year-old, and I'm not as young as I used to be. That's for sure."

There was a slight pause, then Judith said, "You haven't by chance heard anything out of Nadia yet, have you?"

"No—no, I haven't."

"That's too bad. For her sake as well as Davy's,"

Judith added. "The longer she's missing, the more guilty it makes her appear." Judith hesitated. "Ah, Auntie, you will tell me if you do hear from her, won't you?"

"Judith Monroe!"

"Now, now, don't get all insulted. After all, you didn't tell me when Jeanne Dubuisson called that time."

"That was different," Charlotte retorted.

"Not really that much different, but, then, we could argue the finer points all night. Anyway—about Davy. I talked to Mother about keeping him."

"And?"

"Aunt Charley, I know this is an imposition on you, but it might be better all around if Davy could just stay at your house. Just until Daniel makes bail."

"I figured as much."

"I'm really sorry about this, and you know that *I'd* keep him in a heartbeat. But my schedule is so erratic, and what would I do with him if I got called out at midnight on a case or . . ." Her voice trailed away.

Even through the phone line, Charlotte heard the frustration in Judith's tone. "It's okay, Judith. I understand."

"If Mother wasn't so unreasonable, we wouldn't be having this conversation. But she's too busy blaming Nadia for Daniel being in jail, and I just don't think her attitude would be good for Davy right now. I don't mean she would mistreat him or anything, but—"

"Judith, hon, it's okay. Really it is. Believe me, I understand. All too well," she added. "Davy and I will manage just fine. And hopefully Daniel will make bail." Charlotte had more than a few qualms about how she and Davy would manage, but she figured she'd just have to take it one step at a time. After all, it wasn't as if she hadn't done it before.

"There is another option, Auntie."

"If you're going to suggest the child welfare agency, then just forget it. Davy is part of our family now, and we take care of our own."

"Well . . . if you're sure?"

Charlotte wasn't really sure about anything at this point, but what choice was there? And what was the point in worrying Judith more than she already was or making her feel worse than she already felt? "I'm sure enough, hon. Besides, lately I've been thinking a lot about grandchildren. And this will give me a chance to see what it's like, sorta kinda."

"Grandchildren? Oh, yeah, right, Auntie," Judith said. "But there's this teeny-tiny problem. First Hank needs to marry Carol, and, knowing my cousin, he's not in any big hurry."

"Well, yes, marriage to Carol would help."

Judith laughed. "Now all we have to do is convince him. I don't know Carol that well, but I do know she likes kids and she adores Hank. From what I've seen, he couldn't do much better. But, then, almost anyone would be an improvement over Mindy. What a loser she turned out to be."

"I couldn't agree more," Charlotte avowed. Just the mention of her ex-daughter-in-law's name churned up all kinds of mixed emotions within her, anger being the foremost. Mindy had never wanted children, and when she'd found out she was pregnant, she'd gotten an abortion without telling Hank. When he'd discovered what she'd done, he'd been devastated. And furious—so furious that he'd immediately filed for a divorce.

"Auntie, on another subject, there's something you need to be aware of," Judith said, interrupting Charlotte's thoughts. "I spoke to Daniel earlier, and he said that lately Davy has been having some disturbing dreams. They've tried to question him about the dreams, but all they can get out of him is that his daddy—meaning Ricco—comes to see him at night."

Chill bumps chased down Charlotte's arms. "Now that just breaks my heart," she murmured. After what Daniel had told her about Ricco's abusiveness, it was no wonder the little fellow was having nightmares. "If Ricco Martinez wasn't already dead, I'd be tempted to kill him myself."

"Whoa, Auntie! That's pretty harsh, especially coming from you. But I have to admit I know exactly how you feel."

"Well, my daddy—your grandfather—always said, there's a special place in hell for people who abuse little children."

For long moments, neither of them spoke, then: "My grandfather sounds like he was a really good man. I wish I could have known him."

"Me, too," Charlotte murmured. "I wish all of you kids could have known him and your grandmother. They were both wonderful people who always put their family first."

"One last thing about Davy, Auntie, something that might help you out, just in case things don't . . . well, just in case. Davy does go to a day-care when Nadia works. It's the Loving Care Day-Care Center, not far from where Nadia used to live."

A whisper of fear ran through Charlotte. "Are you saying that there's a chance that Daniel might not make bail?"

"No, no. Nothing like that. But with Nadia missing, even when he does make bail, he's going to need some help."

Early Sunday morning, while Davy was still sleeping, Charlotte debated whether to call Madeline or simply wait her out. That she hadn't already heard from her sister didn't surprise her in the least. Madeline was upset, which was understandable, but Charlotte figured she was also pouting . . . again. Even so, Charlotte knew that Madeline was worried about Daniel's situation and probably in need of some sisterly support.

Bracing herself, Charlotte tapped out Madeline's home phone number. After the fourth ring, the answering machine picked up, and Charlotte grimaced. Madeline was screening her calls. When Madeline's answering machine greeting ended and the beep sounded, Charlotte left her own message.

"Maddie, I know you're worried about Daniel right now. I am, too. But I just wanted you to know that I'm here if you need me. I love you." Charlotte waited a moment, in hopes that Madeline would pick up. When she didn't, Charlotte was left with no other choice than to hang up the receiver.

The rest of Sunday passed in a blur for Charlotte. At church she and Davy sat with Hank and Carol. Before the services began, and ever aware that Davy was listening to every word she said, Charlotte quickly updated them as to what was going on as best she could. After church, Hank suggested they all go out to eat.

Carol, sensing that Charlotte needed to talk to Hank, took Davy for a short walk before their meal was served. With Davy out of earshot, Charlotte had a chance to go into more detail with Hank about Daniel's situation.

After lunch Charlotte took Davy home. It always amazed Charlotte how adaptable kids could be. After just one night, Davy had made himself right at home. And he'd become quite the little chatterbox, talking about anything and everything and asking what seemed like dozens of questions.

"Why does Weety have to stay in a cage? Why can't he talk? Where's Mommy? When's Daddy Danol coming to get me? Why can't I go home?"

And then there was Charlotte's favorite, the question he asked most. "What'cha doing, Aunt Chardy?" No matter what she was doing and no matter how many times she explained what she was doing, he'd ask again and again.

By Sunday night, Charlotte was more than ready for a bit of quiet, alone time when she tucked Davy into bed. Just as she'd settled on the sofa with the latest novel by an author named Charlaine Harris, a noise caught her attention. It was the kind of sound that was just enough out of place to put her on guard.

Charlotte glanced up from the novel, tilted her head, and listened more intently. After a moment, she heard the noise again, the faintest of sounds coming from the bedroom where Davy was sleeping.

As quietly as she could, she hurried to the bedroom. Even in the dim glow of the night-light, she could see that the little huddled form beneath the covers was shivering. She walked quietly over to the bed.

Davy had pulled the covers completely over his head, and from beneath the bundle came gulping, sniffling sounds.

"Davy," she called out softly, leaning over the bed as she placed her hand on the bundle. "What's wrong, sweetheart?"

After several long moments, he finally answered, his voice muffled by the covers and pillow. "I-I scared. Want my mommy."

"Oh, honey." Charlotte's heart was breaking for the little boy. She sat down on the bed, reached out, and began rubbing his back. "There's nothing to be scared about." Then she remembered what Judith had told her about the little boy's nightmares. "Did you have a bad dream?"

"Don't know," he answered. "Want Mommy."

"I know you do, sweetheart," she whispered. "But Davy, look at Aunt Charley." She pulled the covers down and turned him over onto his back. Then, propping herself on her elbow, she leaned down close to his face. "Your mommy would want you to be a big boy right now." She kissed his forehead. "And I'm sure she'll be back just as soon as she can." Davy snuggled closer to her. "Tell you what," she continued. "Do you and Mommy say your prayers at night?"

"I say prayers."

"Why don't we say them then, and we'll ask God to bring Mommy home again real soon."

On Monday morning Charlotte's internal clock awakened her around six. The first thing she realized was that Davy was still snuggled close. The second thing that she realized, much to her irritation, was that she had fallen asleep still fully dressed, a sure sign of how tired she'd been, especially since she'd intended on staying with Davy only until he fell asleep again.

Charlotte rarely slept in her clothes, and she never went to bed without washing the day's makeup and grime off her face. Now all she could think about was a shower and clean clothes.

Hoping Davy wouldn't awaken quite yet, she eased out of the bed and placed her still warm pillow up against the little boy to give the illusion that a warm body was sleeping next to him; it was a trick she'd learned when Hank had been a little boy and had insisted on sleeping with her. Most of the time it had worked.

At the dresser, as quietly as she could, she opened a drawer and took out clean underwear. As she opened the closet door, she silently thanked Louis for having greased all the hinges. From the closet, she removed a fresh uniform. Clothes in hand, she tiptoed out of the bedroom and headed straight for the bathroom.

Still hoping that Davy would stay asleep just a little longer, she hurried through her shower and dressed in the bathroom.

In the kitchen, over her first cup of coffee, she debated whether to take Davy to his day-care so she could work, or whether to simply stay home with him. She could cancel working that day without much of a problem. Marian, her Monday client, would understand once she explained the situation. Or she could call Janet to work for her.

Ultimately, she decided that once Davy awakened, just for today, she would let him make the decision. With the two most important people in his young life absent, she felt that his sense of security took precedence over everything else. If he seemed even the least bit hesitant or apprehensive about going to day-care, she'd stay home with him.

When he did awaken a few minutes later, Charlotte broached the subject over their breakfast of oatmeal, toast, and juice.

"Well, Davy, what are we going to do today? What do you think about going to your school, so you can play with the other little boys and girls?"

Without hesitation, he nodded eagerly, and even with his grinning mouth half-full of oatmeal, she was able to understand him when he answered, "I go play with boys and girls."

After Davy finished breakfast, Charlotte kept one eye on the clock as she dressed him. With her guidance and to his delight, she let the little boy help her fill Sweety Boy's food and water container before they left.

The short drive to Loving Care Day-Care Center only took about five minutes. Once there, she parked the van, then she escorted Davy inside. After signing him in, she spoke to the proprietor, Linda Smith, a plump middle-aged woman who had kind eyes and was the quintessence of a grandmother type.

"I'm a bit worried about Davy today," Charlotte told her, and since she'd already decided to keep her explanation as simple as possible, all she added was that Davy was staying with her for a few days while his parents were away. "I'm just worried because he's never been away from his mother for this long a period," she added.

"Now, Ms. LaRue, don't you worry about a thing." Linda Smith reached over and patted Davy on the head. "Me and Davy are old buddies, and he'll do just fine."

Feeling somewhat more at ease, Charlotte left her name, address, and both of her phone numbers, along with instructions that if anything at all happened or if Davy seemed the least bit unhappy, Linda should feel free to immediately call her.

It was close to lunchtime, and Charlotte was in the middle of cleaning the bathroom that Marian's sons used when her cell phone buzzed. She quickly rinsed and dried her hands, then pulled the phone from her pocket. "Maid-for-a-Day. Charlotte speaking."

"Aunt Charley, it's Judith. I'm afraid I have some bad news."

Charlotte closed the toilet lid and sank down on top of it.

Judith's sigh was audible over the phone line and full of frustration. "Bail for Daniel has been denied."

"What?" Charlotte cried. "How can that be possible?"

"Seems that the assistant D.A. convinced the judge that Daniel was a flight risk. He made a pitch about Daniel and Nadia conspiring to get rid of Ricco. And with Nadia missing, he claimed that if Daniel was freed on bail, he would more than likely disappear, too. And that idiotic man who calls himself a judge bought it."

"That just can't be right, Judith. There can't be any evidence, and besides which, Daniel is a respected attorney from a highly respected law firm. He's—"

"I know, I know, Auntie. If you ask me, there's something really rotten going on here. Of course, it doesn't help that the judge is Jonas Tipton, the assistant D.A.'s big golfing buddy."

Charlotte frowned. "I've heard that name before." But where had she heard it? Then, she remembered: something that Bitsy Duhe had told her. "Isn't that the judge who's as old as creation?"

"'Fraid so. Some even say he's a bit senile. And I have to tell you, after watching him in court this morning, I think that old buzzard is more than just senile. I think he's either just plain nuts or else he's on the take."

"Well ain't that just grand?" Charlotte grumbled. "Surely *something* can be done."

"Daniel's firm is working on it, but this kind of stuff takes time."

Time? How much time? And what about Davy? "Have you told your mother about this yet?"

"Not yet, and I'm not looking forward to it. Ah . . . Aunt Charley, you wouldn't consider—"

"No way," Charlotte retorted immediately. "Don't even ask. Your mother and I are barely speaking as it is."

"Sorry. I thought it was worth a shot."

By the time Charlotte finished cleaning Marian's house and was on her way to pick up Davy at the day-care, she'd resigned herself to the fact that the whole fiasco about Ricco could very well turn into a long-term legal battle, a battle for Daniel and Nadia's very lives.

Even when they won the battle, and she had to think they would win or else go crazy, there would be grave damage. Daniel's professional reputation, as well as Nadia's, would suffer. And what of their marriage? Even the best of relationships sometimes fell apart when faced with far fewer obstacles than they were facing.

And then there was the damage to Davy to consider. All within a day's time, his mother had disappeared, his new stepfather had been arrested, and both were suspects in the murder of his father. To top it off, he was staying with someone he barely knew. There was no telling what kind of long-term effect that could have on the little boy.

And if Nadia and Daniel don't win the battle? "Oh, dear Lord," Charlotte murmured, cringing at the thought as she pulled into the driveway of the Loving Care Day-Care Center. What if, God forbid, Nadia and

Daniel were railroaded through and actually convicted of murdering Ricco? Then what would happen to Davy?

For a long time, Charlotte simply sat in the van and stared into space, her stomach twisted in knots.

One day at a time. The words came out of nowhere, and Charlotte sighed. Getting caught up in the worry game was all too easy, but the truth was, worrying about "what ifs" wouldn't do anyone any good, least of all Davy. Besides, ultimately, the act of worrying wouldn't change the outcome of the situation anyway.

For now, all she could do was take care of Davy as best she could and pray. Right now, the little boy needed all the love and stability he could get. And from the looks of things, the only place he was going to get it was from her.

She could handle it, she kept telling herself as she climbed out of the van. With the good Lord's help she could handle anything. She'd done it before and she could do it again.

As Charlotte entered the day-care, she ignored the little voice that kept reminding her just how long ago it had been since she'd juggled caring for a child and taking care of a business. Then, she hadn't been able to afford such things as day-care though. Thank goodness that wasn't the problem now. Day-care would help a lot, especially since Davy seemed to like it.

As for taking care of a business, one thing she needed to do right away was to see if Janet Davis could possibly take over working for Patsy Dufour in Nadia's place. Now, if only she could remember to call Janet.

Charlotte spotted Davy almost immediately in the play area. He and another little boy were having a tug-of-war over a truck. Both little boys seemed equally determined to take possession of it. She was so busy watching the two that she didn't notice Linda Smith standing off to the side.

Evidently Ms. Smith had been monitoring the boys all along, and when things got a bit too rough, she swooped in like a hawk and took away the truck from both of them.

The look on both little boys' faces was priceless, and Charlotte couldn't help laughing. But even as she laughed, she felt a deep anger taking root within, mostly anger at Madeline for her selfish attitude about Daniel and his new family. But she was also angry with Nadia.

Where was Nadia? Why had she run? And how in the world could she have left her little boy, her own flesh and blood, to be cared for by people he barely knew?

Because she's guilty . . . guilty . . . guilty.

Chapter Ten

The moment that Charlotte turned into her driveway, she spied Louis sitting on the porch swing. She hadn't seen or talked to him since he'd borrowed coffee from her on Saturday morning. Did he even know about Daniel's arrest yet? Did he know that Daniel had been denied bail?

Though Louis gave Davy a cursory, curious look when they approached the porch, the first words out of his mouth confirmed that he did indeed know about Daniel.

"Why didn't you tell me that Daniel had been arrested?"

Charlotte felt her temper rise and could have gladly smacked him for being so insensitive in Davy's presence, but she settled for giving him a pointed, hostile glare instead. Then Davy tugged on her hand.

"What's 'arrested,' Aunt Chardy?"

"Thanks a lot, Louis," Charlotte retorted. Ignoring Louis for the moment, she knelt down beside Davy. "'Arrested' just means that Daniel had to go with the police to explain some things. It's nothing important, hon. Nothing you need to worry about."

"Daddy Danol be home soon?"

"Soon, baby. Real soon." *Please let it be true, Lord.*

Davy seemed to mull over what she'd told him, then his eyes widened. "My see Weety now? Pease," he added, his expression hopeful.

"May I see Sweety now," Charlotte corrected. "And, yes, since you asked so politely, you may go see him. But remember what I told you. You can look, but don't touch. And you can talk to him, but don't stick your fingers in the cage. Okay?"

Davy nodded eagerly. "'Cause Weety bite me."

"Yes, that's right. He might bite you," she repeated, and, still ignoring Louis, she unlocked the door and let the little boy inside. Only when she was assured that Davy was occupied with watching Sweety Boy did she finally turn her attention back to Louis.

She'd fully intended giving him a piece of her mind

for being so thoughtless around Davy, but Louis beat her to the punch.

With hands held up defensively, palms out, he said, "I know, I know. Sorry about that. Guess I just wasn't thinking."

Charlotte decided not to make an issue of his blunder. "Will Richeaux arrested Daniel Saturday afternoon," she said curtly. "I didn't tell you because"—she motioned toward the living room where Davy was chattering away to Sweety Boy—"I've had my hands full. So—" She narrowed her eyes. "How did you find out?"

"I read about it in the *Picayune* this morning."

Charlotte groaned. "Oh no. I didn't get around to reading the paper this morning. Shoot! I was hoping that it wouldn't get in the paper quite so soon."

"So what's happened since Saturday? And why is Davy with you?"

Even with the late afternoon sun peeking beneath the overhang of the porch, the temperature was mild. Since Charlotte thought it best if Davy didn't overhear their conversation, she motioned toward the swing.

After making sure that the door was cracked open enough that she could hear Davy, she seated herself beside Louis in the swing. Then she explained the events of Saturday, ending with Judith's call that morning.

"As for Davy, there's no one else to keep him," she said. "It was either I take him or he would be turned over to the welfare system."

Louis shook his head. "What a mess! Somebody

needs to do something about that old geezer Jonas Tipton."

"Tell me about it," Charlotte retorted. "Personally, I'd like to hang him up by his toenails."

At that, a grin tugged at Louis's lips. Then he sobered. "And there's been no sign or word from Nadia?"

Charlotte shook her head. "Nary a peep out of her. I'll be honest with you. I've known her now for several years—since Davy was born—and I can't imagine what she was thinking, leaving him like that. It's just not like her."

"Yeah, well, that's all fine and dandy, but what's got me puzzled is Will Richeaux. You can bet if he's pushing things—and it sounds like he is—then there's a reason behind it."

"Well, I'll tell you one thing right now. There's no way that Nadia could have murdered Ricco Martinez. Why, she wouldn't hurt a fly."

"Wouldn't hurt a fly, huh? But she'd abandon her child and her husband when they needed her the most. Just walk out on them without a word. Haven't you learned by now that people aren't always what they seem?"

Charlotte recognized Louis's sarcastic comeback for what it was, a not so subtle dig meant to remind her that once before she'd thought that someone she cared about was innocent. But she'd been wrong. Almost dead wrong.

Was it possible that she was wrong again?

"Think about it, Charlotte," he told her. "It could be

the Dubuisson scenario all over again—just with a slightly different twist."

Charlotte cringed, thinking about the Dubuisson family, and how, in spite of Hank warning her against getting personally involved with clients, she'd ended up smack in the middle of things when Jackson Dubuisson had been murdered. Though it pained her to admit it, she knew that there was a possibility that Louis could be right.

"But if it makes you feel any better," Louis continued, "if Nadia did kill Ricco—and, to set the record straight, I'm still not convinced she did—I don't think Daniel had anything to do with it."

"Of course Daniel isn't involved in such a thing!" she snapped. The very idea was preposterous. Then she tilted her head and narrowed her eyes. "Why aren't you convinced? About Nadia, that is?"

Louis shrugged. "Given the circumstances of Ricco's remains being found in that urn, and considering that he was involved with the cemetery thefts to begin with, it makes a lot more sense that his death is related to all of that stuff. Then again, maybe it's meant to look like that to cover up the identity of the real murderer."

Louis shoved himself out of the swing. "Tell you what, though. I still have a few connections, so maybe I'll nose around and see what I can find out."

"Oh, Louis—" Before Charlotte thought about what she was doing, she reached out and squeezed his arm. "I wish you would. I know I'd feel a whole lot better knowing you were involved. And, if—as you pointed out—Will Richeaux is pushing it, then that means he won't be actively looking for the real murderer."

Louis covered her hand with his free hand. "I think the big question right now is, why is he pushing it?"

As soon as Louis left, Charlotte went inside. But even as she gently coached Davy in the proper way to pet a parakeet, she kept mentally rehashing the conversation she'd had with Louis as well as berating herself for her impetuous impulse in squeezing his arm.

"That's right, honey," she told Davy. "Be very gentle with him."

While she encouraged Davy, her thoughts continued to stay on Louis. She was both glad and relieved that he had decided to check things out for himself. Most times, he aggravated the stuffing out of her, but despite their differences, she was confident that if anyone could find out what was going on, Louis could. And with Judith nosing around, too, surely Nadia and Daniel would be exonerated soon.

"Careful, Davy," she cautioned when the little boy got a bit too eager with the petting. "Remember he's a lot smaller than you are and can be hurt a lot easier."

"Like this, Aunt Chardy?"

Charlotte nodded, but, again, Louis came to mind. Maybe she should just pretend that nothing happened. After all, by today's standards, her impulsive gesture meant nothing. Women and men touched each other casually all of the time and didn't mean anything by it. *Just stop being such an old prude, Charlotte LaRue.*

Sweety Boy was slowly but surely getting used to

Davy being around. Though he was still a bit leery of the little boy, he didn't act nearly as defensive as when he was around Madeline and Louis. And he never tried to bite Davy. Even so, Charlotte wasn't quite ready to trust him and Davy alone together yet.

"Time to close the cage door now," she told Davy. "And time for a new adventure," she added when she saw him poke out his lower lip in a pout. "I believe it's time for *Sesame Street*," she told him as she hurried over to the television, turned it on, and switched the channel to the PBS station.

The little boy's eyes lit up and, childlike, he instantly forgot Sweety Boy. "Elmo! Elmo! Elmo!" Davy cried, scrambling over to the television.

Charlotte laughed. "I take it you like Elmo."

The little boy plopped down on the rug within a foot of the TV screen, much too close in Charlotte's opinion.

"Tell you what," Charlotte said as she picked him up and positioned him a few feet farther back. "I need to make a phone call, so you sit right here and watch Elmo. After I make my call then I'll fix us something for supper. Deal?"

Already engrossed with the antics of Big Bird dancing across the screen, Davy totally ignored her.

With a grin pulling at her lips, Charlotte walked to the desk and placed a call to Janet Davis.

Janet answered the call almost immediately.

"Hi, Janet. This is Charlotte. I was wondering if you could help me out for the next couple of weeks on Tuesdays and Thursdays."

There was a slight hesitation on the line, a hesitation

127

that, in Charlotte's experience, probably meant that Janet's answer would be no.

"Ah—Charlotte, I'm glad you called," Janet finally said, her tone regretful. "I meant to call you, but things have been so hectic around here I haven't had a chance. You know I would gladly help out if I could, but I won't be able to work for at least the next two or three weeks. There's been an accident. Harry misstepped coming down the stairs, and he's messed up his ankle—broke it in two places."

"Oh my goodness, that's terrible."

"Considering that my husband is a horrible patient, yes, it is terrible," Janet agreed. "Anyway, that happened on Friday, and he had to have surgery that night. Last night, the doctor said he could come home from the hospital today. But it's going to be a while before Harry can put any weight on that foot, and I have to take him in each day for some physical therapy."

Charlotte frowned. "Please give Harry my best, and don't worry about work. I'll manage."

"Thanks, Charlotte. How about I give you a call when Harry is well enough to navigate on his own."

"Good enough," Charlotte answered. "Be talking to you. Bye now."

Charlotte slowly hung up the receiver. The only thing left to do was either figure out how she could pull a double workload on Tuesdays and Thursdays or simply tell Patsy she couldn't provide maid service for her for a while.

Charlotte shook her head and thumbed through the Rolodex until she found Patsy Dufour's phone number.

Patsy's answering machine clicked on after the fourth ring, and Charlotte ground her teeth in frustration.

Once the beep sounded, Charlotte left her message. "Patsy, this is Charlotte LaRue. I'm having a scheduling problem, but I wanted you to know that I'll try to be by a little after lunch tomorrow to clean. If this isn't acceptable, give me a call at home tonight or call my cell phone number tomorrow." Charlotte rattled off the two phone numbers, then she hung up the receiver and headed for the kitchen.

Now all she had to do was to figure out what she was going to fix for supper, something that she hoped a little three-year-old boy would eat.

Usually Charlotte like to read a bit in bed at night before going to sleep. With Davy sleeping in her bed, she'd had to settle for reading in the living room instead.

Charlotte had just decided that she would read one more chapter before calling it a night when the phone rang. The noise both startled her and frightened her. It was already past nine, and in her experience, any calls that time of night were never good news.

She grabbed the receiver. "Hello."

"Charlotte, hang up the phone, but turn on your cell phone, and I'll call back."

"Nadia?"

But it was too late. Nadia had already disconnected the call.

Chapter Eleven

F or several moments Charlotte simply stared at the receiver. The caller had been Nadia. Of that she had no doubt. But why the cell phone business?

The cell phone. Charlotte slammed the receiver back down and scrambled for her cell phone. Almost the instant that she switched the POWER button on, the little phone jangled to life. She pressed the TALK button.

"Nadia?"

"Yeah, it's me, Charlotte."

"What on earth? Where—"

"Just listen a minute. Please," she added with emphasis, her voice low. "I'm afraid the police might have your regular phone tapped, so I thought it would be safer to talk over the cell phone."

Charlotte had never considered such a thing, and just the thought of someone listening in on her conversations raised her hackles. She began pacing the living room. "I'm not sure," she said, "but I think the authorities can also trace a call through a cell phone."

"Maybe . . . but I'm on a cell phone too, and I figured if I was moving around, they wouldn't be able to get a good fix on me."

"Where are you? Why on earth did you take off like that?"

"I-I can't tell you where I'm at." Her voice broke. "Oh, Charlotte, I-I've made such a mess of everything." For long seconds, only the barely audible sound of Nadia's soft sobs came through the line.

"S-sorry," she finally stammered.

Charlotte wavered between sympathy and anger: sympathy for a confused young woman who had suffered at the hands of an abusive man who also happened to be her son's father, and anger on behalf of Daniel and Davy.

Anger won. "I'm not the one you need to apologize to," she lashed out. Then, realizing how loud she was talking and afraid she might awaken Davy, she lowered her voice. "Daniel was left holding the bag, and Davy—that poor little boy—over and over, he keeps wanting to know where his mommy is. Just what am I supposed to tell him?"

"Then Davy is with you?"

"Yes, he's with me," Charlotte snapped. "It was either that or the Child Protection Agency."

"Thank you," Nadia whispered, tears in her voice. "I've been so worried about him. How—how is he?"

"Just how do you think he is? How would any little three-year-old be if his mother abandoned him without a word of explanation?"

"Oh, Charlotte, please don't be so angry with me. Please let me try to explain."

"So explain. I'm listening."

"I-I *thought* I was doing the right thing. I really did. And—and I didn't have a choice."

"There's always a choice."

"No, no, there's not. Not always, and not this time. We both know that the first person the police would suspect is me. I thought that if I left—just disappeared—then they would concentrate on me and leave Daniel out of it." She hesitated. "You have to believe that I would never purposely hurt Daniel. I love Daniel, and, other than Davy, he's the best thing that's ever happened to me. But I also figured that even if, by some remote circumstance, Daniel got arrested, his firm would get him out on bail." Her voice trailed away.

"Didn't exactly work, though, did it?" Nadia whispered after a pause. "But, Charlotte, either way, *I* couldn't risk going to jail."

Charlotte frowned. "Wait a minute. Back up a bit. You know about Daniel being denied bail?"

"Yes, I know."

"But how? I only found out myself this morning."

"I—I have my sources. But how doesn't matter. I need you to understand, Charlotte. No matter what, I still can't go to jail."

"But what about Daniel? What—"

"I'm pregnant," Nadia blurted out. "Daniel and I are going to have a baby."

Charlotte was stunned into silence. Sinking down onto the sofa, she stared at the opposite wall with unseeing eyes. No wonder, she thought. The elopement. The hasty marriage. Nadia's so-called stomach virus. In retrospect, it all made sense . . . maybe more sense than it should.

God forbid, what if Madeline had been right all along about Nadia? What if Nadia had killed Ricco? And what if she'd latched on to Daniel as insurance, just in case she was found out. Who better to have for a husband than a highly respected attorney, especially someone like Daniel, who was also considered a good catch by any woman's standards. After all, getting pregnant to trap and hold a man was the oldest trick in the universe.

Charlotte suddenly felt her face grow warm with shame for even thinking that Nadia would be capable of such elaborate manipulations. *And since when has Madeline ever been right about anything?*

"Please tell me you understand," Nadia begged. "Please don't think I'm a horrible person."

"Does Daniel know? About the pregnancy?"

"Yes, of course he knows. But no one else does. We were going to announce it at the reception party we were planning for next month."

There was one other question that Charlotte had to ask, and though it pained her, the only way to ask it was to just do it, straight out. "Nadia, did you kill Ricco?"

"No!" she cried. "Even through the worse times, it never entered my mind to kill him. All I could think about was getting away from him, getting him out of my life. Charlotte, I swear to you, I had nothing to do with his murder."

Charlotte wanted to believe her. With all of her heart she wanted to once again be able to trust her instincts when it came to the people she cared about. But *once bitten, twice shy.* And she'd been bitten before badly.

"If anyone had Ricco murdered," Nadia continued, each word dripping with bitterness, "it had to be Lowell Webster."

Once again, Charlotte was stunned into silence. *No way.* "Are you talking about *the* Lowell Webster?" The man was almost an icon in New Orleans, for Pete's sake—in the whole of Louisiana, for that matter.

133

"You got it," Nadia retorted.

How was that possible? Charlotte wondered. Lowell Webster was a self-made millionaire with a sterling reputation that was beyond reproach. Numerous articles had been written about him, how he had worked his way out of the quagmire of a childhood of poverty and turned a failing import-export company into a huge success. But it wasn't just the fact that the man was wealthy. He was respected and beloved due to his numerous philanthropic gifts to the poor. He was also the most favored candidate for the next New Orleans' mayor's race.

"What on earth makes you think that Lowell Webster murdered Ricco? Why would a man like Lowell Webster have *anything* to do with the likes of someone like Ricco Martinez in the first place?"

"Nothing directly," Nadia answered. "I don't have any real proof. But Lowell has a son, Mark, and Mark Webster is nothing like his father. In fact, he's probably just the opposite of everything his father supposedly stands for. But Mark is Lowell's only child, and Lowell would do anything to protect him."

Charlotte frowned. "Maybe you'd better explain."

Nadia sighed. "It's a long story." She cleared her throat. "According to Ricco, he and Mark met while they were both serving time in a Florida juvenile detention center when they were teenagers. Believe it or not, Ricco came from a well-to-do family in Miami, but he got mixed up with the wrong crowd. He was in the detention center because one night, for kicks, he and some of the gang he belonged to robbed a liquor store

134

and got caught. Mark was in the center because he'd been busted for running drugs from Florida to Louisiana. And get this. Mark's father thought he was on his high school senior trip.

"Anyway, while they were in detention, Ricco and Mark struck up a friendship of sorts. Mark was released first, but he told Ricco to look him up when he got out.

"When Ricco did get cut loose, he tried to go home. Ricco's story was that his father wanted to teach him a lesson and wouldn't have anything to do with him. He supposedly told Ricco that he had shamed the family and from now on he could fend for himself. At least that's what Ricco claimed.

"After Ricco's so-called rejection by his father, he hitchhiked to New Orleans and found Mark. Mark warned Ricco never to mention their detention in Florida. He said that his father had pulled in favors to get him released and was still angry about him getting caught in the first place."

"Okay," Charlotte told her. "That explains why Ricco knows the Websters, but it still doesn't explain why they would want him dead."

"According to Ricco, Mark was into some pretty nasty business. The cemetery thefts, for one. But he was also a big-time gambler. And Ricco was right in the thick of it with him. Whether it was the cemetery business or something else, you can bet that Ricco knew too much about something. Again, I can't prove it, but I figure that Lowell was simply trying to clean up another mess his son had made so it wouldn't come back to haunt him when he runs for mayor."

The revelation about the Websters was almost more than Charlotte could comprehend. "That's all well and good," she told Nadia, "but I have to admit, I find it all a bit hard to believe. And unless you convince the police of what you just told me, they're going to continue thinking that you're the one guilty—either you or Daniel. Right now, as best as I understand it, the authorities aren't even considering that anyone else could be guilty. You need to turn yourself in."

"I can't do that," Nadia whispered. "Not yet. If I can't even convince you—"

"I didn't say you haven't convinced me," Charlotte retorted. "I simply said I find it hard to believe."

"Well, it's for sure I won't be able to convince the police. I'm a nobody. My word against a man like Lowell Webster or even his son? No way."

"At least tell me where you're staying," Charlotte urged. "In case of an emergency with Davy or Daniel," she added.

"I-I can't do that, either. I know you, Charlotte. You'd think you were doing what's best for me, and you'd tell Judith."

"But, Nadia—"

"No buts. You know that's exactly what you'd do. But I'll call again. I promise. And Charlotte, thanks again for taking Davy in. I can't think of anyone I'd rather he stay with. And please tell Davy and Daniel that I love them both."

"Nadia, you—" The line went dead. Charlotte pulled the phone away from her ear and glared at it. Nadia had hung up on her.

If ever Charlotte had felt like swearing, she felt like it right then and there. She was also tempted to pitch the cell phone just as far as she could throw it. Barely able to control her rising temper or her trembling hands, she switched off the phone and stuffed it back inside her purse.

If only she could switch off her brain as easily, she thought as her mind swirled with bits and pieces of her conversation with Nadia.

Could she believe Nadia? *Should* she believe her? *Innocent until proven guilty . . . innocent until proven guilty . . .*

Once before she'd believed in someone she'd been close to, believed with all of her being. Charlotte squeezed her eyes shut and rubbed her forehead. But she'd been wrong that time, and just thinking about it was giving her a headache. Maybe a cup of hot cocoa would help—that and an aspirin.

A few minutes later, seated at her kitchen table with a cup of warm cocoa, she tried to sort out her feelings.

Just the facts, ma'am. The line from the old sixties TV series *Dragnet* popped into her mind and made her smile. So what were the facts?

Charlotte grabbed a pen and spiral notebook she kept on the kitchen counter. She began jotting down the things she knew to be true.

Fact one: The remains of Ricco Martinez were found in an urn that belongs to Patsy Dufour. Charlotte's pen hovered over the sentence. No, that wasn't truly a fact. Despite the evidence of the billfold, there was no forensic proof that the bones belonged to Ricco. Not yet.

Charlotte scratched through Ricco's name and penned in the word *someone* instead. Then she wrote the word *billfold* and put a large question mark beside it.

For several seconds she stared at what she'd written. Adding an *a* on the next line, she wrote: *Patsy purchased urn at warehouse on Tchoupitoulas. Probably the same warehouse where stolen artifacts were found. Name of new owner? Old owner?*

Next she wrote, *Fact two: Nadia disappears.* Beside it she wrote, *Why?* Then she added *Guilty? Or simply scared? Pregnant?* She skipped a line and wrote, *Fact three: Daniel arrested.* Under *Fact four*, she wrote, *Daniel denied bail.* Beside it she scribbled, *Why?*

Fact five: Nadia calls and claims that Lowell Webster and son, Mark, are involved.

Charlotte narrowed her eyes as she stared at the words, *Nadia calls.* Was it possible that the police had tapped her home phone, or was Nadia being paranoid? Charlotte rolled the pen between her thumb and fingers. Maybe she should ask Judith. Judith could find out for sure.

Charlotte slowly shook her head. No, she couldn't risk asking Judith. If she asked Judith, then she'd have to explain why she was asking. With Judith being a police detective, the whole situation might force her into a compromising position, or at the very least pose a conflict of interest since Judith was her niece and Nadia was now Judith's sister-in-law.

Besides, if her phone wasn't already bugged and she revealed that Nadia had called her, then for sure the police would put a tap on it. If not her home phone, then they might begin monitoring her cell phone, if that was possible.

Charlotte frowned. Was it possible? she wondered. She couldn't recall such a thing being done in any of the mystery books she'd read or on any of the television shows she'd watched. Even so, she knew that there was something about certain frequencies, some kind of electronic technical stuff. . . .

Charlotte sighed heavily. *You're getting sidetracked.* She stared at her list of facts. Then she wrote, *Fact six:* But her eyes kept going back to *Fact five.*

If Nadia's claim was true, if a man of Lowell Webster's wealth and influence was responsible, then Nadia was right to be skeptical about the police believing her. Given Lowell Webster's political connections and influence, Daniel and Nadia's prospects for being cleared would be almost impossible.

Impossible . . . impossible . . .

"No, not impossible," Charlotte said with determination and conviction. "Never," she added fiercely, her gaze scanning the facts she had written.

She tapped the pen on the blank line below *Fact five.* Then, slowly and precisely, she wrote *Fact six: Will Richeaux.* Under *Fact six* she added: *You can bet if he's pushing things, there's a reason behind it,* words that both Judith and Louis had spoken.

But what reasons? Charlotte stared at the list, but in her mind's eye, she was reliving the day that the bones had been discovered. Three days had passed since Friday, but Charlotte could still picture Patsy Dufour's strange reaction to Will Richeaux when he'd entered the room. Then there was his odd behavior toward Patsy as well.

Patsy had been frightened at the sight of him. But why? Why would the sight of Will Richeaux frighten her? In Charlotte's experience, people were usually frightened of someone because they either knew them personally or knew something about them. If Patsy and Will knew each other—and Will had indicated that there had been a previous incident—that could very well explain his behavior toward Patsy.

Charlotte scribbled down: *Ask Patsy about Will Richeaux.*

When she realized what she'd written, she took a deep, fortifying breath. Under ordinary circumstances, she would never consider questioning a client about their personal business. Doing so meant breaking her standing rule of minding her own business, and minding her own business did not include gossiping or being a busybody. It was a rule she'd tried to live by for most of her life, and a rule she enforced when it came to her maid service. Each of her employees was warned from the beginning of her employment that such infractions would not be tolerated and were grounds for immediate dismissal.

Charlotte tapped the pen against the notebook. But this was different. Wasn't it? This didn't involve just her maid service. This involved family; it was personal and was certainly a far cry from ordinary circumstances. And, like it or not, she was already involved. Besides, what was the alternative? Sit around and do nothing? Ignore everything?

Charlotte shook her head. No way could she just sit back and do nothing, not when her beloved nephew and his new family were in so much trouble.

Even so, the thought of prying into Patsy Dufour's life made her squirm with discomfort. No matter the reasons, it just didn't feel right.

With a sigh, Charlotte rolled her head first to one side, then the other, stretching the bunched-up muscles in her neck. What she needed was a good night's sleep. Things always looked different the morning after a good night's sleep.

Charlotte stood, and, after turning off the overhead lights in the kitchen and living room, she tiptoed into her bedroom. In the bedroom, she paused by the bed and stared down at Davy, who was curled up smack in the center.

Ever since the little boy had been staying with her, she hadn't really gotten a good night's sleep. For one thing, she wasn't used to another person being in the house. For another thing, she was used to sleeping alone, and though Davy was just a small little boy, like a lot of children, he tossed and turned . . . and kicked. And she had a sore back to prove it.

Charlotte reached for the alarm clock. She really needed to set the clock a bit earlier than usual so she could get a head start on the day before Davy awakened. But if she set it at all, the jangling sound was sure to awaken Davy, too.

After briefly debating the pros and cons of moving Davy to the spare bedroom, she decided it would be much easier all the way around if she simply moved the alarm clock instead and slept in the other room herself.

On Tuesday morning, Charlotte was once again able to get her shower and dress before Davy awakened. The coffee was brewing, and she figured that if she was very quiet, she might even have enough time to have a first cup and scan the newspaper headlines before the little chatterbox got up.

As quietly as she could, she unlocked the front door and walked out onto the porch. For a change, the Doberman across the street simply stared at her through the fence and didn't growl or bark.

Once she'd retrieved the newspaper, she stood for a second staring up at the morning sky. The sun was just beginning to peek over the tops of the trees. According to the temperature gauge hanging on the porch, it was a glorious sixty-five degrees, the perfect weather to take a walk.

Charlotte sighed. The cooler weather wouldn't last. With a shrug, she went back inside. By noon it would heat up to the high seventies, possibly the low eighties. But none of it mattered anyway.

Now that she had Davy, it was going to be almost impossible to take a walk, even in the evenings. His little legs were too short to keep up with the pace she liked to set, and though she'd considered pushing him in one of those umbrella strollers, the sidewalk was much too uneven for her to consider it.

When Davy did awaken, over breakfast, once again Charlotte asked him if he would like to play with the kids that day. His eager nod was a huge relief. After dropping the little boy off at the day-care, she drove to the home of Bitsy Duhe, her Tuesday client.

Bitsy lived on the same street as the famed author, Anne Rice. Though Charlotte much preferred mystery novels to the horror genre, she greatly admired the author and had had more than one fantasy about being hired to clean for her.

Bitsy Duhe's home was a raised-cottage style, and, like Bitsy herself and most of the other homes in the Garden District, it was very old and very grand.

Depending on her mood, Charlotte sometimes dreaded Tuesdays. In most of the homes that she had cleaned over the years, the clients busied themselves with other things while Charlotte worked, and they were content to let Charlotte go about her business without interfering. But not Bitsy. There had been more Tuesdays than Charlotte cared to count when Bitsy had followed her from room to room, all the while chattering away about people that Charlotte either just knew vaguely or had never heard of. And on those particular days, Charlotte had to remind herself that Bitsy was simply lonely.

Edgar Duhe, Bitsy's husband, had once been the mayor of New Orleans, and he and Bitsy had led an active social and political life. But Edgar had died three years earlier, and since his death, Bitsy no longer attended many social functions due to her advancing age. That, added to the fact that the only family she had were a son and two granddaughters who all lived out of state, left Bitsy with far too much time on her hands. To fill that time, Bitsy kept the phone lines hot, checking in with her old girls' network of friends on the latest gossip going around or the latest scandal.

By the time Charlotte had unloaded her supply carrier and locked the van, she wasn't in the least surprised to see Bitsy waiting for her at the front door.

"Good morning," Charlotte called out as she climbed the steps to the porch.

As usual, Bitsy was fully dressed in one of her mid-calf-length, floral patterned dresses, and every purple-gray hair on her head was in place. She was a spry, bird-like woman with a face that had surprisingly few wrinkles considering her age, and Charlotte could only hope she would look that good herself when she reached her eighties.

Bitsy smiled and returned Charlotte's greeting. "Good morning to you, too." But her smile faded quickly. "Oh, Charlotte, dear, how *are* you?" She stepped back inside into the foyer and Charlotte followed her. "I've been so worried about you and that nice young nephew of yours." Bitsy closed the front door.

Though Bitsy's words and tone sounded sympathetic enough, and she probably meant well, Charlotte braced herself. The eager sparkle in the old lady's faded blue eyes was all too familiar; it was a look that meant that Charlotte was in for the third degree.

"Such a shame," Bitsy said, sighing heavily. "Just a crying shame, what with him just getting married and all. Of all things, someone like him being charged in a murder. Ridiculous! That's what it is. Just ridiculous!" She looped her arm through Charlotte's. "Now I want you to just forget about cleaning for the moment and come on back to the kitchen with me." She tugged on Charlotte's arm, leaving Charlotte little choice but to go along with her.

"That new juicer I ordered—you know, the one I told you about last week—well, it finally came yesterday, and I just finished squeezing some fresh orange juice. We'll have a nice glass of juice before you get started."

Bitsy hadn't mentioned ordering another juicer, but Charlotte didn't bother to correct her. Of late Bitsy had grown really touchy about her ability to remember things. That the older lady had bought yet another kitchen gadget didn't surprise Charlotte in the least, though. Bitsy was obsessed with any and every kind of new gadget that came along, and if memory served her, by last count Bitsy already owned at least two juicers.

Bitsy's attempt at subterfuge didn't fool Charlotte in the least. Having a glass of juice was just an excuse for the old lady to interrogate her in order to have more grist for the gossip mill. Charlotte choked back a groan. From her past experiences of dealing with Bitsy, she'd learned that it was much easier and saved time to simply go along with her than to protest.

Once in the kitchen, Charlotte set down her supplies, then seated herself at the breakfast table. "Just a small glass, please," she told Bitsy. "I have another job after I finish here, so I really need to get started."

Bitsy frowned as she handed Charlotte a large glass of juice. "Another job? Anyone I know?"

Too late, Charlotte realized her mistake. "Patsy

Dufour," she answered reluctantly, knowing she'd just given Bitsy the opening she needed.

If possible, the spark in Bitsy's eyes grew even brighter. "Yes, siree, such a crying shame about all of that," she said. "Why, I heard that Patsy almost had a nervous breakdown, right then and there, screaming like a banshee and carrying on. And who could blame her? Bad enough that all those artifacts were stolen in the first place. But to end up with one in your own back-yard, then to find out that there were human bones in it." Bitsy shuddered and shook her head. "I'd probably have had a heart attack."

Charlotte decided against confirming or denying Bitsy's version of what had taken place; instead, she took a healthy drink of the juice. Then she made the mistake of swallowing wrong and almost choked.

"My goodness, Charlotte, don't be in such a hurry." Bitsy motioned at the glass in Charlotte's hand. "Just sip it."

Charlotte coughed and tried to clear her throat.

"And speaking of those stolen artifacts"—Bitsy shoved a large scrapbook halfway across the table— "I've been keeping up with all the news stories." She reached over and tapped the scrapbook with her fore-finger. "Kept everything that's been written up about them right in there." Barely missing a beat, she con-tinued. "I understand that Patsy told the police that she bought the urn out of that old warehouse on Tchoupi-toulas—the one they're turning into condos." Again she shook her head. "Doesn't surprise me in the least, I'll tell you, given Patsy's political alliances."

Charlotte wrinkled her nose, and in spite of her resolve to keep her mouth shut, her curiosity got the best of her. "What on earth does Patsy Duhe's political alliances have to do with turning the warehouse into condos?"

"Not that. My goodness, Charlotte, pay attention. I'm talking about Lowell Webster. Patsy would do anything to cast aspersions on that lovely man."

Charlotte grew even more confused. "Lowell Webster?"

Bitsy's eyes widened. "Now, come on, Charlotte. Surely you know who Lowell Webster is."

"Yes, yes, of course I do, but what has Lowell Webster got to do with Patsy?"

"Why just about everything. They've been enemies for the longest."

"Enemies?"

Bitsy gave her an exasperated look. "Yes, enemies, Charlotte. Enemies since way back, when they were both students at Tulane. And until recently—until he sold it—that warehouse belonged to Lowell." She tapped the scrapbook with her forefinger. "There was an article all about it."

Bitsy pursed her lips. "And another thing. I don't care what anybody says, Lowell just couldn't have had anything to do with that thieving gang of thugs who stole all of that stuff." She shrugged. "But that's what happens when a good man like Lowell decides to run for office around here. If they can't find something legitimate against him, they make something up, anything to ruin his good name and reputation.

"Well, I'm here to tell you, New Orleans would be dadgum lucky to get a man like Lowell Webster for mayor. If my Edgar were still alive—God rest his soul—he'd be supporting Lowell one hundred percent."

Trying to follow Bitsy's logic was like swimming underwater in a muddy swamp. "Now let me get this straight," Charlotte said, still trying to make sense out of Bitsy's diatribe. "You're claiming that Patsy purposely indicated that particular warehouse just because Lowell Webster happened to own it once."

"Why, I wouldn't be a bit surprised," Bitsy answered with a satisfied smirk. "Nothing would please her more than to see Lowell's good name dragged through the dirt. And another thing. It wouldn't surprise me in the least to learn that all that screaming and carrying on she did was all a big put-on—just an act. Yes siree, I'd bet my last dollar that she was lying through her teeth about where she got that urn."

"Now, Bitsy, don't you think that's a little far-fetched, like some sort of conspiracy theory or something?" The moment the words left Charlotte's mouth, Bitsy's reaction made her wish she could take them back.

The older lady's lower lip quivered and she blinked several times. "I may be getting old, Charlotte, but I'm not senile—not yet. Contrary to what *some* people think, my mind works just fine."

"Of course it does," Charlotte quickly reassured her. Growing senile was one of Bitsy's biggest fears, right along with being forced to leave her home due to her age or due to her inability to care for herself.

Charlotte patted the old lady's hand. "Don't mind me. I'm still upset about Daniel's situation." She stood. "But right now, I really must get busy and earn my pay."

Though Bitsy gave a wan smile and nodded, Charlotte could tell that the old lady's feelings were still hurt. "And by the way," she added. "I really believe your new juicer works a lot better than those others. The orange juice was wonderful."

As Charlotte had hoped, her compliment was just what the elderly lady needed to hear. Her eyes brightened and she gave Charlotte a huge grin. "It does work better, doesn't it," she said.

I'd bet my last dollar that she was lying through her teeth about where she got that urn. Like a pesky fly, Bitsy's comment about Patsy kept buzzing through Charlotte's thoughts throughout the morning, as did the fact that, yet again, Lowell Webster's name had been brought up in a conversation.

By noon, she had finished at Bitsy's, and the older lady seemed to be in a better mood by the time Charlotte was ready to leave. As Charlotte packed the last of her cleaning supplies back into her supply carrier, she heaved a heavy sigh. All morning long she'd waged a mental debate with herself. Like it or not, for once she was going to have to bend her own rules about prying and gossiping.

There was no other way around it. Two lives were at stake—four, if she counted Davy and the new baby. If she was going to help Nadia and Daniel, she had to get

149

certain information, and there was only one way to get that information. A little prying into Patsy Dufour's life was a small price to pay to get to the truth . . . wasn't it?

Now all she had to do was figure out how she could bring up the subject of Lowell Webster to Patsy without seeming too obvious or too—Charlotte shuddered—too nosy.

Chapter Twelve

Ordinarily Charlotte allowed herself at least a thirty-minute lunch break when on the job. To save time, she decided that for today she would eat the sandwich she'd brought with her in the van, en route to Patsy's house.

By the time she reached Patsy's, she was still chewing on the last bite of the turkey sandwich as well as mentally chewing on the best approach to use to initiate a conversation with Patsy about Lowell Webster.

As she drove past the entrance gate a flash of white at the top of the gate caught her eye. She also noticed that Patsy's Mercedes was missing from where it usually sat in the driveway.

After parking the van alongside the curb, Charlotte unloaded her supply carrier, locked the van, and trudged back to the entrance gate, all the while telling herself that Patsy's car could be in the shop for repairs.

The flash of white turned out to be an envelope taped to the gate, and it was addressed to Charlotte. With a sinking feeling, Charlotte set the supply carrier down on the sidewalk and pulled the envelope loose from the tape. Inside was a brief note from Patsy.

Sorry I couldn't give you more notice, Charlotte, but something unexpected came up. I'll see you on Thursday instead.

Patsy.

Still glaring at the note, Charlotte felt her temper rising. On the street just a few feet away from the sidewalk, cars and trucks whizzed by, and somewhere down the block a lawn mower roared to life, but the noise was nothing compared to the angry roar in Charlotte's head.

The sound of voices were what finally broke through to her, reminding her where she was. Out of the corner of her eye, a movement caught her attention.

Tourists. A whole group of wide-eyed, camera-toting tourists, hanging on to every word that the tour guide was telling them, were walking straight toward her.

"Humph! If they only knew," she muttered. Clutching the note and envelope, Charlotte executed an about-face. Trying her best to ignore the tourists, she side-stepped around the group and stomped back to the van. With each jarring step she took, she fumed. All she could think about was how she'd planned and prepared, then rushed around the entire morning, just so that she could work Patsy into her schedule.

Inside the van, she slammed the door shut so hard that the vehicle rocked from the force. Using both hands, she crushed and wadded the note and envelope into the size of a Ping-Pong ball. Then, in a fit of anger and frustration, she tossed it over her shoulder into the back.

By the time that she pulled into her own driveway a few minutes later, her initial anger had passed, leaving only a deep-seated feeling of shame.

Although it pained Charlotte to admit it, she knew that most of her anger and frustration had nothing at all to do with Patsy canceling without notice and everything to do with her own plan to poke and pry into Patsy's life being thwarted. Just the thought of prying into Patsy's personal life was shameful enough, but now she would be forced to wait two whole days before she could question her about Lowell Webster. Two whole days . . .

Charlotte suddenly went stone still. *Davy!* She'd completely forgotten about picking up Davy at the day-care.

Charlotte immediately shifted into reverse, then froze. With a groan of disbelief, she smacked her forehead with the heel of her hand. "What a dingbat," she muttered. With a shake of her head, she shoved the gear shift back into park and switched off the ignition.

There were still at least three hours to go before it was time to pick up Davy, but because she'd gotten so flustered about Patsy canceling the job, she'd also gotten confused about the afternoon schedule.

Serves you right. Charlotte ignored the voice of her conscience and climbed out of the van and locked it. On legs that felt weighted with lead, she slowly made her way to the front steps. Maybe Hank was right after all. Maybe it was all getting to be too much for her to handle. Day in and day out . . . juggling schedules, cleaning, keeping the books.

Maybe it was time she thought about retiring, like Hank wanted her to. He'd been after her for months, offering to subsidize her income. But Charlotte shuddered at the thought of retirement as she unlocked the front door. "And maybe you just need to screw your head back on straight," she murmured, stepping inside and closing the door behind her. She glanced over at Sweety Boy's cage. "What do you think about that, Sweety?"

For an answer, the little bird squawked, ruffled his feathers, and flapped his wings. It was a ritual designed to get her attention, and a part of his normal routine each time she returned home,

Ignoring him for the moment, Charlotte set her purse down, stepped out of her shoes, and slipped on the pair of moccasins she kept by the front door. Still deep in thought, and more out of habit than anything else, Charlotte finally moved over to the little bird's cage and stuck her forefinger through the wires. Sweety Boy immediately sidled up to her finger and rubbed his head against it.

Ordinarily Charlotte would have tried to coax the parakeet into talking, but for the moment she was unable to work up enthusiasm for anything, let alone making another unsuccessful attempt to teach the bird to talk.

Not for the first time, she wished there were such a thing as a switch or button that she could turn or push to instantly clear her mind of all the clutter.

Suddenly Sweety Boy squawked and began making clicking noises. Then, as plain as day, he said, "Pretty boy. Sweety Boy's a pretty boy."

Charlotte's eyes widened with surprise and delight. "Oh, Sweety," she whispered. "Oh my goodness, you did it! You really did it!"

For long seconds, all she could do was stare at the little bird in awe. For months she'd been trying to get him to talk, and though he had said a few words here and there, he'd never said a complete sentence despite all her coaxing and pleading.

"Just goes to show," she finally murmured. "You shouldn't give up. There's always hope." Charlotte blinked several times as sudden realization washed through her: giving up was exactly what she'd been subconsciously doing in regard to Daniel and Nadia's situation.

She gently rubbed the little bird's head. "Good boy. Sweety's a very good boy."

Fueled with new resolve, Charlotte turned away and, hands on hips, began pacing the length of the living room. As the old saying went, there was "more than one way to skin a cat," more than one way to find out what she needed to find out. All she had to do was figure out how.

Abruptly, Charlotte stopped in her tracks. "Tulane," she murmured. "Of course! That's it!" Bitsy had mentioned something about Patsy and Lowell Webster both attending Tulane.

A slow smile spread over Charlotte's face as a mental image of a woman's face formed in her mind. "Yep! There's more than one way to get some answers," she murmured. And she knew just the person to get them from. "Thanks, Sweety," she whispered.

Charlotte looked up the phone number she needed, then tapped it out. Four rings later, the call was answered with a firm, "Hello."

"Professor Mac, this is Charlotte."

The professor laughed. "Why, of course it is. I'd recognize your voice anywhere." Never one to mince words, the professor got right to the point. "I hope this call means you're finally going to pay me a visit. It's been a while, you know."

"Yes ma'am, it has, and I apologize. But if it's convenient, I would love to drop by, say, in about ten or fifteen minutes?"

"Well, stop wasting time and come on over."

The phone clicked in Charlotte's ear, and with a grin on her face, she hung up the receiver.

"See you later, Sweety," she called out as she grabbed her purse. "You be a good little birdy while I'm gone." When Sweety squawked and ruffled his feathers, Charlotte giggled as she locked the front door behind her, then hurried to her van.

The Italianate-style mansions marked the second great period of affluence for the Garden District, the first being the Greek Revival style. Located on St. Charles Avenue, the Maison Rochelle, with its segmental arches, octagonal bays, and paired scroll brackets was one of the more elaborate examples of the Italianate style.

Maison Rochelle had been built in the 1870s, and though Charlotte had never met the most recent owners, multimillionaires Margie and Clarence Rochelle, she'd often heard of their philanthropic educational endeavors through her other clients.

After Clarence's death and in his honor, Margie had turned the monstrous old house into a retirement facility that catered mostly to an elite group of teachers and college professors.

As Charlotte pulled alongside the curb in front of the Maison Rochelle, she checked the dashboard clock for the time. She figured she had about two and a half hours, three at the most, before she needed to pick up Davy at the day-care, plenty of time to find out what she needed to know from Dr. Emma Claire McGee.

Known affectionately as Professor Mac to the many Tulane University students who had taken her freshman English course, Dr. McGee had finally retired. A year after retirement, she'd sold her home and moved into Maison Rochelle and had lived there for the past ten years.

Charlotte owed her very livelihood to her beloved Professor Mac and had tried to visit her at least once every two months or so since her retirement. But it had been a while since Charlotte had seen the elderly lady, and in light of the reason she'd come this time, she felt a pang of guilt for not getting by more often.

Two tiers of steps led up to the porch of the home, and midway Charlotte paused a moment to soak in her surroundings.

The grounds surrounding the grand old house were meticulously groomed and lush with a variety of blooming flowers, various tropical plants, and several species of trees. A couple of the live oaks were reputed to be almost as old as the house itself. The sweet smell of roses, gardenias, and magnolias hung heavily in the air, and Charlotte had often thought that if she could bottle up the combined scents, she could make a fortune. With a sigh of pure pleasure, she finally continued up the steps.

Once on the porch, she paused again, but as she turned to admire the grounds one last time, she suddenly grinned, then rolled her eyes.

In the huge oak near the front that draped over St. Charles Avenue were several strands of purple and green beads still clinging to one of the limbs. Though Mardi Gras had been over for weeks, it wasn't unusual to see the beads dangling from power lines or tree branches, especially along St. Charles Avenue, one of the main routes for the parades. In their enthusiasm, the Krewe members who rode the tall floats sometimes got a bit wild with their aim as they tossed the beads into the crowds that lined the streets. Even so, each time Charlotte spotted the gaudy throws that were left in the aftermath, the sight always made her smile.

"Nowhere but in New Orleans," she murmured as she turned away and walked to the front door.

Inside the facility, the first floor was divided into single, private rooms for the residents who could no longer care for themselves. The second floor, along with the renovated stable, contained small apartments for those residents who were still mobile enough to only need someone to look in on them a couple of times a day. Ms. Margie Rochelle had renovated and still maintained the carriage house located behind the big house for her own use.

Once inside, Charlotte checked in at the reception desk near the front of the wide, marble-floored entrance hall. The ceiling of the hall soared two stories high, the perfect setting for the magnificent staircase near the rear of the hall. The grand, winding staircase was a masterpiece of design and craftsmanship, its beauty unsurpassed by any that Charlotte had ever seen in the many homes she'd cleaned over the years.

The only modern concession that had been made to the entrance hall was a glassed-in elevator installed to the right of the staircase to accommodate the aging tenants in the home.

The thirty-something woman manning the reception desk smiled warmly at Charlotte. "May I help you?" she asked.

The woman had a certain sophisticated, well-groomed look about her that made Charlotte suspect that she was one of the many Junior League volunteers who often helped out at the retirement facility, volunteering tirelessly with their time and their money.

Charlotte nodded and smiled back. "My name is Charlotte LaRue, and I believe Dr. McGee is expecting me."

"Why, of course, Ms. LaRue. I've already prepared your visitor's pass." She held out a small card. "Dr. McGee left instructions for you to go right up just as soon as you arrived."

"Thank you." Charlotte slipped the card into her

purse. To save time, she decided to take the elevator up to the second floor.

At the door to Professor Mac's apartment, Charlotte rapped lightly. Within seconds the door swung open, and Charlotte realized that the professor must have been standing near it, waiting for her arrival.

"My goodness, do come in, Charlotte," the professor gushed. "It's so good to see you again."

"It's good to see you, too," Charlotte answered.

Professor Mac was just a bit shorter than Charlotte, and the years had been kind to her. Except for her gray hair and a face that had aged with grace, there had been little change in her looks in all the years that Charlotte had known her.

The professor stepped backward to allow Charlotte entrance, and only then did Charlotte notice that she was now using a walker. She motioned toward the walker. "I see you have a new friend."

The professor rolled her eyes and her smile turned into a grimace. "Don't remind me. That doctor of mine insists I use the silly thing." She waved her hand. " 'Just for balance, my dear,' " she mimicked in a deep voice that made Charlotte laugh. "But enough about that for now," the older woman said. "I've brewed us a nice pot of tea, so come on in and catch me up on what's been happening with you."

Noting that the professor didn't seem to really need the walker, Charlotte followed her over to the sofa in the living area.

"Now you just have a seat," the professor told her, pointing at the sofa, "and I'll get our tea."

Eyeing the walker, Charlotte asked, "Do you need some help?"

The professor shook her head. "My goodness, no."

Then, to Charlotte's amusement, she made a big production out of folding up the walker and leaning it against the wall. "I told him I didn't need this thing," she grumbled, "but just in case he decides to pop in unexpectedly"—she winked at Charlotte—"I always use it whenever I answer the door." With a saucy grin, she stepped over to the kitchenette that was off to one side of the living area.

Charlotte glanced around the room, her eyes noting that even with the stacks of books that covered almost every available surface, the room was neat and dust-free. The air smelled faintly of disinfectant; it was a scent she recognized immediately, and she wondered if it was the same brand that she used.

"Looks like their housekeepers are doing a good job for you," she commented.

"Oh my, yes," the professor called out from the kitchen. "Those people drive me crazy with their constant cleaning. And speaking of cleaning—" Carefully balancing a tray containing cups, a teapot, and what looked like a plate of old-fashioned tea cakes, she walked toward Charlotte. "How's Maid-for-a-Day doing? Has that son of yours talked you into retiring yet?"

"The business is fine, and, no, I haven't given in yet."

"And I guess you're still cleaning, too."

Charlotte nodded. "No reason not to."

The professor set the tray down in between two stacks

of books on a low table in front of the sofa. "Just as stubborn as ever, huh, Charlotte?" She poured the tea, then handed Charlotte one of the china cups. "But that stubbornness has served you well all these years, hasn't it? Sugar or cream?" She waved a hand. "No, never mind. I forgot that you don't use either one in your tea." Then, without missing a beat, she said, "I still say you should have kept going to school, but there was no reasoning with you back then, either."

Charlotte took a sip of the tea to hide her smile. It was the same conversation they'd had for more years than Charlotte cared to remember, but she didn't mind in the least, nor did she argue or defend the decision she'd made after her parents' deaths. At the time, she'd been a single mother with a small child and a teenage sister to support; she'd had little choice and limited financial resources to draw on, none of which included money for continuing at Tulane University.

Once the professor had failed to talk her out of quitting school, she had been the one to suggest that Charlotte could earn quite a bit of money if she didn't mind cleaning other people's homes. Then she'd gone a step further and recommended Charlotte to several of her wealthy friends in the Garden District.

"But that's all water under the bridge now," the professor continued. She leaned forward and placed her hand on Charlotte's arm. "So, tell me, what's all this nonsense about your nephew?" She shook her head and made a tut-tut-tut sound. "I swear, a body can't believe a word of what they read in the papers or hear on the news these days. Why, that young man is no

161

more guilty of murder than I am."

Charlotte silently breathed a quick prayer of thanks for the perfect opening she'd been given. "I'm so glad to hear you say that," she said. "And you're right, of course. It's not true. None of it. And once again, I find myself in need of your help."

For the next few minutes Charlotte explained the events leading up to Daniel's arrest and ended by telling the professor what Bitsy had mentioned about bad blood between Patsy Dufour and Lowell Webster.

"Bitsy said that both of them had attended Tulane," Charlotte added. "And I thought you might remember something about them—something that might explain why Bitsy thinks they're enemies and why Nadia thinks Lowell Webster is somehow involved."

The professor pursed her lips, and for several moments she stared at Charlotte, deep in thought. "It's been a long time," she finally said, "but I do remember Patsy and Lowell. Let me see, now. As I recall, Lowell was an excellent student, but Patsy was only average. I always thought it had to do with the difference in their upbringing. Lowell was there on a scholarship and loans, while Patsy's folks paid her way through." She paused, then nodded. "If I remember right, those two dated for a while, but, then, my memory isn't what it used to be." She suddenly brightened. "Tell you what, though, you might find out more from Jane Shaw—well, she's not a Shaw anymore. I believe her name is Calhoun now."

"Jane Calhoun? *The* Jane Calhoun who lives on First Street?"

The professor nodded. "If she's married to Glen Calhoun, then that's the one. Jane and Patsy were as thick as thieves back then. They were sorority sisters and gave me fits in class with all of their shenanigans."

Charlotte grinned. She could hardly believe her ears or her luck. For a short period of time, she'd once worked for the Calhouns, right up until Glen Calhoun had been severely injured in an accident, one that had left him permanently impaired. After the accident, Jane had decided that they needed live-in help, so she would have more time to take care of her husband, and she'd reluctantly had to terminate Charlotte's services.

Charlotte shook her head. "Know what? You're amazing, Professor Mac. How on earth do you remember all of that stuff?"

The professor lips thinned into a sad little smile. "I don't remember like I used to. But to answer your question, I never married and didn't have any children of my own, so my students became my whole life—my surrogate children, so to speak. And a mother never forgets her children," she added. "But here now"—she reached down and picked up the plate of tea cakes—"you simply must try one of these. This recipe's been handed down in my family for at least three generations that I know of."

And that's the end of that subject, thought Charlotte, as she selected one of the smaller tea cakes. Hoping it didn't contain too much sugar, she took a small bite, but as she chewed, out of the blue, an idea began to form, and she surreptitiously glanced at her watch. If she left now, she might have just enough time to run by Jane

Calhoun's before she had to pick up Davy.

Ordinarily she would never consider just dropping in on someone without calling ahead first, but the gut feeling that time was of essence just wouldn't go away. On the other hand, if she left now, the professor might get her feelings hurt over such a short visit.

What to do? What to do? "Mm, these are delicious," Charlotte murmured, wondering what kind of excuse she could use to leave right away. Then the perfect pretext came to her. Even as the half-lie took form, the tiny voice of her conscience cried out, *Liar, liar, pants on fire. First gossiping about a client, and now lying. Shame on you.*

Though Charlotte cringed inside, she swallowed hard and ignored the nagging voice in her head. She made a show of holding out her left arm to check her watch. "My goodness, just look at the time," she said. "I almost forgot. I really hate to, but I'm going to have to leave. Daniel's little stepson is staying with me, and I have to pick him up at day-care."

Hoping the professor wouldn't notice, as Charlotte leaned forward to place her cup back onto the tray, she slipped the rest of the uneaten tea cake into her pocket, then stood.

The professor stood, too. "Oh, that's so nice." She sighed. "A little boy in the house must be lots of fun. But here—wait a second." She scooped up the plate of tea cakes. "Boys are always hungry, so let me just wrap a few of these in some foil for you to take with you."

Minutes later the professor returned with the foil package of tea cakes. When she handed them over to

Charlotte, she tilted her head and smiled. "Tell you what, Charlotte. Why don't I give Jane a call for you and let her know you're coming?"

Charlotte's cheeks suddenly felt as if they were on fire, but, then, she shouldn't have been surprised. The professor had always been far more intuitive than her students had given her credit for.

Charlotte wanted to thank her old friend, but the words stuck in her throat and all she could do was nod.

Chapter Thirteen

Charlotte's cheeks were still warm with embarrassment when she pulled into Jane Calhoun's driveway. How could she have forgotten just how astute and forthright the professor could be—and how unselfish and giving?

Not only had the professor phoned Jane to let her know that Charlotte needed to talk to her, but she'd paved the way by taking the time to explain exactly why Charlotte needed to talk to her.

Jane and Glen Calhoun's home was what was commonly referred to as a transitional-style house, a combination of the Greek Revival and the Italianate styles. The double-galleried house, along with its perfectly manicured gardens, was set back from the street and surrounded by a cast-iron fence designed in a rare cornstalk pattern.

Just as Charlotte entered through the gate of the elegant fence, the front door swung open. Jane Calhoun, a tall, slender woman in her mid-fifties, stood in the doorway with a smile on her face. "This is such a pleasant surprise," she called out. "It's been ages since we talked, and it's really good to see you again, Charlotte. I just wish it were under better circumstances. Come on in."

Charlotte returned the smile as she climbed the steps. "Considering the reason for my visit, it's very gracious of you to agree to see me on such short notice."

Jane stood back to allow Charlotte entry. "Don't be silly, Charlotte. We're old friends."

Once inside, Jane directed Charlotte to the formal sitting room. "I don't know how much I can help, but I'm more than happy to do what I can for Daniel." She motioned for Charlotte to sit on the sofa. "You may not know this, but Daniel helped me out of quite a bind two years ago."

"He did?" Charlotte eased down onto the sofa and shook her head. "I guess I didn't realize that you even knew my nephew."

Jane sat in a chair opposite Charlotte. "Oh my, yes. He got me out of a really sticky situation. I was having some work done on the house, and one of the contractors fell off a ladder—well, he didn't really fall—but anyway, he claimed he did, claimed he hurt his back. He was making all kinds of noises about suing me but offered to settle privately. Said if I just paid him outright, he wouldn't drag me into court.

"Well, a neighbor recommended I talk to Daniel, and within a week that contractor was singing a different tune. Come to find out, I wasn't the only client he'd pulled that on. Daniel did some checking around and found out that he had a scam going, and once Daniel confronted him, the man—"

Suddenly distracted, Jane glanced toward the doorway. "Oh, hello, honey."

Charlotte turned to see a tall, muscular man leaning heavily on a cane. The left side of his face and his throat were still scarred in spite of the extensive reconstructive surgery he had gone through, and his left arm, totally useless since his accident, rested in a sling.

Jane stood and walked over to where he was standing. "You remember Charlotte, don't you, dear?"

He gave Charlotte a lopsided grin and nodded.

Jane patted him on the back. "It's not quite time for your walk yet, honey. Is there something else that you need?"

Glen Calhoun replied, but his response was too soft and garbled for Charlotte to understand.

Evidently, Jane had no problem understanding him, though. She turned to Charlotte. "Would you excuse me a moment?"

Within a few minutes Jane returned. "Sorry about that," she said as she seated herself. "Poor thing, he's made a lot of progress, but he still needs assistance at times doing certain things."

"He looks well," Charlotte commented. "A lot better than the last time I saw him."

Jane nodded. "He has good days and bad days still, but for the most part, he's adjusted as well as could be expected."

"And you? Have you adjusted?"

"I'll admit I was pretty bitter for a while there." Jane

paused. Then her eyes crinkled and she smiled. "But with a little help from Father Thomas and the support of some really good friends, I think I've adjusted pretty well for a spoiled-rotten socialite. And speaking of spoiled socialites"—her smile faded—"Professor Mac said you needed some information on Patsy Duhe." Her voice took on a wistful tone. "You know, once upon a time, Patsy and I were really good friends, but . . ." Her voice trailed away. "Not anymore," she finally murmured. "Patsy's a prime example of what bitterness can do to a person. Such a shame, a crying shame. But, as the old saying goes, 'there but for the grace of God go I.' "

Funny, Charlotte thought. She'd never really thought of Patsy as being bitter or spoiled. A bit odd, yes. And maybe a little spoiled. But bitter? "I take it that her bitterness has something to do with Lowell Webster."

Jane nodded. "Of course, that's only my opinion. But Lowell was the love of her life, or so she thought. They met at school—sat beside each other in Professor Mac's class. Patsy fell head over heels in love with him almost from the moment she laid eyes on him. He wasn't exactly my ideal, but for Patsy he was everything she wanted in a man—handsome, intelligent, attentive, and wealthy, or so she thought.

"The one thing she didn't know was that he was also an accomplished liar. He'd presented himself as the only son of wealthy parents who lived abroad when all along he was nothing more than a scheming opportunist, just a dirt-poor boy from the wrong side of the tracks who was there on loans and a work scholarship.

But Patsy represented everything he wanted for the moment." Jane motioned with her hands. "Wealth, acceptance in the right social circles—that kind of stuff. Plain and simple, he used her. From the beginning, he never had any intentions of the relationship being permanent. Marriage didn't fit into his plans—at least not right then. And neither did a baby."

"A baby?" Charlotte whispered. "Patsy had a baby?"

"Patsy got pregnant," Jane corrected. "It was the happiest I'd ever seen her, for a while anyway. Unfortunately, Lowell didn't feel the same. When she told him about the pregnancy, instead of asking her to marry him as she had hoped, he insisted that she get an abortion."

Charlotte gasped, unable to believe her ears. "That must have been horrible for her."

"Yes it was, but that's not the worst of it. For weeks Patsy refused to believe that he really meant it. She kept making excuses for him and hoping that he would change his mind once he got used to the idea." Jane shook her head. "He didn't. And in the end, she finally agreed. By the time that she realized he'd never intended on marrying her in the first place and that he'd just been using her to make society connections, it was almost too late, though."

Charlotte stiffened and a chill ran through her. "She had an abortion?"

Jane shrugged. "What choice did she have?"

Choice? Charlotte forced herself to swallow the sharp retort that was on the tip of her tongue, and she slowly counted to ten instead.

Once upon a time, she, too, had been faced with a

similar situation. She had once found herself unmarried and pregnant. The only difference was that Charlotte knew that the love of her life would have wanted their baby—if *he'd* had a choice. Unfortunately for both of them, Vietnam had taken away his choices about anything, along with his life. Even so, the thought of aborting her baby had never once entered her mind. She'd as soon have torn out her heart.

"When Patsy did finally relent," Jane continued, "the so-called doctor that Lowell found to perform the abortion botched it and botched it good." Jane visibly shuddered. "Patsy almost hemorrhaged to death," she whispered. "And then infection set in." She cleared her throat. "As a result, once she recovered she learned that she would never be able to conceive another child." Jane paused and sighed heavily. "That's when the bitterness set in. That's when she swore that one day Lowell would pay for what he'd done to her."

After Charlotte left Jane Calhoun's, Jane's revelations about Patsy and Lowell were all she could think about. She could understand Patsy being bitter, and she could even understand her blaming Lowell—but only up to a point. After all, no one had put a gun to her head and forced her to sleep with Lowell in the first place. And in spite of Jane's belief that Patsy didn't have a choice about the abortion, Charlotte disagreed. It was true that Patsy didn't have an easy choice, but she'd had a choice. She could have chosen life, life for her baby, whether it was with her or with one of the many eager couples who would have gladly given the baby a loving home through adoption.

That's when the bitterness set in. That's when she swore that one day Lowell would pay for what he'd done to her. Jane's words played through Charlotte's mind as she pulled alongside the curb in front of Loving Care Day-Care. For long moments she sat staring straight ahead.

Thirty years was a long time. Was it possible for a person to hold on to bitterness for that length of time?

Possible? Yes, came the answer. *The same way it's possible for you to still love a man who's been dead for over forty years.*

So, if that was possible, then, logically, it stood to reason that Patsy could have been simply biding her time, waiting for the perfect opportunity to pay Lowell back.

And what of Lowell? If what Jane said about him was true, and Charlotte had no reason to doubt that it was, then Lowell Webster was the worst kind of liar and a far cry from the pillar of society that most people believed him to be.

If his own flesh and blood had meant so little to him that he could ruthlessly dispose of it without a qualm, how much less would someone mean to him that he thought might be a threat to his ambitions? Someone like Ricco.

For most of her life, Charlotte had unfailingly adhered to the philosophy that there were two sides to every story. *Judge not lest you be judged.* So, did Lowell have a side? she wondered as she slowly climbed out of the van. Had there been circumstances that could possibly

171

explain his actions or motivations involving Patsy? Charlotte couldn't see how; still, anything was possible. But how on earth could she find out for sure?

Charlotte climbed the steps to the porch. In the past, she'd always considered herself a pretty good judge of character. Until the Dubuissons.

But that was different, she argued with herself. With the Dubuissons she had become personally involved with the family, whereas she had never even met Lowell Webster. Since she didn't know the man, it stood to reason that she should be able to be objective about him.

If only she could figure out some way to make contact with him or be around him, she felt sure she could learn more about him. Just simple observation could sometimes tell you a lot about a person. But how on earth could she, a mere maid, hope to make contact with him? After all, they certainly didn't travel in the same social circles.

Chapter Fourteen

When Charlotte entered Loving Care Day-Care, there were only a few children in the large playroom, and those that were there were seated around a television set watching Barney. The only adult in the room was a young woman who looked to be an older teenager.

"May I help you?" she asked.

Charlotte nodded and smiled. "I'm here to pick up Davy Martinez."

"He's probably with the others out back on the playground," the girl offered. "Just go that way." She motioned toward a door.

The door opened to a short hallway, which led to another door. The moment Charlotte stepped outside she was greeted by sheer bedlam. The playground was a small area enclosed by a chain-linked fence that appeared to be about six feet tall. Noisy children of all shapes and sizes squealed and laughed as they clamored for turns on the various jungle gym equipment and the riding toys.

It took Charlotte a few minutes to locate Davy, but she finally spotted him sitting alone in a sandbox in a corner of the play area near the back fence.

As she made her way through the children, she noticed that although Davy was surrounded by plastic buckets, shovels, miniature dump trucks and draglines, he wasn't playing with any of the toys. Instead, he was staring through the fence toward the narrow alley that ran alongside the playground.

"Davy!" Charlotte called out. "Time to go."

When Davy turned his head toward her and frowned, Charlotte tried telling herself that he was probably just disappointed that his mother wasn't the one who had come to get him, and his disappointment had nothing to do with her personally. At least she hoped that was the case.

Charlotte knelt down beside the little boy and smiled at him. "Hey, buddy, you ready to go?"

"Where's Daddy?"

"Ah . . . he's still busy, trying to help the police," she told him, unable to think of anything else at the moment. There was simply no other way that she could think of to explain about Daniel being in jail. "But he'll be home real soon," she hastened to add and prayed it was true. "Until then, though, he wants you to stay with me. Remember? Me and Sweety Boy," she said, hoping to distract him.

He stared at her for what seemed like forever, then he finally nodded.

"Good. Let's go." Taking Davy firmly by the hand, she led him back through the maze of children to inside the house, where she signed him out. Though he went with her without protest, the solemn expression on his little face worried her. Any minute she expected him to burst into tears. Only when she'd settled him in the van did he finally speak again. She breathed a sigh of relief as he began chattering away, telling her all about how some kid named Tommy had bit another kid and left a big boo-boo on his arm.

During the drive home, Charlotte made noises to reassure Davy she was listening to him, but she was only half listening. Her thoughts kept swirling around Lowell Webster and the possibility that he'd either murdered Ricco himself to cover for his son Mark or he'd had him murdered.

But even if she found a way to meet Lowell, to be around him, what then? What purpose would it serve? It wasn't as if she could just come right out and ask the man if all the gossip she'd heard about him from Nadia and Patsy was true. And she certainly couldn't ask him outright if he'd murdered Ricco Martinez. Even if there was a way of asking him, he'd be a fool to admit to any of it, given his present political ambitions.

The more Charlotte thought about it, the more frustrated she grew. Davy was still chattering away when she pulled into the driveway. As she switched off the engine, out of nowhere a possible solution to her dilemma dawned on her, a way to spy on Lowell without him even knowing who she was or that she was spying. And she knew just the person who could help her out.

When Charlotte and Davy entered the house, Sweety Boy began his usual chatter and squawking, vying for attention.

"Play with Weety, Aunt Chardy? Me play with Weety?"

Charlotte set her purse down. "Tell you what," she said as she slipped out of her shoes and pulled on her moccasins. "Aunt Charley needs to make a few phone calls first. If you'll be a good boy and watch TV for a little while, then I promise I'll let Sweety out of his cage. And if you're very, very good, I might even let you pet him."

Davy grinned from ear to ear and thumped himself on his chest with his fist. "I be good."

"I know you will. You're a good boy," Charlotte told him as she turned on the television and settled Davy in front of his favorite afternoon show.

Satisfied that he'd be content for a little while, she headed for the phone. But as she drew near the desk, her footsteps slowed, and she began to have qualms about the solution she'd come up with and about contacting her old friend Carrie Rogers.

Involving Professor Mac and Jane Calhoun was one thing. At least they knew Daniel and had sympathy for his situation. But what she was contemplating doing now was a different matter. Carrie didn't know Daniel, and she didn't know about his predicament. Even so, if anyone had an "in" with whoever cleaned Lowell's offices, Carrie would.

Still Charlotte hesitated. First gossiping, and now lying and subterfuge as well. Just how far was she willing to go, and where would it all end?

Charlotte glanced over at Davy, but in her mind's eye she was seeing Daniel holding Davy with one arm, his other arm wrapped around Nadia, all three of them standing at the foot of her table on Easter Sunday as Daniel announced that they were now a family.

The truth. It will end with the truth. Ruthlessly tamping down her feelings of guilt, she turned her attention to the phone. Beside the phone, the light on her message machine was blinking. At first she tried to ignore it.

Just do it. Make the call before you lose your nerve. But the blinking light beckoned, and she hesitated. What if the call was news about Daniel or Nadia? Or it could be business.

If you had Caller I.D., you wouldn't have to wonder who had called. She had considered having Caller I.D. service installed, but since she already had the answering machine, she'd never been able to justify the added expense—until now. Maybe it was time to reconsider.

176

"Probably just one of those stupid telemarketing calls," she muttered. But there was only one way to find out. With an exasperated sigh, she tapped the MESSAGE button of the answering machine.

"Hi, Charlotte, it's me."

Madeline.

"Sorry I wasn't here when you called Sunday."

Charlotte rolled her eyes. "Yeah, right," she muttered.

"And I appreciate you keeping Davy," Madeline continued. "I—I just couldn't handle everything at the time. I've been so upset and worried about Daniel, I can hardly think straight. Anyway, I thought you might like to know that I was able to see Daniel today. It—it wasn't easy seeing him there . . . in that—that place." Her voice choked up, and it was a moment before she continued her message.

"Oh, Charlotte, what are we going to do? Daniel says everything will work out, but what if it doesn't? What if—" She choked up again. Then, after a brief pause, she continued, her voice almost a whisper. "Daniel told me about Nadia—about her being pregnant. He also told me he was worried about her and Davy." Madeline stopped to clear her throat. "In fact," she said, "that's one of the reasons I called. I can help out with Davy . . . if you need me to." She paused as if waiting for an answer, then said, "Well, just let me know. Call me, okay?"

The machine beeped, signaling the end of the message. With mixed emotions churning inside, Charlotte glanced over to where Davy sat entranced with the TV actions of Barney, the big purple dinosaur.

Charlotte wanted to believe Madeline was sincere, wanted to believe the best about her sister with all of her heart. But how could she? From the beginning, Madeline had made it crystal clear how she felt about Nadia and Davy.

More than likely, the reason she was changing her tune had more to do with Daniel shaming her into making the offer to help. Either that, or Daniel had laid it on the line to his mother: my way or the highway type of stuff. It was a sure bet that Madeline's offer wasn't out of the goodness of her heart. Madeline thought only about her own welfare, and in Charlotte's experience a leopard didn't change its spots, at least not overnight.

Charlotte worried her bottom lip with her teeth. She could take Davy to Madeline. Doing so would certainly make her own life less complicated. But how would yet another upheaval in his young life affect the little guy, especially since he seemed to have finally adjusted to staying with her?

On the other hand, maybe she was letting past experiences with her sister prejudice her judgment. Maybe, just maybe, once Madeline was around Davy and saw what a darling little boy he was, she might have a change of heart.

And maybe pigs can fly.

Tormented by conflicting emotions, Charlotte closed her eyes and shook her head.

When in doubt about what to do, do nothing. Charlotte wasn't sure where she'd heard the adage or if she'd read it somewhere or whether she'd simply made it up herself, but regardless, she decided that it was good advice.

Besides, if she could somehow prove that Nadia and Daniel had nothing to do with Ricco's murder, then she wouldn't have to make a decision at all. "The sooner this mess gets straightened out," she murmured, "the sooner everything can get back to normal."

Lowell Webster. Charlotte couldn't help feeling that he was the key. *And if he isn't?*

Ignoring the pesky little voice inside her head, she reached for the Rolodex. Once she'd located the card she was searching for, she tapped out the phone number listed on the card.

A woman answered the call on the third ring. "Big Easy Janitorial Services," she said. "Keeping it clean is our business."

"Hi, this is Charlotte LaRue. Is Carrie Rogers in?"

"Oh, hi, Ms. LaRue. If you'll hold a second, I'll check."

The line clicked, and as Charlotte was treated to an earfull of Dixieland music, she thought about Carrie.

They had met years ago. Like Charlotte, Carrie had also built up a thriving cleaning service, but Carrie had favored commercial services as opposed to Charlotte's preference for domestic services. And Carrie had done extremely well. Her business had grown to the point where she had contracts for some of the largest office buildings in the New Orleans CBD area.

Through a mutual friend, Carrie had heard about Charlotte, and she'd tried to persuade Charlotte to work for her as one of her top managers.

At the time Charlotte had been tempted to take Carrie up on her generous offer, but the thought of being confined behind a desk all day had held little appeal, despite the generous benefits of the job. Besides, she truly loved the old homes she cleaned, loved the personal, hands-on aspect of her work. In the end she'd decided that she'd be much happier working for herself.

Abruptly, the music stopped and a booming voice cried out, "And just what, pray tell, do I owe the honor of a call from you for? Don't tell me you've finally changed your mind about working for me."

Charlotte laughed. "And be filthy rich like you? No way. Why, I wouldn't know what to do with all the money I'd make."

Carrie snickered. "Yeah, right! So, what's up, Charlotte?"

Charlotte sobered quickly and swallowed hard. "I need some information, Carrie, and I figured if anyone can tell me what I need to know, you can." Before she could chicken out, she rushed ahead. "The no-questions-asked kind of information," she explained. "And you have to promise that you won't tell anyone about this conversation."

"No-questions-asked, huh? Sounds intriguing. You haven't, by chance, found another dead body, have you?"

Charlotte cringed at the reminder of the horrible experience she'd had at the Deviliere house just a few months earlier. "Not exactly. Like I said, no questions asked."

"Well, phooey, that's no fun."

"Carrie!"

"Hey, just kidding, Charlotte. To tell the truth, it gives me the willies just thinking about *anyone* finding a dead body."

"Me too," Charlotte agreed.

"Okay, so just what is it that you need to know?"

"Will you promise not to tell anyone that we talked or why?"

"Sounds serious."

"It is," Charlotte confirmed.

"Okay, okay, you've got my promise."

"Well . . . I was wondering if you might just happen to clean the offices of A to Z Import-Export?"

Carrie whistled through her teeth. "Oh, wow, you're talking Lowell Webster, aren't you? Don't I wish I had that contract, but, no, unfortunately for me, I don't clean his offices."

"Do you know who does?"

"Why sure. Zachary Carter has that contract, darn his hide. You remember Zack, don't you?" Without waiting for an answer, Carrie continued. "We both bid on it, you know, but Zack had someone on the inside, and he won the bid."

Like the blade of a sharp knife, disappointment sliced through Charlotte. She did remember Zachary Carter. Remembered him well. And the memories weren't good. "Well . . . thanks anyway," she finally said, feeling as if she'd just hit a brick wall. "I was really hoping that you had the contract, and that I could find out the cleaning schedule for A to Z."

"Nope! Don't have the contract. *But,* I do just happen

to know the schedule. You see, Zack and I have . . . well, we've sorta been seeing each other, even talked about a merger." She laughed. "A merger of more than one kind, if you get my drift."

Charlotte had to bite her tongue to keep from giving her opinion about Carrie's so-called merger. It hadn't been that long that she'd had a bit of experience with Zachary Carter herself. Even now, each time she thought about him, it left a sour taste in her mouth. The man was nothing but an opportunist. A charming one, but a self-serving opportunist nonetheless. Warning Carrie would do no good, though. Carrie was just stubborn enough to ignore any warnings or advice once she made up her mind about something.

"It seems that Mr. Webster doesn't want anyone in his offices unless he or one of his managers are around," Carrie said. "So Zack's people have bankers' hours, or almost. They work from nine A.M. till five P.M. on Tuesdays and Thursdays."

Relief washed through Charlotte. "Thanks, Carrie. That's exactly what I needed to know."

"Glad I could help, but, Charlotte . . ." Carrie hesitated a moment, then cleared her throat. "You aren't planning anything that's, well, you know, illegal or anything, are you? I mean, like it's none of my business, and I can't imagine you would—not really—but—"

Carrie's insinuation left Charlotte stunned, and suddenly she felt like crying and laughing all at the same time. "No," she quickly reassured her friend. "Nothing illegal. I promise." she added forcefully.

"Whew! That's a relief. Like I said, I can't imagine

you would, but I had to ask."

After saying her good-byes and hanging up the receiver, Charlotte slid her hand inside her apron pocket and fingered the envelope and note that Patsy had left her. She was supposed to work for Patsy Thursday morning. "Well, too bad," she muttered. For once she would just have to be late. And if Patsy didn't understand, then, tough!

But as Charlotte turned away from the phone, doubts about what she was planning assailed her. Thursday was only two short days away, but those two days suddenly seemed like an eternity. *Plenty of time to change your mind, and plenty of time to lose your nerve.*

"Too much time," Charlotte murmured as she headed for Sweety Boy's cage. Meanwhile, she still had to make good on her promise to let Davy pet Sweety Boy.

Chapter Fifteen

Ordinarily being wishy-washy was not a part of Charlotte's nature. If nothing else, running her own business had taught her that being informed and being decisive were the keys to success in almost any venture. By the time Thursday morning rolled around, though, she had changed her mind at least a thousand times. One minute she was ready to charge right in and just do it. The next minute she found herself second-guessing the validity of the plan to the degree that she was ready to throw up her hands and just forget the whole thing.

Then she would think about Daniel locked up in jail

and about Nadia, pregnant and wandering around homeless, and the whole cycle would begin again.

To carry out her plan meant that she needed to be at Lowell's offices by eight o'clock at the very latest. It wasn't until she had actually dropped off Davy at day-care that she decided once and for all to go ahead with it.

"What's the worst that can happen?" she muttered as she drove down St. Charles Avenue toward the Central Business District. She was pretty sure that they wouldn't call the police and have her arrested, not for just being in the office. After all, she could always claim she'd gotten lost.

Worst-case scenario, they would escort her out of Lowell's offices. And yes, it might be embarrassing, or she might be labeled as weird or nosy, but being a bit embarrassed or being labeled nosy wasn't going to kill her. At least she hoped not.

Charlotte suddenly shivered, thinking of Ricco being murdered and stuffed inside the urn to rot until there were only bones left. She shivered again. Even if Lowell had murdered Ricco, he had no reason to kill *her,* and certainly not in broad daylight.

Charlotte shook her head, as if the action would clear away the morbid thoughts. "You're really being ridiculous to even think such a thing," she muttered as she approached the high-rise where A to Z's offices were located. For one thing, she had no concrete proof that Lowell Webster had anything to do with Ricco's death, no evidence at all that he was anything but what he presented himself as being. All she really had was hearsay about a woman who'd claimed to have had an affair with him. No proof. Just gossip and rumors . . . so far.

One Shell Square was located on Poydras Street, smack in the heart of the New Orleans Central Business District. One of the largest office buildings in the city, it was also reputed to be one of the tallest.

When Charlotte had first come up with her idea, her plan had seemed simple enough. She would pretend to be an employee of Zachary Carter's cleaning service, show up an hour earlier than the regular cleaners showed up, and observe and listen to the goings on in the office. After all, no one paid attention to maids and janitors, so there was no telling what she might learn. Hopefully, she'd see or overhear something that might help her learn the true character of Lowell Webster. And once inside, she would play it by ear and hope she didn't get caught.

Charlotte had phoned the A to Z offices the day before and inquired about their exact location in One Shell Square, so once she'd parked and had armed herself with her supply carrier, she already knew which bank of elevators to take after she entered the building.

After a dizzying ride up to the forty-first floor, she headed for the A to Z suite of offices. Upon entering the reception area, the first thing Charlotte noticed was how clean and orderly the area looked. As far as she could tell, there wasn't a speck of dust anywhere.

The next thing she noticed was the decor. In keeping with the import-export theme, the walls were hung with large posters depicting scenes from several foreign countries; they reminded her of a travel agency office she'd once been in.

A centrally located desk was made of teak, and the armchairs that lined the walls of the room were padded. The colors in the fabric covering the chairs coordinated perfectly with the colors in the carpet and the walls.

Everything was perfect, just what she'd expect of someone of Lowell's status and reputation—except that there was no one manning the desk. But someone had been there. The computer was on, and steam rose from what appeared to be a cup of coffee sitting next to the keyboard. There was also an array of folders and papers scattered about the desk.

"Probably taking a potty break," she murmured. Then she suddenly grinned at how quickly she'd reverted to a child's vernacular since Davy had been staying with her.

But the clock was ticking, and as she glanced at her watch, her grin faded. There was no time to dilly-dally around, waiting for the receptionist to return, not if she was going to pull this thing off. Ignoring the butterflies in her stomach, she ventured down a wide hallway. On either side of the hallway were several closed doors; in the center of each door was an engraved brass name-plate. It was at the very end of the hallway that she finally found a door with Lowell Webster's name on it.

Charlotte stepped closer to the door. Barely breathing and with her head cocked to the side, she listened for any sounds that might indicate that someone was inside the office.

She could hear muted voices, but she couldn't make out what whoever was in the office was saying. Her heart thundering in her chest, she stepped even closer

186

and placed her ear right up against the door.

Suddenly everything happened at once: somewhere a phone rang; down the hall an office door slammed. At the same time, Lowell Webster's office door abruptly swung open.

Startled, Charlotte automatically jumped back just as a woman emerged from Lowell's office and stepped forward. Within the blink of an eye, the two were almost nose to nose.

As if choreographed, both women took a step backward, putting more distance between them.

"I—I was just about to knock," Charlotte blurted out. Raising her forearm, she feigned a knocking motion with her fist, as if the demonstration would give credence to her lie.

"Who are you?" the woman demanded, glaring at her.

Charlotte swallowed hard and willed her legs to stop shaking as she lowered her arm. The woman appeared to be in her early thirties, and though some might consider her beautiful, she reminded Charlotte of a Shakespeare quote she'd once read, something about beauty being a witch.

Charlotte motioned toward her supply carrier. "Janitorial service," she blurted out. "I-I'm here to clean."

With a frown firmly in place and a suspicious glint in her eyes, the woman eyed Charlotte up and down. "You're early," she snapped. "And I don't remember seeing you before." She waved her hand at Charlotte's clothes. "Where's your uniform?"

So much for not noticing the janitor or the maid. Intimidating didn't begin to describe the woman, and for a second, thoughts of abandoning the whole scheme right then and there flitted through Charlotte's head. *And if you keep acting like you're guilty of something, she'll think you are.*

Gathering her courage, Charlotte straightened her spine and raised her chin a notch. "I haven't been here before," she retorted sharply. "I'm a substitute. The regular person who cleans is sick. And they don't provide uniforms for last-minute substitutes," she added. "Now, if you'll just kindly direct me to which office you'd like me to start on first, then I'll get busy."

Abruptly a man appeared behind the woman, and Charlotte immediately recognized him from the photos she'd seen of him in the newspapers.

Of medium height and build, Lowell Webster was an attractive man in his early fifties with thick salt-and-pepper hair worn just a bit longer than a military cut. His face was relatively unlined, and even from a distance his piercing blue eyes had a mesmerizing quality about them. She could easily imagine a younger Patsy Duhe falling head over heels in love with him.

"Is there a problem here, Kimberly?" he asked.

The woman he'd called Kimberly turned to face him, but not before Charlotte witnessed the miraculous transformation that came over her.

Within the space of a heartbeat, Kimberly's whole countenance changed to what could only be described as sickeningly ingratiating. "No problem, Mr. Webster," she said sweetly in a lilting voice. "Just a slight mixup with the cleaning service. Sorry we disturbed you."

Almost bowing and posturing, Kimberly backed out

188

of the doorway, her action forcing Charlotte to move too or else get stepped on.

Lowell tilted his head to one side and peered over Kimberly's shoulder at Charlotte. "Well, send her in," he said. "My office is a mess." With that, he did an about-face and went back to his desk.

Pivoting to face Charlotte, Kimberly once again made a transformation. The hard-edged look was back, along with her disapproving frown. "Well?" she snapped. "You heard what Mr. Webster said, so why are you just standing around?"

Suddenly feeling contrary, and just to aggravate the silly woman, Charlotte snapped to attention, gave her a stiff, three-fingered salute, and said, "Yes ma'am. Right away, ma'am."

The moment the words left Charlotte's mouth, she immediately regretted the impulse. *Really stupid, Charlotte. That was a really stupid thing to do.* The woman was suspicious enough already, and the last thing she should have done was antagonize her or draw more attention to herself.

And she regretted her actions even more when the woman narrowed her eyes and gave her an *I'll get you* look just before she stalked past Charlotte and marched down the hallway.

Charlotte figured she'd better hurry and make hay while the sun was shining, because she had a funny feeling that it wouldn't be shining long.

Though Lowell Webster's office carried out the same decorating scheme as the reception area, it was far larger. A bank of windows took up one wall, lending a spectacular view of the skyline. A row of file cabinets and a bar area, complete with a small refrigerator, lined yet another wall, and along the third wall was a computer center and a doorway that Charlotte suspected led to a private bathroom. In the center of the room was a massive desk, the top covered by folders and papers; facing the desk in a conversation cluster were a small sofa, two matching high-backed club chairs, and a octagonal-shaped coffee table.

Lowell was in deep concentration, studying some papers on his desk, but he raised his head long enough to tell her, "You can start in there." He motioned toward the door near the computer center, then he bent back over the papers again.

As she'd suspected, the door led to a bathroom. Though Charlotte pulled the door closed behind her, she left it cracked just enough so that she could still hear what was going on in the office.

The bathroom was almost as large as the one in her house. Not only did it contain a lavatory and toilet, but an oversized shower as well. Beside the shower was what appeared to be a small closet.

Curious, Charlotte opened the door. Just as she'd suspected, there were a couple of suits, some shirts, and sweat suits hanging inside on a rod. On the floor a pair of dress shoes and a pair of tennis shoes peeked out from beneath the hanging clothes.

Ever aware of the passing time, with a shake of her head, she closed the door, set her supply carrier on the floor, and pulled on a pair of rubber gloves.

The first thing she did was pour a healthy measure of

pine cleaner into the toilet bowl. Leaving it to soak, she Windexed the mirror and the faucets, then wiped down the sink and the shower. She'd just begun to scrub the toilet when she heard the phone ring in Lowell's office. It rang a second time before he finally answered it.

"Yeah, Kimberly." He paused. "No, I've told you before that I don't want to talk to him." There was a moment of silence, then he said, "No! Hell, no! I don't want him coming up here." After another short silence, Lowell let loose a string of curse words. "Okay, okay," he finally relented. "I'll talk to him. Put him through."

Charlotte tapped the toilet brush against the rim, and after quickly rinsing it under the faucet, she placed it in the sink to drip-dry. Barely breathing, she tiptoed closer to the door so she could hear better.

"How many times have I told you not to call me here?" Lowell snapped at the caller. There was a slight pause; then, his voice rising in anger with each word, he began ranting. "I don't want to hear it. That woman is out to ruin me—has been for years. Why the hell didn't you get rid of her, too, along with that two-bit hustler she hired?" Another pause. "Yeah, yeah, I've heard it all before," Lowell snapped at the caller. There was another silence, then, "Tell you what, buddy," he said, his voice dropping to a soft, menacing drawl, "if I go down, I'm dragging you with me." Again his voice rose to a shout: "And the next time I hear from you, it had better be good news or else!"

The crack of the receiver being slammed down jolted Charlotte into action. After what she'd just heard, the last thing she needed was for Lowell to suspect that she'd been listening in on his conversation. In hopes of allaying any suspicions that she'd been listening, she quickly flushed the toilet.

With her insides churning and her mind swirling with bits and pieces of the conversation she'd overheard, Charlotte decided she should wait a few minutes before she left the bathroom.

She eased over to the toilet, closed the lid, and sat down.

That woman is out to ruin me—has been for years. "That woman" had to be Patsy . . . didn't it? Of course there was always the possibility that he'd been talking about someone else, maybe even his wife, but Charlotte didn't think so. Everything that she'd read about his wife indicated that she was his biggest supporter.

Why the hell didn't you get rid of her, too, along with that two-bit hustler she hired? Charlotte shivered. If "get rid of her" meant what she thought it meant and "that woman" was indeed Patsy, then Patsy was in big trouble.

Another thought brought a frown to Charlotte's face. Again assuming "she" was Patsy, then it stood to reason that the "two-bit hustler" could be Ricco.

Charlotte reached up and rubbed the bridge of her nose. Trying to figure out this mess was giving her a headache. After a moment, she realized that it had been a while since she'd heard any noise coming from the outer office. Maybe Lowell had left, and maybe it was time for her to be thinking about doing the same.

Relief washed through her when she saw that the office was indeed empty. Since she hadn't heard Lowell leave, she figured he must have left when she flushed the toilet.

Charlotte stared longingly at the door that led out into the hallway. If her suppositions were right, then she'd heard what she came to hear, or at least enough to confirm in her own mind that Lowell was capable of almost anything, including murder. And if she had any sense, she'd leave now, just as fast as her legs could carry her.

Charlotte closed her eyes and willed her heart to slow down. *No. Too suspicious. It would look too suspicious to leave now.*

Taking a deep breath, she quickly set about dusting and straightening the office. Just as soon as she finished up Lowell's office, she'd make up some kind of excuse, then hightail it out of there.

She had just begun dusting the file cabinets when she heard a commotion in the outside hallway.

"She's in there," Charlotte heard Kimberly say as the door abruptly swung open.

Charlotte was speechless when the uniformed security guard stepped into the room. Her eyes widened in recognition, and her heart began pounding in her chest. What on earth was Louis Thibodeaux doing there?

Chapter Sixteen

T he shocked expression on Louis's face was almost comical, but laughing was the last thing Charlotte felt like doing at the moment.

Louis pointed at Charlotte. "Is this the woman?"

Kimberly gave Charlotte a Cheshire-cat grin; then she

turned to Louis and nodded. "That's the one. I took the liberty of phoning the janitorial service we use. They assured me that the regular cleaning lady was on her way, and they also confirmed that they hadn't sent out any substitutes today. I don't know what this woman thinks she's doing here, but I want her removed from these premises immediately."

Louis took a step closer to Charlotte, his eyes narrowing with suspicion, and Charlotte's mind raced with possible excuses she could use.

The best defense is an offense. In for penny, in for a pound. Placing her hands on her hips, she glared at Louis. "What's going on here? Isn't this Mr. Lawrence Webster's offices?"

The look Louis gave her said she wasn't fooling him in the least. "No, this is Mr. *Lowell* Webster's offices."

Charlotte feigned surprise and embarrassment. "Oh, my goodness." She turned to Kimberly. "I'm so sorry. I thought this was—I mean—this is such a huge building and all, I guess I got confused." She bent down and picked up her supply carrier.

To Louis, she said, "If it isn't too much trouble, maybe you could direct me to Mr. Lawrence Webster's offices? I'm sure they're wondering why I haven't shown up yet."

Louis rolled his eyes, but he held out his arm anyway. "Be glad to, ma'am," he drawled.

With one last faked apologetic look at Kimberly, Charlotte gladly took his arm and let him escort her out of the office.

Louis didn't utter a sound all the way to the elevator.

Nor did he say anything while they both watched the panel above the elevator doors as they waited for it to arrive.

Finally the bell dinged, and when the elevator doors slid open, a lone woman stepped out wearing a uniform with a Zachary Carter's Janitorial Services logo on the front. For a second, Charlotte was tempted to tell the woman that Lowell's bathroom had already been cleaned, but Louis was nudging her toward the inside of the elevator.

Oh well, too bad. With a sigh, Charlotte gave the woman a quick smile, and with Louis right on her heels, she stepped inside.

Louis punched the GROUND FLOOR button, and once the elevator doors slid closed, he turned to face her. "There is no Lawrence Webster office in this building," he said. "As you well know," he added pointedly. "And you didn't fool anyone back there with that trumped-up excuse about the names. For Pete's sake, woman, Lowell Webster's name was right on his office door in plain sight."

Charlotte's cheeks grew warm and she groaned. "Oops! Forgot all about that," she muttered.

Louis glared at her. "Want to tell me what's going on here?"

For a split second Charlotte considered trying to bluff her way through the situation. But only for a second. Trying to bluff Louis would be like lying to the pope during confession. Not an advisable thing to do.

"If you'll walk me to my van, once we're out of the building I can explain," she finally told him.

"Yeah, I'll just bet you can," he said, sarcasm oozing with each word. "I can't wait to hear this one."

Spring had always been one of Charlotte's favorite times of the year. Outside the sun was shining, promising to be another beautiful morning, but all that Charlotte could think about was the phone conversation she'd overheard in Lowell's office.

While Charlotte and Louis walked, she did her best to explain, beginning with the call she'd received from Nadia. By the time they reached the van, she had finished her explanation with recounting her visit to Jane Calhoun.

Charlotte unlocked the back door of the van. "After talking to Jane, I wasn't sure who or what to believe," she said as she loaded her supply carrier into the van. She stepped aside to close the door. "I just thought that—"

Louis suddenly grabbed the door and slammed it so hard that a passing couple stopped to gawk.

Oblivious to the couple, Louis took a menacing step toward Charlotte. "Thought what, Charlotte?" The harshness of his voice shocked her to her toes, especially since, up until that very second, he hadn't given the slightest indication that he was anything but mildly interested in what she'd been telling him.

"Let me guess," he drawled sarcastically. "You thought you could just waltz in there, and Lowell Webster would outright confess to being a prick, or—no, wait: you thought he'd just outright confess to being a murderer!"

"No, of course not," she sputtered. "I—"

"You never learn, do you, Charlotte?" He shook his head. "The Dubuisson mess was bad enough, and now this! Do you have any idea who you're messing with? Lowell Webster could eat you up, spit you out, and never blink an eye, not to mention that he's got a whole army of lawyers who could keep you tied up in court for the rest of your natural life on defamation of character charges alone."

He poked her shoulder with his forefinger, then leaned down until he was right in her face. "Stay out of it, Charlotte. Let the police do their job. Let Judith handle it. If Daniel is innocent, then—"

"Just what do you mean 'if'?" Charlotte snapped. But she didn't give him time to answer. She'd tried hard to control her temper during his tirade, tried hard to ignore the fact that he was almost shouting at her and treating her as if she didn't have the sense God gave a goose. But enough was enough. There was no way she could ignore his sneering remark about Daniel.

"There is no *if!*" she yelled at the top of her lungs. "Daniel is innocent!" She poked him hard in the chest. "Do you hear me, you—you—you chauvinist pig? My nephew is innocent!"

With the heels of both hands, Charlotte hit him square in the chest to shove him out of her way. Caught off guard, he stumbled back long enough for her to get around him, and she hotfooted it to the driver's side of the van.

She wrenched the door open, scrambled inside, and slammed it shut. In the side-view mirror, she saw him heading toward the driver's side of the van. For good measure, just in case he decided to try to keep her from leaving, she hit the automatic door lock.

By the time she jabbed the key into the ignition switch, he was right beside her window.

"Charlotte!" he yelled. "Open this door!" He pounded on the glass.

Ignoring him, Charlotte switched on the engine, and the van roared to life. With one last contemptuous glare at him, she stomped on the accelerator, forcing Louis to either move or get bumped. He jumped back, and with the tires burning rubber, Charlotte pealed out into the street.

Brakes squealed and car horns blared in protest at being cut off, but Charlotte was oblivious to everything but the anger burning a hole in the pit of her stomach.

The short drive to Patsy Dufour's house passed in a haze of fury, laced with humiliation. To even think that she'd ever, for the slightest moment, considered Louis Thibodeaux as someone she could possibly spend the rest of her life with only fueled her anger even more. And she *had* thought about it, thought about it more than once.

"Well, no more!" she muttered. One thing she didn't need in her life was some overbearing know-it-all who had no conception of what family loyalty was all about.

The fact that he'd disowned his own son, his only child, should have given her a clue. Oh, he'd had his so-called reasons, reasons he thought justified what he had done.

Stephen had been a problem child. Louis's wife,

unable to cope with their son's problems and no longer able to tolerate the long hours required by her husband's job as a homicide detective, had deserted them both, leaving Louis to deal with Stephen by himself.

Then, when Stephen was a teenager, he'd gotten mixed up with a group of homeless runaways. One night Stephen and a couple of boys from the group mugged a tourist. The tourist died from injuries they'd inflicted on him, but before he'd died the man had been able to give a description of Stephen and one of the other boys. As a result, they had all been caught, convicted, and imprisoned.

For Louis, his son's conviction and imprisonment had been the last humiliating straw in a hayfield of problems. He'd disowned Stephen and had had no contact with him for over twenty years.

Only recently, due mostly to Charlotte's influence and encouragement, had Louis finally made the move to reconcile with his son. As a result, he now had a relationship with his little granddaughter as well.

Charlotte sighed as she parked the van on the side street that flanked Patsy Dufour's property. Reasons or not, she still couldn't conceive of abandoning your own flesh and blood.

She switched off the engine but sat staring straight ahead. If she were honest, though, Louis's lack of family loyalty was just one of the many symptoms of a larger problem between them. She'd called him a chauvinist pig, and she'd meant it. The crack he'd made about the Dubuissons had been totally uncalled for and had only confirmed what she already knew about him but had chosen to ignore.

"Lord save us from the male ego," she muttered as she finally climbed out of the van and stomped around to the back to collect the cleaning supplies she would need.

The fact that she, a rank amateur and a woman to boot, had been the one to ultimately solve the Dubuisson murder for him was something he was never going to forget, or forgive. He simply couldn't let it go. Never mind that the whole thing was over and done with.

Charlotte slammed the back door, locked the van, then headed for the gate. At least she could be thankful that she'd been spared from having to testify at the trial. Even now, just the thought of all the publicity that the trial would have attracted made her cringe. But at the last moment, thanks to some plea bargaining between the district attorney and the Dubuissons' defense lawyer, her testimony hadn't been necessary after all.

Charlotte paused at the gate. As a witness, she had been expendable, and the sad fact of the matter was that everyone, no matter who they were, was expendable. No one wanted to admit it, but, then, no one liked to face reality, either, especially if that reality included the death of an illusion about themselves.

A heaviness settled in Charlotte's chest. Had she been fooling herself all along? Had a relationship with Louis just been an illusion? Had she been so desperate for male companionship that she'd ignored the reality of who he really was?

Charlotte squeezed her eyes shut and took a deep breath. Maybe, just maybe, like Scarlett in *Gone With the Wind*, she could "think about that tomorrow."

Taking a firm grip on the gate, she shoved it open. And in spite of the urge to simply turn around, go home, and bury herself beneath the covers of her bed, she forced herself to march up the sidewalk toward the porch. For today, she still had a job to do, and in light of what she'd overheard in Lowell Webster's office, there were more important, more urgent matters to consider than her relationship with Louis Thibodeaux.

At the front door Charlotte raised her hand to ring the doorbell, then froze, her forefinger just inches from the bell.

Out of nowhere, it occurred to her to wonder why Patsy had canceled the Tuesday cleaning on the spur of the moment, without prior notice or a reason. Could it have been because Charlotte's nephew had been arrested for Ricco's murder?

Not likely, but possible, Charlotte decided. After all, Patsy was, as Jane had pointed out, a spoiled socialite. She might not want to be associated with anyone who had a jailbird in the family. And though Charlotte couldn't recall offhand if she'd ever mentioned Daniel as being her nephew, she was pretty sure that Nadia had probably done so.

But there was another possibility, too. What if Patsy had conspired to taint Lowell's reputation and used Ricco to do it, maybe even paid someone to murder him and put him in that urn. Knowing that Daniel, who was innocent, was Charlotte's nephew, Patsy might not want Charlotte around as a reminder.

Suddenly the front door swung open, giving Charlotte a start. As if her thoughts had conjured Patsy up, there she stood in the doorway.

"I thought I saw you drive up," Patsy said. "Come on in." She stepped back to allow Charlotte to pass.

Because Patsy seemed the same as always, Charlotte began to have second thoughts about the reason Patsy had canceled on Tuesday. As usual, she figured she'd let her imagination get out of hand.

But if nothing was different, then why did she feel so uneasy, so self-conscious all of a sudden? Whether the reason was because of the gossip she'd uncovered about Patsy and Lowell or because of what she'd overheard in Lowell's office, she couldn't be sure.

Probably just guilt, she concluded as she followed Patsy down the hallway. Guilt because she'd broken one of her cardinal rules and had given in to the temptation to gossip and be an all-around nosy busybody.

"I have to leave in a few minutes," Patsy said once they were in the kitchen. "I'll probably be gone most of the day, but I should be back by the time you finish up."

Charlotte had always found the physical labor involved in cleaning to be soothing, and by the time Patsy returned from her errands after lunch, Charlotte was packing up her supplies, and her melancholy mood, along with her paranoia about Patsy, had abated somewhat.

At the van, she had just finished loading her supplies

when her cell phone rang. Charlotte slammed the back door of the van closed, retrieved her phone from her purse, and pressed the TALK button.

"Maid-for-a-Day. Charlotte speaking," she said as she walked around to the driver's side.

"Aunt Charley, it's me."

Judith. Now wouldn't it be just like Louis to call and blab about her early-morning escapade in Lowell Webster's office to Judith.

"I hope I haven't caught you at a bad time, Auntie."

"No, hon. I'm just finishing up at Patsy Dufour's house." Though tempted to outright ask Judith if Louis had called her, Charlotte held her tongue. If by chance, he hadn't, then Judith would want an explanation as to why she'd asked in the first place.

"Well, I don't have but a minute to talk," Judith continued. "But I wanted to let you know that I plan on picking up Davy to give you a break tonight."

Charlotte frowned and leaned against the van. "Are you sure, hon? He really hasn't been any trouble."

"I'm sure," Judith replied. "I figured he and I would spend tonight at Mom's, just in case I get called out. I think she's ready now to take on some of the responsibility for him."

Charlotte narrowed her eyes. "Did your mother put you up to calling me?"

"Well, I—yes, ma'am, she did."

"Because she knew that I'd give her the third degree," Charlotte grumbled. "She hasn't exactly kept it secret how she feels about Daniel's marriage or his new stepson."

"If it will make you feel any better, I'll be there to run interference, Auntie."

"I suppose I have very little choice in the matter, as I'm sure that your brother insisted that she take her turn or else." Knowing how forthright Daniel could be, Charlotte was positive that was exactly what he'd done.

"I'm pleading the fifth on that one," Judith responded, which in and of itself, was an admission, Charlotte figured.

"Ah, Judith, what about his clothes and his toothbrush? And his toys," she added.

"We'll just make do for tonight, and if things work out, then I'll pick them up tomorrow. But right now, I do have to run. Love you, Aunt Charley. And we'll be talking."

"Love you too, hon. Bye now." Charlotte slowly lowered the phone and pressed the button that ended the call. Slipping the phone into her purse, she shoved away from the van and climbed inside.

She'd only had Davy a few days, and she should be grateful for a break. So why did she feel as if she were abandoning him? Why the sudden feeling of loss? And why, after over twenty years of living by herself, did the thought of returning to her empty house alone suddenly bother her?

Charlotte started up the van and pulled away from the curb. Maybe she should give Hank a call tonight. Talking to her son might help. And even better, maybe it was time for her to come right out and tell him she wanted a grandchild instead of just hinting around about it.

"Yeah, right," she muttered. "Even the thought of such a conversation with her uptight son brought a smile to her lips, a smile that lasted all the way to Milan Street.

As she approached her house, her smile quickly faded. Sitting on the front-porch swing was Louis Thibodeaux. Charlotte grimaced, and only then did she face the real truth about the reason for her depressed mood.

Chapter Seventeen

"**R**idiculous," Charlotte muttered. But even as she tried to deny that Louis was the reason for her melancholy mood as well as the main reason she hadn't wanted to go home, the thought of another confrontation with him was more than she could handle at the moment.

For a split second she was sorely tempted to simply keep on driving past her house. But to what purpose? She'd have to go home eventually anyway.

Charlotte slowed the van and turned into her driveway. Unlike Nadia, she'd never believed that running away from a problem solved anything. Avoiding Louis wasn't the answer. Besides, the house belonged to her. And there was nothing written in stone that said she had to talk to him right that moment. Later, when she'd had time to deal with her feelings about the situation, then she'd talk to him.

The minute she switched off the engine, she grabbed her purse, climbed out of the van, and hurried around to the back door. Once inside, she locked the door and headed straight for the shower.

Even with the shower running full blast, she heard him pounding on the front door. Too bad, she thought. He could pound on it until his knuckles bled for all she cared, but she wasn't talking to him until she was good and ready.

The pounding finally stopped, but by the time she'd dried off, the phone was ringing. Her first instinct was to answer it, just in case the call was about work or news about Daniel. Grabbing her robe, she hurried into the living room just as the answering machine picked up the call.

After the initial greeting, the machine beeped, and, "Charlotte, this is your friendly chauvinist pig calling."

In spite of herself, a grin pulled at Charlotte's lips, and she unconsiously began fingering the satin trim of her robe.

"I know you're home," he continued, "and I know you're avoiding me on purpose."

"You got that right," she muttered, glaring at the machine.

"I guess I can't much blame you after this morning, but all I want is to apologize. Honest."

Her fingers stilled, then balled into a fist. "Too bad," she grumbled.

"I guess I—" He hesitated for what seemed like forever, then, "Just give me a call when you're ready to talk."

"Don't hold your breath," she told the machine as it beeped and clicked off. Oh, she'd call him eventually.

There was no way of avoiding it forever. But only when she was good and ready.

Without Davy around, the house seemed strangely quiet and empty that evening, and Charlotte couldn't help worrying about him and wondering how he was adjusting to his new surroundings. Even Sweety Boy seemed to sense that something was amiss. Inside his cage he paced restlessly back and forth along his perch.

"Aw, you poor thing." Charlotte approached his cage. "Maybe you need some exercise. Want out for a while?" She opened the cage door, and the little parakeet immediately made a dash for the opening.

The moment Sweety Boy was free, Charlotte watched in amazement as she followed his flight from room to room. Was it possible that Sweety was searching for Davy?

Only after he'd been in each room did he finally settle down enough to light on the cuckoo clock above the sofa, his favorite out-of-cage perch. After watching the antics of the little bird, Charlotte concluded that, yes, such a thing was possible. Like her, the little bird missed Davy.

During the long evening, Charlotte tried her best to occupy herself with a bit of reading and television, anything to keep from dwelling on Davy, or on Louis, or especially on the conversation she'd overheard in Lowell Webster's office.

She was mentally and physically tired, and to add to her problems, her blood-sugar level was higher than normal. Since she couldn't think of anything that she'd eaten that could have caused the higher level, she figured the reason had to be stress.

Time and time again she found herself heading for the phone with the intention of calling her sister to check on Davy. But each time she walked away without doing so. For all intents and purpose, Madeline was his grandmother now, and the sooner the two of them got used to each other without interference, the better.

Exhausted, she'd finally made up her mind to simply go to bed, but as she was coaxing Sweety Boy back into his cage, the phone rang.

Charlotte recognized Nadia's voice right away. "Turn on your cell phone," Nadia told her. Then she hung up.

Just like the first time, almost the second Charlotte switched on the cell phone, it rang.

"How's Davy?" Nadia asked immediately, her voice anxious and tearful.

Charlotte settled on the sofa. "He seems to have adjusted okay, but he still asks about you and Daniel."

"Is he in bed yet? I—I'd really like to talk to him. I really *need* to talk to him, Charlotte. I miss him."

Charlotte wanted to point out that Nadia should have thought about that in the first place. But she didn't. What purpose would it serve except to alienate Nadia? And in spite of her initial feelings of anger, pity welled up within Charlotte.

"I know he'd love to talk to you too, hon, but he's not here tonight," Charlotte told her. "Judith called earlier today and said she was going to pick him up from daycare. The two of them were going to spend the night at Madeline's."

When long moments passed without Nadia saying anything, Charlotte grew afraid that she might hang up. "Nadia, I'm pretty sure it was Daniel's idea for Davy to stay with Madeline. They need to get used to each other. But there's something else I want to talk to you about, so please don't hang up."

There was more silence, then Charlotte heard what sounded suspiciously like soft sobbing. "I'm sorry, Charlotte," Nadia finally said, her voice barely above a whisper. "I know you're right. And Daniel's right. And it's not fair for me to expect you or anyone to take care of Davy, but it's just that—that I know you better than I know Daniel's mother, and I miss my little boy so much." After another long pause, she finally continued. "So what was it you wanted to talk to me about?"

"I've been nosing around," Charlotte told her. "And I've found out some stuff about Patsy Dufour. Now, I want you to think, and think hard. Did Patsy know Ricco? Had they ever met or come in contact with each other?"

"No, I don't think so. But why do you want to know? The only way she knew anything about him was through me."

"I'll get to the whys in a minute," Charlotte said. "But right now, can you remember what you said to her about him?"

"Well . . . yes. I confided in her once right after Ricco had had one of his—his tirades. Just before he was arrested for the cemetery-theft thing, he'd had a fight with Mark over some money that Mark owed him. I figure it must have been a lot of money because afterward, Ricco got drunk. And by the time he came home, he was in a real mean mood and . . . well, I—anyway, I ended up with some bruises I couldn't hide with makeup."

Charlotte shuddered and empathy welled within her. It still amazed her how a woman could stay with a man who beat up on her.

"I had to work the next day," Nadia went on. "And of course Patsy noticed the bruises and asked me what had happened. I was so embarrassed and ashamed that at first I tried to make excuses, but one thing led to another, and I ended up telling her all about Ricco, then blabbed about his fight with Mark.

"Lord knows, I didn't mean to, but I was so upset and she seemed so sympathetic. Why, I even told her about Ricco and Mark's time together in that Florida juvenile detention center."

"Why didn't you say something about this before now?"

Nadia cleared her throat. "I-I told you. I was ashamed . . . and embarrassed."

"No, not about that. I'm talking about the fight between Ricco and Mark. Don't you see? If Ricco and Mark had a fight, then Mark could have had a motive to kill Ricco. Something like that would take the heat off you and Daniel."

"I did think about that, Charlotte, but it's only my word against his. Only hearsay," she emphasized. "And just who do you think the cops are going to believe? Me or the great Lowell Webster's son?"

"Hmm . . ." Charlotte frowned and worried her

bottom lip with her teeth. "Guess you have a point there," she finally said. "But even so, I think it bears looking into. Maybe Judith could put a bug in the right person's ear."

"Oh, Charlotte, I don't think that's such a good idea. I don't want anyone else I love to get into trouble."

"Listen, hon, don't underestimate your sister-in-law. I'm here to tell you she's one tough cookie. She's been a cop long enough to—"

"Charlotte, I hate to interrupt, but I've got to go."

"Nadia—"

"Someone's coming. Got to go now. I'll call again."

"Nadia, wait—" But it was already too late. Nadia had already hung up the phone.

Someone's coming. So who could have been coming? Charlotte wondered. Who could have spooked Nadia into cutting off the call? But even more puzzling, where was Nadia? Where had she been calling from?

"Probably just saw a patrolman or something," Charlotte muttered, recalling that in their other conversation Nadia had told her she moved around while on the cell phone.

Charlotte turned her own phone off and shoved it into her purse. She eyed the phone on the desk for a moment, then had second thoughts about using it. If, as Nadia had suggested, her phone was tapped, then maybe she should use her cell phone to call Judith about this particular matter.

Digging the cell phone out of her purse again, Charlotte glanced up at the cuckoo to check the time. Telling herself that nine o'clock was not too late to be calling

211

her niece, especially about something so important, she turned the phone back on and punched in the numbers of her sister's phone.

The phone was answered on the second ring, and Charlotte sighed with relief when she recognized Judith's voice.

"Hi, hon, it's Aunt Charlotte."

"Oh, hi, Auntie. What are you doing calling this time of night? As if I didn't know," she added, a smirk in her voice.

Charlotte grinned. "Well, Miss Smarty Pants, since you know so much, how is the little rascal?"

"He's doing just fine. I put him to bed about an hour ago, so he's all tucked in and fast asleep."

"And your mother?"

"She's just fine, too. In fact, I think she actually enjoyed having a little one around for a change. She keeps making references to when Daniel was a little boy, and how much Davy reminds her of Daniel."

"Well, that's certainly a good sign. I'm glad that things seem to be working out. But listen, Judith, I have something I think you should know. Something that just might help Nadia and Daniel."

Chapter Eighteen

Early Friday morning the phone rang just as Charlotte was leaving. Tempted to let the answering machine catch the call, Charlotte hesitated at the door. Then, with a resigned sigh, she executed an about-face and trudged back inside. Whether it was her superstitious nature or simply her innate sense of duty and responsibility, she wasn't quite sure, but whichever it was, she'd always found ignoring a ringing phone almost an impossibility.

"I almost made it," she told Sweety Boy as she passed his cage. The little parakeet did little more than flutter his wings in response. With a shrug, Charlotte picked up the receiver. "Maid-for-a-Day. This is Charlotte."

"Hey, Aunt Charley, I'm glad I caught you before you left."

"I was on my way out the door," Charlotte told her niece.

"Sorry about that," Judith apologized, "but I thought I'd better let you know that Mother wants to keep Davy again tonight. In fact"—Judith lowered her voice to just above a whisper—"she's acting really weird. She's even called in sick so she can spend the whole day with him. Says—and I quote—'the poor little guy needs special attention right now.' She's planning on the zoo this morning, McDonald's for lunch, then a movie this afternoon. And Auntie, she's even going around humming kiddy songs."

Charlotte widened her eyes. "Humming?"

"Totally weird, huh?"

Charlotte was at a loss for words.

"Anyway," Judith went on, "Whatever the reason for her sudden change, I only wish she could have had an attack of it when Daniel and I were growing up."

At that, Charlotte grinned. "I suspect that all grown-up children wish the same thing," she said. "I also suspect that what's happening to your mother is what's referred to as the joys of becoming a grandmother."

Charlotte was certainly glad and relieved to hear about Madeline's supposed change of heart, and she truly hoped it was genuine, for Davy's sake. Yet a perverse part of her couldn't help wondering if, in some odd way, her sister saw herself as some sort of competitor vying for Davy's affections. Madeline had made it no secret that though she appreciated Charlotte's help in the early years in raising her children, and she recognized the influence Charlotte had on Judith and Daniel's upbringing, she also resented it.

"Well, whatever it's called," Judith said, "the important thing is that Davy is getting some good positive attention from her. One last thing, Auntie, then I've got to run. I'm going to look into that matter we talked about last night, first thing this morning. I think you're on to something and it bears further investigation."

"I'm so glad you think so, and I'd give anything to be a fly on the wall when you tell Will Richeaux about that fight between Ricco and Mark Webster. You will let me know what he says, won't you?"

"Yes ma'am. But I wouldn't get my hopes up too much if I were you, Auntie. Given my past relationship with Will and considering my personal interest in this case, he isn't going to be too inclined to listen to much of anything I have to say."

"Good or bad, I still want to know, so call me immediately—either on my cell phone or at home."

"Be glad to." Then Judith laughed. "Just one thing, though. In order for me to call you on your cell phone, you have to turn it on and leave it turned on."

"J-u-d-i-t-h!"

"Okay, okay. Just kidding you a bit. Anyway, I'll either call or leave a message if I learn something good. Otherwise, how about I drop by your place later this afternoon—that is, unless you have plans for the evening."

"No, no plans, and coming here would be even better. I could order us a pizza for dinner and fix a nice salad to go with it?"

"Sounds great! Bye now."

"Good luck, hon."

Within minutes of hanging up the phone, Charlotte once again headed out the door to go to work. As she was backing out of the driveway, she noted that Louis's blue Taurus was missing.

Charlotte frowned. Come to think of it, she didn't remember hearing him leave earlier, not since she'd been up, which meant he must have left before she got up.

But not even thoughts about Louis could quell the excitement that hummed through her veins. If Judith could steer the investigation in another direction, if she could give the powers that be another suspect besides Nadia and Daniel, maybe, just maybe, the D.A. would reconsider the charges against them. It was even possible that Daniel could be free by that very afternoon.

"Yeah, right," Charlotte muttered as she turned onto Prytania. From what she'd heard about the wheels of justice, they never turned that fast, not without a million complications to slow them down. Even so, ever the optimist, she still couldn't help hoping and dreaming a bit. Maybe by that very afternoon, there would be cause for celebration. Maybe they could even have a pizza party for the whole family. . . .

Charlotte's Friday client, Marian Hebert, owned her own real estate company. Marian had scheduled an early luncheon date with a potential client so had left the house around eleven.

Outside the sun was shining, and, for a change, the humidity level was bearable. It was such a beautiful day that when Charlotte's noon lunchtime rolled around, she decided it would be a nice break to sit out on the Hebert's front porch while she ate.

Hoping that the fresh air and sunshine would sooth her strained nerves, Charlotte tried to relax as she unpacked the small insulated bag that held her lunch. She'd already checked her cell phone half a dozen times that morning just to make sure it was working, but surely one more time wouldn't hurt, she decided.

Had Judith been able to talk to Will Richeaux yet? she wondered as she tapped out her home phone number as a test call, then hit the SEND button. And if Judith had talked to Will, what had been his reaction? Positive or negative?

The buzz in her ear told her that the cell phone was working, and Charlotte quickly punched the END button before her answering machine at home picked up the call.

The thought crossed her mind that Judith could have decided to leave a message on her answering machine. Even now there could be a message waiting at home.

Charlotte glared at the cell phone. She knew that there

was a way to check for messages on the answering machine by phone. According to the instruction booklet, all she had to do was punch in a number code. Too bad she could never remember her code.

With a shrug, she put away the cell phone. "Patience is a virtue," she muttered. She'd just have to have patience. But meantime, she still had bathrooms to clean and a load of clothes that needed folding and putting away.

Spurred on by the thought that the sooner she finished, the sooner she could leave, she gobbled down the chicken salad that she'd brought with her.

On the off chance that Judith might come by a bit early, and with dreams of both Judith and Daniel waiting for her on her porch swing, Charlotte rushed through the remainder of her cleaning tasks at Marian Hebert's house.

Neither Judith nor Daniel were waiting on her porch when she pulled into her driveway around two. But Louis was.

By the time she switched off the van and opened the door, he had already rounded the back of the van.

He stopped within two feet of the driver's door. "It's time we talked," he said, getting straight to the point.

Her mind racing to find a plausible excuse for not talking to him, Charlotte climbed out of the van and slammed the door.

The minute she slammed the van door, he placed fisted hands on his hips and, glaring down at her, he said, "Just how long are you going to pout?"

"Pout? I'll have you know I don't pout."

He nodded. "Oh yes you do. You definitely pout. Lately I've become an expert on women pouting. But I think you even have my little granddaughter beat."

Charlotte shook her head at his comparison of her to his four-year-old granddaughter. "Oooh, that was a low blow, Louis."

At least he had the grace to look contrite, whether he truly was or not. "Yeah, I guess you're right," he said a bit sheepishly. "Sorry. But I've already apologized for the other day, so what's it going to take for you to get over it?"

Charlotte was tempted to tell him that what it would take hadn't been invented yet, but she held her tongue. Ever conscious that there could be a message from Judith waiting for her inside, she said, "How about I simply tell you that I accept your apology? Will that satisfy you?"

"Only if you mean it."

He had her there. Did she mean it? Or was she being the hypocrite that Madeline had once accused her of being.

"And another thing," he said before she could reply, "Where's the kid? I haven't seen or heard him now in a couple of days."

"Davy is with his grandmother," she replied impatiently.

Louis frowned and tilted his head to the side. "His grandmother?"

"Madeline," Charlotte clarified.

"You let him go with *her?*"

Charlotte held up her hand. "I know, I know. You don't have to say it. But, for your information, it was Judith's idea, and one, I might add, that seems to have worked a miracle."

"Now this I've got to hear," he said, motioning for her to walk with him to the porch. "I've brewed a fresh pot of coffee, and on my way home I picked up a freshly baked angel food cake from Gambino's. Could I bribe you into having some, so you can tell me about this miraculous change in your sister? Also, there's another matter I need to talk to you about."

Angel food cake? When Charlotte had first been diagnosed as a diabetic, she'd had a couple of sessions with a dietician to find out what kinds of foods she could eat. From the dietician, she'd learned that a small piece of angel food cake was allowed once in a while. But how did Louis know that?

As if he'd read her thoughts, he said, "You can eat angel food cake, can't you? That's what the book said."

"The book?"

Louis hesitated, then lowered his gaze to stare down at his shoes. "Yeah," he muttered. "I checked out a book at the library on diabetes and read up on it." Glancing up, his tone almost defensive, he said, "I figured if I'm going to cook for you once in a while, I needed to know what kinds of food you can eat."

For long moments, Charlotte couldn't seem to utter a sound. The man was an enigma, a living, breathing Jekyll and Hyde. One minute he'd make her so angry that she could chew nails, then he'd turn right around and apologize in such a way that *she* was the one who ended up feeling guilty.

Charlotte sighed. She figured if she lived to be a hundred, she'd never understand him . . . or understand her attraction to him. "I'd love a cup of coffee and a piece of that cake," she finally said. "But I'm expecting an important call, so just give me a minute to check for any phone messages."

With Louis's nod, Charlotte hurried to her front door, unlocked it, and went inside.

Ignoring Sweety Boy's squawking bid for attention, she headed straight to the desk. Catching sight of the small, unblinking light on the answering machine, disappointment ripped through her. No messages. A heaviness centered in her chest, and Charlotte collapsed on the sofa. Why hadn't Judith called yet?

Chapter Nineteen

Charlotte kept telling herself that there could be all kinds of reasons why Judith hadn't called. Maybe Judith hadn't been able to talk to Will Richeaux yet, or maybe she got caught up in another case.

Or maybe she had talked to him, and he had chosen to ignore what she'd told him. "No," Charlotte muttered, denying the possibility. Surely there was no way he could ignore such an important lead . . . was there?

Charlotte closed her eyes and, tilting her head first to one side, then to the other, she stretched the taut muscles in her neck. She could sit there and second-guess reasons till doomsday, but until she heard from Judith, there was no use in even trying to speculate how Will Richeaux would react to the information. Best to stop borrowing trouble and get her mind on something else.

With a groan, she opened her eyes and shoved herself up off the sofa. Louis was waiting, and having coffee and cake with him would at least serve as a diversion. Almost anything had to be better than sitting around, stewing and wondering about Judith and Will Richeaux.

Louis had left the front door ajar, so after a quick rap on the door frame, Charlotte let herself inside.

"Back in the kitchen," he called out.

The one time that Charlotte had visited Judith at the Sixth District police station was before Louis had retired. When she'd seen how messy he kept his desk, she'd been appalled. And she'd worried about renting to him for just that reason.

Charlotte glanced around the living room and was pleased once again to see that, unlike the desk he'd had at work, he kept his living space neat and orderly. Everything looked to be relatively dust-free and, judging by the condition of the floors, he had recently swept and mopped.

Because she had rented the double already furnished, she knew that Louis had decided to store most of his furniture. But when he'd moved in he'd brought several choice pieces with him, including a well-worn recliner, a bookshelf full of books, and a gun cabinet, along with some paintings and sculptures. He'd also brought along his large-screen television and a state-of-the-art stereo system that took up almost a complete wall.

She'd only been inside his half of the double one other time, when he'd invited her to dinner. *I figured if I'm going to cook for you once in a while, I needed to know what kinds of food you could eat.*

Charlotte's head swirled with confusion as she suddenly recalled what he'd said on the porch. Had he meant that he would be pursuing a relationship with her now?

"Really strange," she whispered with a bewildered shake of her head. He'd been acting weird ever since her sixtieth birthday bash—ever since he'd kissed her. She wasn't exactly sure what she'd expected to happen after he'd kissed her, but what she hadn't expected was for him to act as if it had never happened. The man was truly an enigma.

With another shake of her head, she took a moment to admire the paintings he'd hung on the walls. And, like the first time she'd seen them, she was struck again by their beauty.

Louis's son was an exceptionally talented artist whose work was featured in his wife's art gallery down in the Quarter. All but one of the paintings were magnificent oils of Louisiana wildlife scenes that Stephen had painted while he was in prison. The one exception was a hauntingly sweet portrait of Louis's little granddaughter.

When Charlotte entered the kitchen, the rich aroma of freshly brewed coffee filled the air. "Have a seat," Louis told her, nodding toward one of the chairs at the table as he poured the coffee.

A grin tugged at Charlotte's lips when she saw the

table. Louis's penchant for the more refined things in life was totally incongruous with his chauvinistic attitude and his gruff, manly persona. Yet another sign of his Jekyll-and-Hyde personality, she decided as she seated herself in the chair that he'd indicated.

The small table was covered with a white linen tablecloth. In the center of the table was a crystal vase that contained a single red rose. Next to the rose, he'd placed the angel food cake on a pedestal-type cake server made of cut glass. The table was set with silverware, creamy white china cups and saucers trimmed in gold, and dessert plates that matched the cake server.

"This looks lovely," she told him.

Not even his gruff "Thanks" could hide how pleased he seemed that she'd noticed his efforts.

"So did you get that call you've been waiting for?" he asked as he sliced the cake.

"Unfortunately, no," she answered, unable to hide her disappointment.

"Must be important." He placed a small slice of the cake on her dessert plate.

The last thing Charlotte wanted to talk about was the call from Judith, and the last person she wanted to discuss it with was Louis.

She cut into the cake with her fork. "This cake looks delicious," she said, and in an effort to delay answering him, she popped the bite of cake into her mouth.

Louis simply shook his head. "Don't want to talk about the call, huh?"

"Well, I—"

He waved a hand. "Never mind for now. Like I said

earlier, I have something I need to discuss with you, then you can tell me all about your sister's miraculous transformation. I'll be leaving for New York tonight, and I'll be gone for a couple of weeks."

Charlotte frowned. "New York?"

"It's a special assignment for the security company I work for. Anyway, I'm having my newspaper stopped, but I was wondering if you'd mind getting my mail. I could have it stopped too, but I'd rather not have it piling up at the post office."

Charlotte shrugged. "No need to. I can keep it for you until you get back. That way it can pile up at my house instead." Charlotte grinned, then said, "So . . . just what is this special—"

A sudden sharp rap at the front door echoed throughout the house, and Louis and Charlotte turned their heads toward the hall doorway.

"Hey, Lou, you in there?"

The unexpected sound of her niece's voice chased everything else out of Charlotte's head.

Finally. Maybe now she could find out about Will Richeaux's reaction to being handed a new suspect.

"Yeah, Judith," Louis called out. "We're in the kitchen."

Charlotte blinked, and her gaze slid quickly to Louis. *But not here, and not now.* There was no way she wanted to discuss any of this in front of Louis, especially after the fiasco at Lowell Webster's office.

Within seconds Judith walked through the door, and Charlotte's insides began to knot with dread.

"Oh, hey, Aunt Charley. I was hoping that 'we' meant

that you were over here, too." She leaned down and hugged Charlotte, and when she pulled away, she said, "I'm not interrupting anything, am I?" She eyed the table setting, cleared her throat, then waggled her eyebrows. "If I am," she teased, "I can always come back later."

Louis rolled his eyes, and Charlotte gave Judith what she hoped was a stern, disapproving look. Much to Charlotte's chagrin, ever since Judith had first introduced Charlotte to Louis, she seemed to take some kind of perverse pleasure in teasing both of them.

"No, Miss Priss," Charlotte retorted. "You're not interrupting anything but coffee and cake."

Unfortunately. The second the word popped into her head, Charlotte stiffened. *Where on earth had that come from?*

"Louis was just telling me that he'll be out of town for the next couple of weeks," Charlotte quickly added.

"And as long as you're here," Louis drawled, "you might as well join us." He waved at one of the chairs. "Have a seat, and I'll get an extra cup and saucer."

"Well . . . if you're both sure I won't be in the way."

"Judith!" Charlotte and Louis protested at the same time.

"Okay, okay," she said, laughing. "Make sure you bring an extra dessert plate, too. That cake looks yummy." With an exaggerated wink at Charlotte, Judith seated herself. "So, Lou, where are you off to?" she asked.

Louis set her coffee and a dessert plate in front of her. "Out-of-town security job in New York."

Judith raised her eyebrows. "Sounds interesting."

Louis shrugged, but when he didn't comment any further, Judith gave him a curious look. When he still didn't elaborate, she said, "Must be some kind of top-secret or hush-hush job, huh?"

"Not really," was all he said.

With a shrug of her own, Judith turned to Charlotte. "Afraid I don't have good news, Auntie."

Charlotte panicked. *Please, not in front of Louis.* Trying her best to be inconspicuous, she shook her head once in a feeble attempt to discourage Judith from saying anything further.

Though Judith gave Charlotte an odd look, she didn't take the hint. "I told him about the fight," she said. "And he got all in an uproar and told me to stay out of his case. Claimed he already knew about the fight, and there was nothing to it, that it had no bearing on the case."

Judith turned to Louis. "Aunt Charley uncovered some important information concerning Ricco's murder," she explained. "Seems Ricco and Mark Webster had a big argument about some money owed to Ricco. We were both kind of hoping that it might be enough to take the pressure off of Daniel and Nadia."

When Louis nodded slowly and narrowed his eyes, Charlotte held her breath, waiting for what she was sure would be another explosion from him about minding her own business.

"I assume the 'him' you're referring to is Will Richeaux," Louis said to Judith in a deadpan tone of voice.

"Unfortunately, yes."

"Do you think he was telling the truth?"

Judith pursed her lips and shook her head. "Of course not. That jerk wouldn't know the truth if it bit him on the butt."

"Who didn't know that?" Louis said, his voice dripping with sarcasm. "So, let me take a wild guess here. If I know you and how you operate, I'd venture to guess that you decided to do a little investigating, or should I say interrogating, on your own, in spite of what Richeaux said?"

Judith simply shrugged, neither confirming nor denying Louis's conclusion.

"Well, little girl, what did the big bad Mark Webster have to say for himself when you questioned him?"

Judith shot Louis a twisted, cynical smile. "You think you're so smart, *old man.* But to answer your question, he didn't say diddly-squat. He got all indignant on me. Claimed I was harrassing him. But before he clammed up, he threatened to sic his lawyer and the chief on me. That alone is enough to make *me* suspicious."

For long seconds Louis and Judith stared at each other. Neither said a word, and Charlotte could feel the tension between them clear to her toes.

Judith was the first to break. "Well, what did you expect me to do, Lou?" She threw up her hands. "What?" she repeated. "This is my brother's life they're messing around with, and I don't intend to sit by, quietly twiddling my thumbs while they railroad him to death row."

With a sigh that spoke volumes, Louis turned his

steely eyed stare on Charlotte. "Meddling again, Charlotte." It was a statement, not a question. "And where, pray tell, did you learn about this supposed fight between Ricco and Mark?"

Judith frowned and turned to stare at Charlotte, too. "Yeah, come to think of it, how did you find out about that fight?"

Busted. Charlotte stiffened. Glaring first at Louis, then at Judith, she raised her chin defiantly. "I'd rather not say," she told them in an attempt to bluff her way through the situation.

Louis heaved a weary sigh. "Which could mean only one thing." He rolled his eyes, then glanced at Judith. "She's talked to Nadia."

"You don't know that," Charlotte blurted out.

Louis shrugged. "No, I didn't before—not for sure—but I do now. Doesn't matter, though. It's a logical conclusion." He held up a hand and ticked off each finger as he spoke. "For one, she works for you, so she'd trust you. Two, you've been taking care of her kid. And, three, she'd want to check on him if she's any kind of decent mother at all."

"Is that true, Auntie? Have you talked to Nadia?"

"And what if I have?" Charlotte argued, figuring there was no use now in denying it. "So what?"

Judith's expression grew tight with strain. "Well, Auntie, for one thing, I distinctly remember that I asked you to let me know if she called you. For another thing, they've probably tapped your telephone. Then, to top it off, there's a minor little matter they call aiding and abetting, which happens to be against the law. You do know that every cop in the city is looking for her, don't you?"

"Of course I know," Charlotte shot back.

Louis cleared his throat. "And do you also know that you can go to jail over this?" he drawled.

Cornered, Charlotte went on the defense. "Oh, for Pete's sake!" She glared first at Louis, then at Judith. "Do you both think I'm that stupid? For your information, I did not call Nadia. She called me—on my cell phone," she stressed. "Not my home phone, which I'm sure is bugged. And just in case you're wondering, and I'm sure you are," she added sarcastically, "I don't know where she is. So, see? Nobody has grounds to accuse me of anything."

"Oh, Auntie," Judith said with a groan. "With the right frequency, cell phones can be monitored, too."

"Humph!" Louis grunted and waved a hand at Charlotte. "And that's not all she's been doing," he told Judith. "Why don't you ask her about the little visit she paid to Lowell Webster's office?"

If possible, Judith looked even more horrified. "Oh, Aunt Charley, you didn't. Please tell me you didn't. What on earth were you thinking? And just what in the devil did you hope to accomplish?"

"So what? So what if I did?" Charlotte retorted. "It's a free country, last I heard. And it's nobody's business but my own who I see."

Judith just groaned again and shook her head. "Wait till Hank hears about this one. Don't you realize you just can't go around—"

"That's enough!" Charlotte objected. "From the both

of you," she added as she abruptly shoved out of her chair and stood. "Like I said, it's a free country. Tell you what, though." She motioned at Louis. "Why don't I let Mr. Blabbermouth tell you all about it. Oh—and another thing—you can get your own pizza tonight." With one last glare, first at Judith, then at Louis, Charlotte turned and stomped out of the kitchen.

"Wait—hold up, Auntie. Don't get mad."

"Charlotte!" Louis called out.

But Charlotte ignored both of them as she marched down the hallway. The second she stepped through the front doorway, she reached back, grabbed the doorknob, and, just for good measure, slammed the door hard.

Chapter Twenty

"The very idea!" Charlotte muttered, as she unlatched the door to Sweety Boy's cage early Saturday morning. After her confrontation with Judith and Louis Friday afternoon, she'd gone straight home. There, she'd locked and bolted the front door, and for the remainder of the evening, she'd ignored their repeated phone calls.

She knew she was overreacting, but she couldn't seem to help herself. Not even the knowledge that Louis was leaving and wouldn't be back for two weeks was enough to cool her anger. He'd left around nine, and all she'd felt was relief.

Then she'd gone to bed. But she'd ended up tossing and turning all night. Even now, almost a whole day later, each time she thought about how Louis and Judith had ganged up on her, treating her like she didn't have the sense God gave a goose, it stirred up hurt and indignant feelings all over again.

Charlotte extended her forefinger inside the cage, and once Sweety Boy hopped on, she eased the little bird through the door. Finally free, he immediately took flight. After fluttering around the living room a few minutes, he landed on the cuckoo clock.

Charlotte smiled up at the little bird, but her smile quickly faded. "You know, Boy, I just don't understand it," she told him. "Just because I'm a maid and not some big hotshot police detective doesn't make me an idiot. You'd think they would want all the help they could get."

With a frustrated shake of her head, Charlotte removed the soiled paper from the birdcage and stuffed it into a garbage bag. Then she removed the water and food containers. "And here I thought we were all supposed to be on the same side," she murmured. "Daniel and Nadia's side. Guess that's what I get for thinking, huh, Boy?"

Charlotte took out the perch and swing. Setting them aside, she lined the bottom of the cage with clean paper. Once she'd scrubbed the perch and swing in soapy water and rinsed them thoroughly, she dried them off, then affixed them back inside the cage.

With one last eagle-eyed inspection of the now-clean birdcage, she attached a new cuttlebone and replaced the water and food containers.

For long moments afterward, she simply stood there, staring out the window. The sun was shining, and what bit of sky she could see was blue and cloudless.

Could Daniel see the sky from his jail cell? she wondered. Was there a window in his jail cell?

She closed her eyes and bowed her head. She'd considered visiting him, but even if she was allowed to, she simply couldn't do it. Just the thought of seeing her beloved Daniel locked up behind bars was more than she could bear.

"Wimp," she muttered. "You're nothing but a big wimp, Charlotte LaRue. A coward."

As if Sweety Boy had somehow sensed her morose mood, he flew down from the cuckoo clock and after circling her a couple of times landed on her shoulder. Though Charlotte allowed him to stay there for a few minutes and felt some measure of comfort from his presence, the little bird couldn't be still. He kept prancing back and forth across her shoulder, his tiny claws tickling her through her blouse.

Charlotte held her forefinger near the little bird's feet. "Come on, Boy. Time for me to get off my pity pot and get busy."

Her mind raced ahead to the list of chores she still had to do. There were clothes that needed to be washed, the bathroom needed a good cleaning, and it was way past time to clean the stovetop and oven. There were also receipts from the past week she still needed to record as well—plenty to do to keep her busy the whole day.

"You know the old saying," she told the little bird. "'Busy hands are happy hands.'"

If only it were true, she thought as the little parakeet hopped onto her finger. "Sorry, Boy. I hate to do this to you, but it's also time for you to go back inside your cage."

Several months earlier, Sweety Boy had decided to join her in the shower and had ended up knocked out cold in the bottom of the tub from the force of the spray. She'd been reluctant to let him loose without supervision ever since. And for today, the last thing she wanted to have to worry about was the safety of the little parakeet.

"Now, now, there you go." She eased him back inside his cage and quickly latched the door. With one last glance at the little bird and ignoring his squawks of protest, she turned and headed for the bathroom to gather the dirty clothes.

By midmorning, she had finished most of her personal cleaning tasks and was ready to tackle the neglected bookkeeping. She had just settled at her desk to begin recording receipts when she heard a car pull into the driveway. Moments later a door slammed. Since Louis was gone, the visitor had to be for her.

"Great," she muttered. "Just what I don't need right now."

In no mood for entertaining unexpected company, she was sorely tempted to simply ignore whoever was outside. But in the end her curiosity got the best of her. Just a peek out the window would tell her who the unwanted visitor was. Reluctantly, she shoved away from the desk. Before she could get to the window, though, there was a sharp rap on the front door.

For several moments, Charlotte stood in the middle of the room and debated whether to ignore the unwelcome visitor or to give in to her curiosity again and open the door.

Then the door handle rattled. "Open up, Aunt Charley," Judith's muffled voice demanded. "Enough's enough. I know you're in there, and, remember, I also know where the spare key is."

With a sigh, Charlotte trudged to the front door. Everyone in her family knew that she kept a spare key beneath the fat ceramic frog in the flower bed near the front corner of the house. She supposed she should be grateful that Judith hadn't already used it to let herself inside.

Charlotte unlocked the door and opened it. "What do you want, Judith?"

"I want to apologize, and I want you to stop being so angry with me." Judith shifted from one foot to the other, a sure sign she was under stress. Any time she was nervous, uncomfortable, or in a tense situation, she resorted to what Charlotte thought of as the nervous fidgets.

"But I also figured you'd be interested in knowing the latest development in this Ricco murder mess," she said.

"Now, why on earth would someone like me be interested?" Charlotte retorted.

"Aw, come on, Auntie. Don't be like that."

After a moment, Charlotte finally relented, but only up to a point. "Okay, you've apologized, Judith. Now, if you'll excuse me . . ."

When Charlotte didn't budge or say anything further, Judith crossed her arms and rocked back and forth on the balls of her feet.

"Auntie, can I please come inside?"

It was rare that Judith ever resorted to pleading, and to hear her do so made Charlotte feel like the wicked witch of the West.

Feeling guilty and ashamed, Charlotte shrugged. "Suit yourself." She stepped back, and once Judith was inside, Charlotte closed the door and locked it. Then she faced her niece. "As long as you're here, we might as well have some iced tea." Without waiting for Judith's reply, she turned to head for the kitchen.

"Aw, come on Auntie." Judith cried as she stomped her foot. "Like I said. Enough's enough, and I've had enough of that cold-shoulder routine from my mother to last a lifetime."

Being compared to Madeline brought Charlotte up short and sparked her temper all over again. She whirled to face Judith. "First I get treated like a moron by you and Louis, and now you're comparing me to your mother. Well, for your information, young lady, I am not a moron. And I don't appreciate being compared to your mother, either. I don't deserve that, not after all I've done for you and your brother over the years."

As soon as the words left her mouth, Charlotte immediately wished them back again, and, to add further humiliation, sudden unwanted tears sprang into her eyes. The last thing she'd meant to do was to suggest in any way, shape, or form that she resented her role in Judith or Daniel's lives. Hoping that Judith hadn't noticed her tears, she bowed her head and blinked furiously.

But it was too late. Judith took a firm grip on Charlotte's arm. "Oh, Auntie, don't—I'm so, so sorry. And you're right—you didn't deserve what you got. Not yesterday, and certainly not that crack about my mother. Not any of the rest of it, either," she whispered as her voice trailed away.

It wasn't so much what Judith said, but how she'd said it that made Charlotte's chest grow tight with even more regret and made her wish again that she could take back her angry words.

When she lifted her head to face Judith and saw tears well within Judith's eyes, she pulled her niece into her arms. "I'm sorry too, hon." She hugged her hard. "For yesterday, and for all the yesterdays. You and Daniel are like my own children, and I don't want you to ever think—not for a moment—that I resented helping raise you, because I didn't. I love you and your brother." She pulled away and tilted her head, searching for some kind of response from Judith. But Judith had closed her eyes. "Are you listening to me?" Charlotte asked. "Do you hear what I'm saying?"

After a moment, Judith sniffed, then finally opened her eyes. "I guess deep down, I've always known that, but it's just that—"

"No buts!" Charlotte firmly shook her head. "We're family, and families have their ups and downs, and their squabbles. And they sometimes say foolish things that they don't mean. That's just being human. But that doesn't mean they love each other any less. Okay?"

Only when Judith finally nodded did Charlotte release her. "Now, why don't you go to the bathroom and blow your nose, then tell me about this new development?"

Within minutes, Judith joined Charlotte in the kitchen. "Thanks," she said as Charlotte placed a tall glass of iced tea in front of her. Once Charlotte was seated, Judith began. "I got a call from the chief early this morning. He wanted me to come in for a talk."

"Sounds serious."

Judith shrugged. "Serious enough, I guess. What he called talking ended up being a speech which was really a lecture and warning, one that was short and to the point. It seems that there's been a complaint filed against me by Mark and Lowell Webster—for harassment, of all things. Bottom line, I'm forbidden to go anywhere near either one of them again."

"But I thought you only questioned Mark Webster. So why would Lowell Webster file a complaint, too? Especially for harassment."

Judith shook her head. "Search me. All I did was ask Mark Webster a few pointed questions. I swear, that's all I did."

"So why would they feel the need to file a complaint just because you asked a few questions involving a murder investigation?" Charlotte probed. "Very interesting . . . and suspicious, if you ask me. I hope you reminded that chief of yours that asking questions is what you get paid for."

Judith's face went grim. "Oh, I reminded him all right. But all he did was repeat what he'd said to begin with, only louder. Then he ordered me out of his office." Judith leaned forward. "But that's not all."

"What do you mean?"

"Now get this. I'm on my way out of the chief's office when guess who I run into?" Before Charlotte could respond, Judith answered. "None other than Will Richeaux. Now tell me, Auntie, just what do you think the odds are of that happening bright and early on a Saturday morning? I'm here to tell you the odds are zero, which leads me to believe that Richeaux already knew about my talk with the chief ahead of time." She narrowed her eyes. "In fact, I'd be willing to bet my last dime from the way he was smirking that he's the one behind that meeting and the complaints."

"But why? Just to tick you off because of your—your—"

"Affair, Auntie. The word's affair. And that's certainly a good possibility. Sour grapes and all that. But there's no way of knowing. Not for sure, anyway. And if that's true, why now? It's been months since I stopped seeing him. That's a lot of trouble to go to just to get back at someone who dumped you."

"Hmm . . . maybe not," Charlotte murmured as she stared at her glass of tea and drummed her fingers against the tabletop. If she could believe the gossip, Patsy Dufour had been waiting for almost a lifetime to get back at Lowell Webster. But when Charlotte conjured up a mental image of Patsy, all she saw was the fear on Patsy's face when Will Richeaux had first arrived on the scene the day they'd discovered the bones.

"Ah, Aunt Charley? Hello, earth to Aunt Charley."

Charlotte glanced up and blinked. "Oh, sorry, hon. I was just thinking about something."

"Auntie, what's this?"

The notebook. Charlotte swallowed hard. Judith was staring at the notebook she'd left on the table.

"Oh, that—that's nothing." Charlotte reached for the notebook, but Judith scooped it up first.

"I wouldn't exactly call this 'nothing,'" Judith said, scanning the page. "In fact, I'd call it v-e-r-y interesting, especially this last part here about Will Richeaux." Judith read from Charlotte's notes. "'Ask Patsy about Will Richeaux.'" Judith laid the notebook back on the table. "Why ask Patsy Dufour about him? Is there some connection between the two of them?"

Now what? "Well . . . er . . . there might be."

"What kind of connection? And don't give me any of that client confidentiality crap, either."

"Judith!"

Judith held up a hand. "Okay, okay. Sorry."

"Well, you know I don't like that kind of language."

"Aunt Charley!"

Charlotte waved vaguely at the notebook. "It's probably nothing anyway. Mostly just one of those gut feelings you get sometimes."

Judith rolled her eyes. "Grrrr, this is like pulling teeth. Look, Auntie, knowing you, there has to be *some* reason you got that feeling, so spit it out."

Charlotte shrugged. "It was when he came in the house to question us—you know, after we'd discovered the bones. If you could have seen the look on Patsy's face. It was—she looked like she'd just seen the devil himself. Granted, she was already upset," Charlotte hastened to add, "but this was different."

"Scared?"

Charlotte nodded. "More like terrified."

Judith frowned. "That's not really that unusual, Auntie. Believe it or not, there are some people who are terrified at having to deal with the police, period. Kind of like being scared of an IRS audit."

"No . . ." Charlotte shook her head. "It was more than that."

With a frown marring her face, Judith stared at Charlotte. "But what other reason would she have, then?"

Chapter Twenty-one

*W*hat other reason would she have, then? Charlotte never had answered Judith's question. She'd simply shrugged and said she didn't know. And she didn't know. But even now, long after Judith had left, the question still nagged at her as she slipped on an apron and began cleaning the kitchen.

Maybe she should have told Judith the other stuff she'd learned about Patsy as well, especially the scandal concerning Patsy and Lowell Webster's relationship.

Then again, the scandal about Patsy and Lowell was just gossip. Granted, the gossip came from what she considered reliable sources, but, knowing her niece, Charlotte was sure Judith wouldn't see it that way. She'd see it as just gossip, strictly hearsay.

Besides, after the ridicule and humiliation she'd suffered on Friday from Louis and Judith, she couldn't see submitting herself to that kind of derision again.

As Charlotte loaded the last of her lunch dishes into

the dishwasher, she thought about the other things that Nadia had told her as well. According to Nadia, there was a definite connection between Mark Webster and Ricco Martinez. Nadia had said that Mark Webster was behind the cemetery thefts and he'd involved Ricco. She'd also said that the two men had argued over money that Mark owed Ricco—probably money from some shady deal they had going, or maybe even money they got from the cemetery thefts.

Charlotte poured detergent into the slot in the door of the dishwasher. If she remembered right, it was about that time that Patsy had questioned Nadia about her bruises and found out about the two men's connection.

Patsy again. To Charlotte it seemed that everything kept circling back to Lowell and Patsy. "And where there's smoke, there's fire," she murmured.

But was there fire?

According to Jane Calhoun there was. Jane had said, "That's when she swore that one day Lowell would pay for what he'd done to her."

What if Patsy had finally found the perfect vehicle for revenge after all these years? What if she'd either murdered Ricco herself or had hired someone to murder him, then stuffed him into the urn. Bitsy had more or less implied that Patsy had just been putting on a show with all of her screaming, and a dead body being discovered in a stolen urn in Lowell's warehouse would go a long way toward sullying his reputation and possibly ruining his chances to become mayor.

Charlotte shook her head as she closed the dishwasher door. "Talk about a conspiracy theory," she muttered.

Wouldn't Judith and Louis have a field day with that one? "Wouldn't work, anyway," she murmured, deep in thought. Why would Patsy stuff Ricco's body in an urn then buy the urn for herself? Unless . . . she'd hired someone else to kill him and didn't realize he'd been stuffed into the urn. Someone could have found out and decided to turn the tables on Patsy—someone like Lowell.

Charlotte shook her head. "Too, too weird," she murmured. But even as she dismissed her theory as being too far-fetched, an idea began to form. Whether Patsy had anything to do with Ricco's death or not, she was mixed up in the mess in some way. So why not simply come right out and ask her about Will Richeaux, Ricco, and Lowell Webster?

Yeah, right. And what makes you think she'd give you a straight answer? Charlotte shrugged away the thought and latched the dishwasher door. But for long moments, she stood there, staring out the window above the sink. More than likely, Patsy would either tell her to mind her own business or deny knowing anything at all. She might get upset enough to even fire her.

Then again, if asked the right questions in the right way, Patsy might be just itching to tell someone all about it, someone other than the police.

"Assuming there's anything to tell," Charlotte muttered. Finally dismissing the idea as ludicrous and foolhardy, she turned away from the window and headed for her desk so that she could finish entering the expense receipts into the weekly log.

But once seated at the desk, she hesitated, and the idea

of confronting Patsy with what she'd learned began to take root and grow. Then, like an ugly weed determined to choke off the root, another thought occurred. Even if Patsy wasn't guilty of murdering Ricco, it was clear that she was involved in some way. And if Patsy was involved, confronting her might make her panic. It could be just the thing to push her into doing something rash.

Charlotte shivered, remembering another time she'd confronted a client who had been involved in a murder. She'd had to fight for her life that time.

"But you won," she muttered. *Yeah, and you had nightmares about it for weeks afterward.*

Charlotte drummed her fingers against the desktop. That time she hadn't expected to confront the murderer face to face. She hadn't been prepared. This time would be different. There had to be some way she could prepare for the confrontation—some way to minimize the danger to herself.

Suddenly her fingers went still. Out of the blue, what seemed like the perfect solution came to her. She'd use Judith as her excuse. She'd simply let Patsy know that Judith was expecting her and that Judith knew she was stopping by to see Patsy first.

Then what? Abruptly Charlotte sighed, defeated again. Even if she could get Patsy to talk or confess, it would still be hearsay. Unless . . .

Charlotte reached down, pulled out the bottom drawer of the desk, and rummaged around until she found what she was looking for.

Several years back she'd bought the small, voice-activated tape recorder with intentions of keeping notes on each client's likes and dislikes. She'd used it for a while but had found it much less practical than she'd thought it would be.

Digging into the drawer again, Charlotte found a package of unopened batteries and a blank tape still wrapped in cellophane. Once she'd popped the old batteries out of the tape recorder, she replaced them with new ones. Then she unwrapped the tape and slipped it into the tape player as well.

"Now," she murmured. "All set to go." Pushing the red RECORD button, she began speaking. "Testing, testing. One, two, three, testing." After rewinding the tape, she listened. Satisfied that the tape player still worked, she set it on the desk in front of her.

Then the internal battle began in earnest. For a solid hour Charlotte forced herself to sit at the desk. Entering the receipts didn't take long, but even after she'd finished, she sat there, staring at the tape recorder as she once again weighed the pros and cons of confronting Patsy.

One minute she'd talk herself out of doing such a foolish thing, then the next minute she'd picture her sweet, funny nephew dressed in an ugly orange jumpsuit, sitting in a tiny, windowless jail cell.

When Charlotte opened her front door, she shivered. Though the sun was shining and it wasn't really all that cold, the steady breeze put a chill in the air.

Over the years Charlotte had found that she could stand the heat a lot better than she could stand the cold, so as a precaution, she had slipped on a lightweight jacket before she left. Besides, she figured that since the jacket had deep pockets on either side, it would be easier to hide the tape recorder.

The trip to Patsy's house was only about a ten-minute drive. Plenty of time to change her mind. At least that's what Charlotte kept telling herself as she bumped along the uneven pavement down Milan Street.

She'd considered phoning ahead first, just to make sure Patsy was home, but at the last minute she'd chickened out. She'd also considered making up some kind of excuse once she was there as to why she was coming to see Patsy on a Saturday afternoon. After thinking about it, though, she'd opted to simply wing it.

When Charlotte got to Patsy's house, she noted that Patsy's Mercedes was in the driveway. As she slowed down the van, her foot hovered over the brake, but at the last minute she stepped on the accelerator instead and drove past the house.

Only after she'd circled the block twice more did she finally gather enough courage to pull over and park the van in her usual spot alongside the curb near the corner of the huge mansion.

Before she got out she turned the tape recorder on and slipped it inside her jacket pocket. Halfway to the door, she paused. She'd just about made up her mind to forget the whole thing, to turn around and go home, when the front door swung open.

"Why, Charlotte, this is a surprise," Patsy called out. "What are you doing here on a Saturday afternoon?"

At the sight of Patsy, Charlotte was too stunned to

move or speak for a moment. The woman looked like death warmed over. Her hair had a dirty, dull look about it and hung limply around her face, and she was dressed in oversized, faded jeans and a ratty-looking Saints T-shirt, worn thin from one too many washings. There were dark circles beneath her eyes, and, with no makeup, her sallow face was even more homely than usual.

Charlotte had never seen Patsy look so slovenly. Something must have happened, but what?

As if Patsy had guessed what Charlotte was thinking, she crossed her arms and stared at the floor of the porch. "I was just coming out to check the mail," she said, by way of explanation.

Charlotte forced herself to walk to the steps. "I'm sorry for not calling ahead." She trudged up the steps on leaden feet. "I was on my way to meet my niece for a bit of shopping and decided that this was as good a time as any to talk to you about something. Since your house was on the way, I phoned ahead and told her I'd be stopping by for a minute." The lie caused a twinge of guilt, but Charlotte ignored the twinge and forced a smile. "But if it's not a good time right now," she hastened to add, "I can come back later."

Nervous sweat trickled down Charlotte's back, and she held her breath while she waited for Patsy's response.

Please say it's not a good time . . . please.

Patsy shrugged, gave a wan smile, then motioned for Charlotte to come inside. "Now's as good a time as any. But I hope you're not going to tell me that you've

246

decided to retire. I don't think I could take that on top of everything else that's going on right now."

Charlotte shook her head. "No, nothing like that, but has—has something happened? You seem upset."

"I am. First, there's all of this stuff about those bones, and now, Missy." Patsy backed away from the door opening to let Charlotte inside. "I-I may have to have her put to sleep. Dr. Janseen thinks she might have cancer. . . ." Patsy's voice trailed away as she closed and locked the door.

Charlotte frowned. "Oh, poor Missy. And poor you. I'm so sorry." She followed Patsy down the hallway and into the front parlor. "I know how much that little dog means to you."

Patsy nodded. "She's been my baby for a long time now. Almost twelve years." She motioned for Charlotte to be seated on the sofa. "But she hasn't been eating much lately, and she's been whining and crying a lot. Then, when I noticed some blood in her stools yesterday, I knew something was definitely wrong, and I took her straight to the vet. They kept her for observation and a few more tests, just to make sure."

Charlotte eased down onto the sofa, and not knowing exactly how to respond, she said, "Maybe things aren't as bad as they seem."

Patsy gave a halfhearted shrug and sat in a chair opposite the sofa. "As they say, only time will tell." After a moment, she sighed deeply, then said, "So, Charlotte, what was it you needed to talk to me about?"

For a second Charlotte was tempted again to make up some story about the cleaning schedule for the upcoming week. But like a kaleidoscope, mental images flashed through her mind: Daniel . . . little Davy crying for his mother . . . Nadia . . .

Charlotte swallowed hard. "I'm here to talk about Ricco Martinez's murder. And I'm here to talk about Will Richeaux and Lowell Webster."

What little color Patsy had slowly drained from her face as she stared at Charlotte for what seemed like an interminable length of time.

Though the polite side of Charlotte felt the need to further clarify what she'd said, to further explain, she forced herself to hold her tongue for the moment, mostly to see what Patsy's reaction would be.

Finally, Patsy blinked several times and seemed to get a hold on herself. "Wh-why would you want to talk about those men? Especially to me?" she added.

Charlotte's insides churned. *In for a penny, in for a pound.* Now came the hard part. She sat up straighter and cleared her throat. "Because I think you know all three of them," she said evenly. "And I also think that Will Richeaux and Lowell Webster are connected in some way to the murder of Ricco Martinez."

"Wh-what on earth are you talking about?" Patsy sputtered.

Charlotte held up her hand and ticked off each point with her fingers. "For one, you and Lowell Webster have a history. Number two, you forget, I saw the look on your face when Will Richeaux showed up as the detective in charge. You were scared spitless for some reason, and I want to know why. And finally, last but not least, I know that Nadia told you all about Ricco and

Mark Webster's relationship."

"But—but none of that means anything," Patsy exclaimed. "And how dare you come in here and accuse me like this. I-I—"

Charlotte stiffened. "Oh, believe me. I dare," she retorted sharply. "I dare because two innocent people who just happen to be a part of my family are taking the fall for something they didn't do. And—to set the record straight—I'm not accusing you of anything—not yet. But, one way or another, I *will* find out what I need to know. Now, you can either tell me what *you* know, or you can tell my niece, who, by the way, is also a police detective. So—do you deny knowing Lowell Webster?"

From Patsy's expression, Charlotte could see that she was weighing the pros and cons of answering her. Finally, in a haughty voice so cold it made Charlotte shiver, she said, "I think you already know the answer to that question." Still glaring at Charlotte, Patsy abruptly stood. Then she began pacing. "And further-more," she continued, "I think you already know all about our so-called sordid relationship. But what you don't know is that he ruined my life. Thanks to Lowell Webster, I was never able to have a family of my own."

The more she talked, the more irritated she seemed to become, and Charlotte watched her warily.

Patsy held up two fingers and shook them at Char-lotte. "I've been married twice and divorced twice. You see, both of those men wanted families, wanted chil-dren.

"Oh, in the beginning they said children didn't matter. Yeah, right! Now I know better. Why else would they have both divorced me? And as for Lowell, I've thought about killing him at least a thousand times. *Thought about it,*" she emphasized, glaring at Charlotte. "But thinking about it and doing it are two different things. Besides, killing him is too good for him, too easy."

"So you came up with a way to make him suffer instead."

Patsy stopped her pacing to stand just to the right of Charlotte. She was breathing hard, and there was a strange smile on her lips that raised goose bumps on Charlotte's arms.

Patsy shook her head and gestured wildly with her hands. "Not just suffer. Even that's not enough. With Ricco Martinez's help, I could have ruined Lowell forever like he ruined me. I could have ruined that precious reputation he's so proud of."

Patsy leaned forward until she was just inches from Charlotte's face. She was still breathing hard, and Charlotte got a whiff of something that smelled suspiciously like liquor on her breath.

"I could have ruined his chances of ever being in politics again," Patsy told her. "And I still can!" she yelled in Charlotte's face.

In a sudden, unexpected move, Patsy grabbed a large glass vase on the end table next to the sofa and swung it at Charlotte's head.

Charlotte threw up her hand to ward off the blow, but she wasn't quick enough. When the vase hit her, blinding white pain erupted in her head. The room spun. Her vision blurred. Then there was nothing but the black void of unconsciousness.

Chapter Twenty-two

W hen Charlotte came to, she was flat on her back and there was a dull throbbing in her head. When she opened her eyes, she panicked. Darkness. Nothing but darkness. She blinked several times, but blinking didn't help. Nothing had changed. It was still dark.

Oh, dear Lord, was she blind? Had the blow to her head caused her to go blind?

Closing her eyes again, she reached up and gingerly explored the side of her head with her fingers. Just back from her left temple was a bump that felt like the size of a golf ball. Though the bump was really sore and painful, as far as she could tell there was no blood, which meant that the skin hadn't been broken.

She opened her eyes again, but she was afraid to even move. She thought about trying to get to her feet, but she squelched the instinct for the moment.

"Easy does it," she whispered. "One step at a time."

For now the throbbing was bearable, but she suspected that any sudden movement could change that status. Ever so slowly, ever so carefully, she turned her head first to one side and then to the other, testing the threshold of pain. And that's when she saw it.

Right near her feet, barely visible, was a hair-thin sliver of light just beneath what she figured had to be a door. Her eyes blurred with grateful tears, and she blinked them away. At least now she knew for sure that she wasn't blind.

Think, Charlotte. Think. With her head still pounding,

it was difficult to think of anything but the pain and how frightened she was. Even so, she had to try.

Charlotte concentrated on the light she'd seen, the light beneath the door. But a door to what? Where was she? And, even more urgent, where was Patsy and what did she plan to do with her?

Only one way to find out, Charlotte decided. Shifting her body to her left side, and thanking the good Lord that Patsy hadn't tied her up, she reached over with her right hand and pushed herself up until she could rest on her left elbow.

Her head throbbed, and she felt dizzy, even in the dark, so she waited a moment to see if the sensation would pass.

Once the throbbing lessened, so did the dizzy feeling, and she eased into a sitting position. Again, she had to wait a moment. Encouraged that the throbbing subsided in even less time, she used her hands to explore the area around her that was within reach.

The moment her fingers touched the first prickly object, she immediately recognized it as the bristles of a broom.

The pantry. She had to be in the pantry.

If she remembered right, Patsy kept the broom in the oversized kitchen pantry. By the process of elimination, it made sense that Patsy would have put her in the pantry, since she would have had to drag her to wherever she put her, and the pantry was the nearest closet that was large enough.

A mental image of the walk-in pantry came to mind. All in all, she calculated that it measured about five feet wide and six feet deep. There were narrow built-in shelves that went from the floor to the ceiling on three sides. Each of the side shelves was filled with canned goods and groceries, while the back shelves contained various other miscellaneous items.

Again Charlotte looked back at the sliver of light beneath the door. Was there a lock on the outside of the door? She couldn't remember seeing one, but, then, she'd never really paid much attention to whether it had a lock or not.

She slid herself over to the door and felt around until she located the doorknob. When the doorknob twisted freely, sudden hope sprang in her heart. But when she pushed against the door and nothing happened, the hope died.

Evidently, Patsy must have something blocking it or she'd wedged something against it.

Now what? "Now nothing," she whispered, disappointment knifing through her. If only she had her cell phone, she could call for help. But, darn it all, she'd left it in her purse and left her purse locked in the van.

She could always scream, but the house was isolated from its neighbors. No one would hear her if she yelled her head off. No one but Patsy. And the last thing she wanted was to attract Patsy's attention. There was really nothing she could do but wait. Wait and pray.

Charlotte had no way of knowing how long she sat there, waiting and praying in the dark, and when she first heard the noise, she wondered if she was hallucinating.

Not hallucinating, she finally decided. The footsteps

were real, and so were the voices, and both voices were getting louder by the second, which meant that whoever the voices belonged to, those people were headed for the kitchen.

Again, hope sprang within her. If someone else was there, maybe that person would help her. She scooted nearer the door and pressed her ear against it. Sure enough, she could detect the muffled voices of Patsy and some man.

"What are you doing here?" she heard Patsy say. "What do you want?"

"More to the point, what is Charlotte LaRue doing here?"

Will Richeaux. Even as Charlotte's hope for help died, the hairs on the back of her neck stood on end. But how had he known that she was at Patsy's in the first place?

"She works for me," Patsy answered belligerently. "And since when do the police check up on maids?"

"Since maids get too nosy for their own good," he snapped.

Judith's confrontation with him earlier that morning came to mind, and Charlotte's insides churned. Had he, like Louis, come to the same conclusions about her involvement? How else would he know that she was there? Unless he had followed Judith to her house, put two and two together, then followed her.

Had she been followed? Charlotte had to admit that she didn't know. She'd been too caught up in trying to decide whether to confront Patsy to pay attention to anything else.

"Where is she, and what does she want?" he demanded.

"I told you she *works* for me."

"Not on a Saturday afternoon, she doesn't."

"So? Maybe I hired her to do some extra work."

"Yeah, right, and maybe I'm the king of Rex. Now, answer me. Where is she? And don't lie. Her van is still outside, so I know she's in here somewhere."

"Ouch! Let go of me. That hurts."

"It's gonna hurt a lot worse unless you tell me where that nosy maid is."

Charlotte winced. She shouldn't have cared what Will Richeaux thought, one way or the other. But no one had ever accused her of being "nosy" before, and that hurt almost as much as the lump on the side of her head.

"In there," Patsy screeched. "She's back there in the pantry."

"And just what does that mean?"

"It means she's in the pantry where I put her."

"Where you put her? And why in hell would you put her in the pantry?"

"Ouch! That hurts. Please don't—"

"Then answer the question."

"I-I sort of knocked her out."

"And why would you do that?"

" 'Cause she was asking too many questions . . . about Ricco Martinez."

"What kind of questions?" When no answer was forthcoming, Will Richeaux made a noise of pure frustration. "What's with you, lady? First you try that half-baked scheme with that cemetery junk. Even a moron could have figured out that Ricco Martinez wasn't about to bite off the hand feeding him. What happened? Did he turn on you—try to shake you down?" He laughed, but it was an ugly sound that made Charlotte's stomach turn.

"That's exactly what he did, didn't he? He tried to blackmail you. What'd he do? Threaten to go to the police if you didn't pay up?" Again he laughed. "You should have paid him, you stupid cow. But not because he'd run to the police. Believe me, the police were the last people someone like him wanted to tangle with. You should have realized that he'd run straight to Lowell.

"Well, he won't be running to anyone anymore, will he? I warned you once before about bothering Mr. Webster, but this time you went too far. We had hoped that if and when Martinez's body was found, you'd finally get the message, and everything was working out just fine until that nosy maid started snooping around."

We? Charlotte's heart pounded. Did "we" include Mark or Lowell Webster?

"I knew it!" Patsy screeched. "When I realized that you were a cop, I knew I'd been set up. You're the one who killed him," she accused.

"No—not me personally. I don't usually dirty my hands with that part of the job. Mr. Webster has other people who take care of stuff like that. But now you've gone and jeopardized everything—you and that maid. You've left me no choice."

"Wh-what are you doing? Oh no! Please don't— please, I'm begging you—"

A loud popping sound made Charlotte jump. Oh, dear Lord. Was that a gunshot? If it was, then for sure she'd be the next victim on his list.

Charlotte scrambled to her feet, but the sudden move caused her head to swim. She grabbed hold of the door frame for support until the dizzy sensation passed.

What to do . . . what to do? Any minute Will Richeaux would be opening the door to get to her. If only there was some way to get him first, a way to launch a surprise attack of some kind.

"This is Will. Let me speak to the boss."

Charlotte froze for a second before realizing that he had to be talking to someone on the phone. Had he decided to call Lowell Webster? Good, she thought. She didn't care who he talked to. The longer he talked, the more time she had.

"Yeah, yeah," Charlotte heard him say. "I know what he told you about me calling him there. Just tell him I said this is an emergency."

A memory niggled at the back of Charlotte's head as she frantically ran her hands over the canned goods stacked on the shelves, looking for something, anything she could use as a weapon. Then she remembered what was bothering her. On the day she'd gone to Lowell Webster's office, he'd received an unwelcome phone call while she'd been cleaning his office bathroom. She'd overheard him tell the caller in no uncertain terms that he was never to call him at the office, which meant it was possible that the caller had been Will Richeaux that day. If only she'd realized then . . .

But now wasn't the time to dwell on "if only's." What

she needed now was a weapon. An idea began to form. Although she couldn't recall the name of the movie, she did remember one of the scenes where a teenager who was in jail used his T-shirt filled with canned drinks for a weapon. Why couldn't she do the same?

Listening intently to Will Richeaux, Charlotte slipped out of her jacket.

"Just wanted to let you know I've run into a little problem," she heard him say.

The heaviness on one side of the jacket reminded her that the tape recorder was still in the pocket. Vaguely wondering if it had continued to record, she dug it out of the pocket and shoved it into her pants pocket.

She quickly spread her jacket on the floor, and as she placed several of the canned goods in it, she thought of yet another idea. If she remembered right, Patsy kept a large bottle of cooking oil on the bottom shelf near the canned goods.

Charlotte tilted her head closer to the door and was relieved to hear Will still talking.

". . . one more little problem to take care of . . ." she heard him say. Knowing he was talking about her, her fingers trembled as she quickly ran them along the shelves, searching for the bottle of cooking oil.

How much longer? she wondered, her ear attuned to any noise outside the pantry that would indicate that Will had finished his conversation. And where was that cooking oil?

Bingo! Charlotte's fingers grasped the large plastic bottle she'd found. From the way it felt and the size of it, she was sure that it had to be the oil. She twisted off the top and stuck her finger inside. When she pulled out her finger, then rubbed her finger and thumb together, relief washed through her. As she suspected, she had found the oil.

Using the sliver of light beneath the door for a guide, she stepped over to the door, dropped to her knees, and poured a stream of the oil on the floor along the threshold of the door. Using both hands, she spread it out, careful to keep it on the inside of the pantry.

Satisfied, and ever aware that time was of the essence, she eased back to where she'd left the jacket. Her hands were slick and greasy with oil and were sure to leave stains. Too bad, she thought, as she gathered up the edges of the garment over the canned goods and stood. Having a stained jacket was preferable any day to being dead.

With a grunt, she hefted the jacket full of cans over her shoulder like a bat, then flattened herself against the wall near the door, and she waited. All she could do now was hope that her plan would work.

A sudden click made Charlotte jump.

The tape recorder. It *had* been recording the whole time. Dare she hope that it had picked up some of Will and Patsy's argument? Though it was doubtful that the machine had picked up any of it due to the distance, at least she'd have Patsy's tirade on tape.

The sound of heavy footsteps drew her attention, and as she tensed, she forgot about the tape recorder. She tightened her grip around the gathered jacket but could do nothing to stop the trembling in her legs except to pray that they would hold her up. There was a bumping, scraping sound, then the doorknob twisted, and the door swung open.

"I know you're in there," Will sneered. Then, in a singsong voice, he said, "Come out, come out, wherever you are."

Chapter Twenty-three

With her heart pounding and her knees knocking, Charlotte blinked rapidly in an effort to force her eyes to adjust from the darkness of the closed closet to the sudden, blinding light at the door.

"I said come out of there!" Will snarled.

His hand that held the gun suddenly appeared around the edge of the door, and Charlotte tensed, ready to swing. Then everything happened so fast that all she could do was stand frozen and watch.

The moment Will took a step inside, his foot slipped in the oil. "What the—" With a yelp of surprise, he flung out his free hand for balance but only grabbed air. His feet went out from under him, and as he fell, Charlotte winced when his head hit the edge of the lower shelf with a thu-whacking sound, followed by the rest of his body hitting the floor with a thud.

Charlotte tensed, ready to clobber him with the cans, but she hesitated when she realized that he wasn't moving.

His head was turned to the side and his eyes were closed. When a moment more passed and he still hadn't moved or tried to get up, Charlotte feared he might be dead.

Her gaze slid down to his chest. No, not dead. Not yet. The movement was ever so slight, but he was still breathing. Her gaze traveled back to his face. It was the sight of blood pooling beneath his head that finally spurred her into action. She needed to get out and call for help, but the only way out was the pantry doorway, and Will Richeaux's body was blocking it.

With visions of him regaining consciousness and reaching up and grabbing her any minute, she took a deep breath and jumped over him.

When she successfully landed on the outside of the pantry without slipping or falling, she felt like sobbing with relief. But the relief was short-lived when Will emitted a groan.

Terrified that any minute he would come to, Charlotte dropped the jacket and cans and threw all of her weight against the door. Using the door for leverage, inch by inch, she was able to shove him far enough inside the pantry so that she could get the door closed.

With all of her weight against the door, Charlotte glanced around for something to use to jam the door shut. Patsy had used something, but what?

Then she spied a door guard propped against the wall and grabbed it. She jammed the yoke of the steel rod under the doorknob and braced the gripper base that anchored the device against the floor. She tested the strength of the door guard by pulling hard on the doorknob. Satisfied that the door wouldn't open, she went in search of Patsy and a telephone.

Charlotte found Patsy sprawled on the kitchen floor. From the looks of the blood on Patsy's blouse, Will had shot her in the chest. Since Charlotte couldn't detect any breathing movement, she knelt down and felt for a pulse.

Though Patsy's pulse was thready, she was still alive . . . but just barely. Charlotte jumped to her feet and hurried to the phone on the wall near the cabinet. With trembling fingers she pressed the numbers 9-1-1.

Once she'd given the operator her location and described the emergency, she was told to stay on the line until help arrived. Charlotte ignored the instructions, depressed the switch-hook, and immediately called Judith.

Judith answered on the third ring. "Judith, this is Aunt Charley."

"What's wrong, Auntie?"

"I'm at Patsy Dufour's, and I need you to get here A.S.A.P. Patsy's been sh-shot, and I-I've got Will Richeaux locked up in the pantry. He's injured, too. I've already called nine-one-one, and I'll explain it all when you get here."

"And you? Are you okay, Aunt Charley?"

"No—yes. I mean I'm fine, I think. But, Judith, please hurry."

"Okay, okay, now just calm down. The first thing I want you to do is get out of the house. Go straight to your van, lock yourself inside, and stay there until the police get there. I'm on my way."

Charlotte hung up the phone, then stared down at Patsy.

What goes around comes around, and people get paid back for the things they do. No one would blame her if she did as Judith had instructed and left Patsy, not after what Patsy had done. Charlotte swallowed hard.

She couldn't do it.

For reasons Charlotte couldn't begin to fathom, she couldn't leave Patsy all alone in spite of what Patsy had tried to do to her. Besides which, Patsy was the only one who could corroborate what Will Richeaux had said about Lowell Webster's part in Ricco's murder.

And what about Will Richeaux? Charlotte couldn't explain it, but the thought of leaving *him* by himself didn't bother her one iota. The only feeling she had for him was fear.

Charlotte reached down and smoothed back a strand of Patsy's hair. She figured that Patsy was probably in shock from her wound. And she was probably dying.

Charlotte's mind raced. In all of the movies, didn't they always cover the victim? Maybe to keep them warm or hold in their body heat. Whichever, it certainly couldn't hurt, and it might actually help save her life.

With her ears attuned to any sound from the pantry, Charlotte hurried off in search for something to cover Patsy with.

She found what she was looking for in the sitting room. In a basket beside the sofa was a folded crocheted afghan. She snatched up the afghan and rushed back into the kitchen.

After covering Patsy, there was nothing else to do but wait for help to come. "You hang in there, Patsy," she murmured.

The sound of distant sirens suddenly broke through

the silence. "Thank goodness," Charlotte murmured. With one last glance at Patsy, she hurried to the front door.

Police cars and two ambulances arrived within seconds of each other. When Charlotte saw that Billy Wilson was among the officers striding toward the porch, she almost cried with relief.

"Inside," she told the officers, motioning toward the front hallway. "Straight back, the last door on the left, there's a lady who's been shot. There's also a man—" She cleared her throat. "There's a man locked in the pantry. He's been injured, too. He's the one who shot the lady."

Out of the corner of her eye, Charlotte spotted Judith's car pull in alongside one of the squad cars.

"What happened here, Ms. LaRue?" Billy asked her.

When Charlotte opened her mouth to explain, her knees suddenly went weak, so weak that she could barely stand, and she couldn't utter a word.

"Whoa, now—" Billy grabbed hold of her arm. "Why don't you sit down before you fall down?"

All Charlotte could manage was to nod as she allowed Billy to help her to a nearby wicker chair.

"Hey, Bill, is she okay?" Judith ran up the porch steps. "Is she hurt?"

Charlotte shook her head. "Not hurt, hon," she whispered.

"Probably delayed reaction," Billy offered.

"I'm sure you're right," Judith agreed, then knelt in front of Charlotte. "Auntie, I need to check out what's going on inside? Bill will stay with you until I get back. Okay?"

Charlotte nodded. "Do your job, hon," she murmured. "I'll be okay. I just need a minute."

Judith nodded and stood. "Stay with her for me," she told Billy. Then she disappeared inside the house.

Charlotte wasn't sure how much time passed before the paramedics wheeled out first one stretcher then a second one. But she was aware of Billy Wilson's quiet presence and felt comforted by it as each stretcher was loaded inside a separate ambulance and the ambulances screamed off down the street.

After the ambulances left, the normal flow of traffic on the busy street seemed quiet by comparison. As Charlotte waited, time seemed to drag, her head was throbbing again, and all she wanted was to go home.

Police officers came and went from within the house, and Charlotte was beginning to wonder if Judith was ever coming out. What was taking so long? When Judith did finally appear a few minutes later, Charlotte was so relieved that she felt like crying.

"Here, Auntie, drink this." Judith handed Charlotte a glass of water that Charlotte gratefully accepted. She promptly gulped down most of it.

Judith patted her on the back. "Feel up to telling me what happened now?"

Charlotte sighed, then nodded. As best she could, she went over the sequence of events. When she'd finished, she said, "If Patsy survives, I'm hoping that she will corroborate what I've said. And I'm hoping it will be enough to get Daniel and Nadia off the hook." She paused. There was something else, something that she'd forgotten. Had she left out anything?

Just as she remembered what it was, Judith frowned and reached up and touched Charlotte's head. Charlotte winced.

"Why didn't you tell me you'd been injured?" Judith cried. "I would have had the paramedics examine you."

Charlotte brushed her hand aside. "I didn't tell you because I'm just fine, but there is something else that I need to tell you. I almost forgot." Charlotte reached inside her pants pocket and pulled out the tape recorder. "I recorded all of my conversation with Patsy, and the recorder was still running when Will Richeaux showed up. But I doubt you'll be able to hear what he and Patsy said to each other because of the distance and me being inside the closet and all."

Judith took the recorder. "What am I going to do with you, Auntie?" Shaking her head, she pressed the REWIND button. The tape whirred in the small recorder. "When Lou and Hank hear about this one, they'll both have conniption fits."

Charlotte sighed. "Can we please save the lecture for later? I'm not quite up to it right now."

The tape clicked, and Judith pressed the PLAY button. Charlotte was relieved to hear that the conversation between her and Patsy was clear enough to be understood. Then there was a long space of nothing but some grunting, some scraping, and finally the distinct click of a door being shut.

Unable to suppress a shudder, Charlotte said, "That's

probably when she dragged me inside the pantry." For several minutes, there was no noise on the tape, then there was the sound of a groan. "Guess that's when I regained consciousness."

Much to Charlotte's disappointment, the remainder of the tape was unintelligible. "Well, phooey," she muttered. "Unless Patsy survives, now it's only my word against his."

"Maybe not, Auntie. I'll give it to the lab boys and see what they can come up with. They have ways of enhancing stuff like this so that it's clear as a bell."

Static from Judith's radio interrupted. Judith stepped away toward the other end of the porch to answer the radio page. When she returned, Charlotte could tell from the expression on her face that whatever the message had been it wasn't good news.

"Richeaux didn't make it, Auntie. Seems the blow to the side of his head was worse than they thought. He died before they could get him to the hospital."

"Oh no . . ."

"Aunt Charley, don't—" Judith knelt down beside her and squeezed her hand. "It's not your fault. If anyone's at fault, it was Will Richeaux for being a crooked cop to begin with."

Charlotte heard what Judith was saying, and, while part of her knew it was true, another part of her couldn't get past the fact that she'd helped contribute to a man's death.

"What about Patsy?" Charlotte whispered, trying hard not to think about Will Richeaux.

"She's in surgery. We won't know anything for a

267

while yet. Meantime, I'm going to need you to come to the precinct and give a statement. But only if you're up to it. I really should take you to the emergency room first."

"No!" Charlotte protested. "I don't want to go to the emergency room—not for a silly bump on the head. All I want is to go home. So let's just get this over with and do what has to be done."

By the time Charlotte finished giving her statement at the Sixth Precinct station house, Judith had news about Patsy Dufour.

"She survived the surgery, Auntie," Judith told her as she escorted Charlotte to the elevator. "Once the doctors say it's okay, we'll question her. Probably not until tomorrow morning, though. For now, I want you to go home and try and get some rest." She motioned toward Billy Wilson. "Bill and another officer will take you to pick up your van; then he'll drive you and the van home."

Much of the ride back to Patsy's to pick up her van and then the short drive home passed in a blur for Charlotte until Billy Wilson turned the van into her driveway.

Hank's BMW was parked alongside the curb, and Hank and Carol were seated on the porch swing, waiting for her.

"Just wonderful," Charlotte murmured with a groan as she allowed Billy to help her out of the van. "Just what I don't need right now."

Before Charlotte's feet had touched the ground, Hank was standing in front of her.

"Thanks, Billy," he said.

"No thanks necessary," Billy told him, then he turned and headed toward the patrol car that had pulled in behind the van. "Take care, Ms. LaRue," he called over his shoulder as he climbed inside the patrol car.

"Are you okay, Mom?"

Charlotte nodded. "I'm okay. Just bone-tired, son." And sore, she suddenly realized, but decided against mentioning it. Charlotte gave her son a wan smile. "You didn't have to come over, though."

"Ah, excuse me! My mother almost gets killed and there's no need for me to see about her?" Then, in a move that completely caught her off guard, he pulled her into his arms. "I love you, Mom." He hugged her tightly. "Of course I'd come to make sure you're okay. And, no, I'm not going to lecture you." He laughed. "Not right now anyway." He held her at arm's length. "Besides, Judith would have my hide if I did."

At that Charlotte smiled again.

"Carol and I thought you might could use a bit of pampering after the ordeal you've been through. How does a hot shower, your pajamas, and a hot meal sound? We picked up Chinese on the way here."

"Sounds like heaven," Charlotte told him, tears springing to her eyes. "What did I ever do to deserve a son like you?"

Hank simply shrugged and winked. "Just lucky, I guess."

Charlotte playfully boxed him on the arm. "And so

humble, too," she teased. Then she suddenly sobered. "I just hope it wasn't all for nothing. All I wanted was for Daniel and Nadia to be cleared."

"Me too, Mom. Me too. Now, why don't you come inside, and while Carol warms up dinner, I want to take a look at your head. Judith said that lick you got knocked you out cold."

In spite of Hank and Carol's pampering, after they left Charlotte was unable to get to sleep right away. She tried drinking a glass of milk, and she tried reading, but nothing seemed to help.

Over and over she kept reliving each harrowing moment of her ordeal. And over and over in her mind's eye she kept seeing Will Richeaux slip in the oil and fall. And she kept hearing that awful sound, that cracking sound when his head had hit the edge of the pantry shelf.

Finally, as a last-ditch effort, she gave in and took one of the pills that Hank had left for her.

"Just to help you rest," he'd told her once he'd determined that the injury to her head wasn't critical.

It was the sound of the phone ringing that awakened her on Sunday morning. "Hello," she mumbled into the receiver, noting that daylight was peeking through the miniblinds in her bedroom.

"Charlotte? Did I wake you?"

"Hmm, yeah, Maddie," she answered, still groggy.

"You doing okay?"

"So-so."

"Guess you aren't going to church this morning."

"What time is it?"

"Ten-fifteen."

"Guess not. Had trouble getting to sleep, so I took a pill Hank gave me last night."

"Well, go back to sleep. I just called mostly to tell you that I'm really not up to doing our Sunday family dinner thing, not with Daniel still in jail, and Nadia . . ."

"Yeah, I know what you mean," Charlotte mumbled. "Just as well," she added. "I don't think I'm up to going anywhere, not even for a free meal. Talk to you later."

"Charlotte, wait—don't hang up yet. Listen, I—I just want to—I— Oh, shoot. I'm glad you're okay. I love you. Now go back to sleep."

"Love you too, Maddie. Thanks."

It was almost noon before Charlotte woke up again. She was tempted to pull the covers over her head and stay in the bed, but she forced herself to get up.

By midafternoon, she was on pins and needles. Had Judith been able to question Patsy yet? And if she had, did Patsy corroborate what Charlotte had told the police about everything? Had the police talked to the Websters yet? And the biggest question of all, would Daniel finally be released from jail?

To get her mind off everything, Charlotte tried to read. But concentration was impossible. Then she tried watching television, but there was nothing on but the same old tired reruns she had already seen several times.

She'd just about made up her mind to go for a walk

271

around the block in hopes of working out some of the soreness left over from her ordeal when she heard a car pull into her driveway. Rushing to the window, her pulse jumped when she saw that her visitor was Judith. Charlotte hurried to the door and opened it just as Judith was approaching the steps.

One look at her niece and sympathy welled up within Charlotte. Judith looked tired. Her clothes were rumpled, and there were dark circles beneath her eyes.

"Come in, come in," Charlotte told her. "No offense, but you look like you could use one of those pills that Hank gave me last night to sleep."

"Humph. I wish. No rest for the weary, though." Judith stepped past Charlotte into the living room. "Too much going on."

"Please tell me you have some news." Charlotte closed the door.

"Good news and bad. Got any coffee?"

"No, but I'll make some. I could use a cup myself. Have you eaten? Are you hungry?"

"Just coffee, but thanks."

While Charlotte got the coffeepot going, Judith talked. "The bad news is that the lab boys couldn't enhance the last part of that tape enough to even tell who was talking. Sorry, Auntie."

Disappointment settled in Charlotte's stomach like a rock. "And the good news?" she asked as she turned the coffeepot on.

"Patsy backed up everything you said, especially after I told her that you had recorded everything. She even confirmed what you said about Will Richeaux working for Lowell Webster. But I'm afraid there's even more good news, bad news.

"The Websters *were* questioned," Judith went on. "For all the good that did," she scoffed. "Of course they both denied having anything to do with Will Richeaux. And the powers that be have decided that since the only evidence against the Websters is hearsay, they're laying the blame for Ricco's death on Will Richeaux."

"But that's just not true. What about the phone call Will made right after he shot Patsy? All they had to do was check his cell phone records to verify that he called Lowell. Isn't that hard evidence?

"And the tape," she continued. "Even if it can't be heard, both Patsy and I can verify what Will said when he denied that he had killed Ricco himself. We both heard him as much as admit that Lowell Webster hired someone else to take care of Ricco.

"Then there's the fact that Lowell owned that warehouse where the artifacts were found." Charlotte seated herself at the table. "Besides," she continued, "Will Richeaux didn't even know Ricco, did he?"

"None of that matters, Aunt Charley. They're saying that they have evidence that Will was the one behind the cemetery thefts. Patsy even admitted that Will was the one who sold her the urn. Of course, at the time she didn't know that he was a police officer.

"Remember? You said that when the police arrived after the bones were discovered and she saw Will, she acted funny—like she was scared or something. Well, she admitted that she was scared, scared because she recognized him as the one who had sold her that urn in the first place. Right then and there she knew something was wrong about the whole setup.

"Anyway, the theory they've come up with is that Will killed Ricco to keep him quiet about his involvement with the thefts."

"But that's just not true," Charlotte protested again.

"Sorry, Auntie. True or not, it makes for a much tidier package than dragging someone like Lowell Webster into the mess, especially since Will is dead and can't defend himself. But that's just between you and me, so don't go telling that to anyone else."

"Humph!" Charlotte stood and walked over to the cabinet. "Sounds to me like no one wants to rock the Websters' boat." No one but Patsy, she added silently as she poured two cups of coffee.

Judith shrugged. "Maybe so. But the one thing we have to keep in mind is that at least this way, Daniel and Nadia are off the hook. Speaking of which"—she glanced at her watch—"can I take that cup of coffee with me? I want to be there when Daniel is released."

"Today! He's being released today?" Charlotte felt like laughing and crying at the same time. "That—that's wonderful!"

Judith smiled and nodded. "In just about an hour, I figure. Only problem now is how to get word to Nadia that she can finally come home."

"Maybe Daniel will know where she's been hiding out." Charlotte reached inside the cabinet and selected one of several insulated coffee mugs she kept on hand. Then she dumped the contents of one of the cups into the mug. She handed Judith the mug.

"I hope so, Auntie, but just in case, if she happens to call you again . . ."

Judith's voice trailed off and Charlotte nodded.

Tuesday morning found Charlotte dragging her feet. It was her day to work for Bitsy, and she dreaded having to listen to what she was sure would be endless questions from the elderly lady. But having to contend with Bitsy was just part of her problem, she finally admitted to herself as she headed for the living room.

She should have been satisfied with the way everything had turned out. After all, Davy's precious Daddy Danol was finally home with him. And within an hour of Daniel's release from jail on Sunday afternoon, Nadia had miraculously, if not mysteriously, showed up at home, too.

On Monday evening the family had gathered at Daniel's for an impromptu pizza party celebration. Each time the matter of Nadia's whereabouts was mentioned, though, Nadia had remained closemouthed and promptly changed the subject.

Charlotte, along with everyone else, was left wondering where Nadia had been hiding out and how she'd known about Daniel's release so soon.

But what did it matter in the long run? All that really mattered was that all the little chickies were back in the roost where they belonged.

Charlotte grimaced. So why the nagging feeling that something was still missing?

"'Cause no one should get away with murder," she told Sweety Boy as she checked his food and water containers. As far as she was concerned, that's exactly what had happened in spite of the final police report. By his own admission, she heard Will Richeaux say that he hadn't murdered Ricco, and at the point he'd said it, he'd had no reason to lie about it.

Then who had? *Someone* had gotten away with it. But who?

The obvious answer was Lowell Webster. At least to Charlotte it was.

Charlotte paused to stare out the living room window. The day was overcast, and rain was predicted. But Charlotte was staring with unseeing eyes. In her head, she kept hearing what Will Richeaux had said about Lowell.

I don't usually dirty my hands with that kind of work. Mr. Webster has other people who take care of stuff like that. What other people? she wondered.

Lowell may not have actually murdered Ricco with his own hands, but he'd hired it done; therefore, he was just as guilty as the person who had actually pulled the trigger.

As far as murder plots went, Lowell had planned well. For years Patsy had been a thorn in Lowell's side, and more recently Ricco had become a problem. It made sense that Lowell had decided to take care of both of them in one fell swoop, kill two birds with one stone.

He'd had Ricco murdered and stuffed into the urn, then he'd had Will Richeaux sell the urn to Patsy in hopes that the body would be discovered and that it would serve as a warning for her to back off from her smear campaign. In fact, with everything that had happened, it wouldn't have surprised Charlotte in the least to find out that Lowell had even made sure there was a crack in the bottom of the urn.

The cuckoo clock sounded, and with a shiver Charlotte turned away from the window and glanced at the clock. Time to go to work.

Bitsy was waiting at the door when Charlotte pulled up alongside the curb in front of her house.

"Now, be nice," Charlotte muttered, dreading what she knew was coming as she gathered her cleaning supplies. Bitsy was going to have a field day with everything that had been happening.

"Be charitable. She's just a lonely old lady," Charlotte whispered to herself.

The words proved to be Charlotte's silent mantra as the morning progressed. As she'd expected, Bitsy followed her around almost every step of the way, asking endless questions and chattering nonstop.

But when Bitsy followed her into the bathroom, Charlotte almost lost her temper. Only by concentrating on counting to a hundred was she able to control herself.

By lunchtime Charlotte's patience had worn thinner than a frazzle. Relieved and ever so grateful that the one thing that Bitsy never missed was the midday news, Charlotte took her lunch and headed straight for the front porch.

Outside it was pouring rain, but she figured that on the porch she could at least eat her sandwich in peace.

Besides, the sound of the rain was kind of soothing and relaxing after listening to Bitsy all morning. But, then, almost anything would have been preferable to listening to Bitsy.

As Charlotte settled herself in one of the two rattan chairs, she spread out the contents of her lunch on the small glass-topped table. She had just taken a bite of the turkey sandwich she'd brought with her when the front door swung open and Bitsy stuck her head out.

"Charlotte, hurry! Come see. It's all over the news. Lowell Webster has been murdered!"

Chapter Twenty-four

"Murdered?" Shock waves ricocheted through Charlotte. But before she could question Bitsy, the old lady had already disappeared back inside the house. By the time Charlotte raced to the TV room, the segment about Lowell's murder was over.

"You missed it," Bitsy told her, waving at the television set. "They said he was found dead in his office early this morning. Someone shot him, but according to the reporter on the scene, it was evident that Lowell put up a fight. They said that his office was in shambles, and a trail of blood led out the door to the elevator. They also found a brass letter opener that had blood on it near Lowell's body, so they're pretty sure he stabbed and wounded his killer before he died."

Bitsy moaned and sank down onto the sofa. "I just can't believe he's dead. Who would want to murder such a fine, upstanding man like Lowell Webster?"

Who indeed? Charlotte wondered.

According to the news early Wednesday morning, the police still hadn't uncovered a suspect for the murder of Lowell Webster.

Charlotte switched off the television and headed toward the kitchen for a second cup of coffee. She'd just poured herself a cup when the phone rang.

"Now what?" she muttered. Early-morning calls always meant problems. As she trudged into the living room, she wondered which of her employees wouldn't be able to work today.

She picked up the receiver. "Maid-for-a-Day. Charlotte speaking."

"Charlotte, it's Nadia."

"Oh, hey there. How's everything going?"

"So-so," Nadia answered. "But listen, I'm sorry to be calling you so early, but I wanted to catch you before you left for the day."

"Sure, hon, no problem. What's going on?"

"It's Davy, Charlotte. I'm really worried about him and thought you might could help—you know, since he stayed with you for several days. Anyway, he's had another one of his nightmares, and I was just wondering if he'd had any while he'd stayed with you. Of course he could be having some aftereffects from everything that's happened . . ." Her voice trailed away.

"He did have a nightmare one night," Charlotte offered sympathetically, "but I just figured it was because he was so confused about everything and missing you and Daniel. Weren't you able to get him to tell you what he dreamed?"

"Oh, that's not the problem. It's *what* he dreamed that has me worried. He keeps saying that his daddy came to see him. Of course, he's said that before . . . before all this other stuff happened. But always before he seemed kind of happy about it, so I didn't pay it too much attention. I figured it was just wishful thinking.

"But this time was different. This time he was really upset—sobbing his little heart out. He keeps insisting that his daddy is hurt and that he's bleeding."

"Aw, poor little guy," Charlotte said as goose bumps chased along her arms and a shiver ran up her spine, for she suddenly remembered something that Bitsy had said: *It's believed that Lowell was able to stab and wound his killer with a brass letter opener before he died.*

Was it possible? "No," she whispered, denying the possibility even as everything within her cried otherwise.

"Excuse me?" Nadia responded.

"I—ah—listen, Nadia, I want you to shut the door to Davy's room. Don't let him in there, and don't you go back in there, either. I want Judith to have a look around first."

"But why—" Suddenly Nadia gasped. "Oh, Charlotte! You're not thinking that— No! That's not possible. Ricco is—is—"

"I know, I know. It's too crazy to even contemplate, but that's why I want Judith to take a look around—you know, just in case there might be traces of blood."

"But Ricco is dead . . . isn't he?"

"He's supposed to be, but—I just don't know now. Look, hon, once Judith gets there, why don't you bring Davy and come stay at my house—just until Judith has a look around. No use further exposing him to anything else."

"Oh, dear Lord. You really think he might still be alive?"

"Honestly, I don't know what to think," Charlotte answered, "but, like I said, why don't you and Davy come over to my house for a while. There's an extra key beneath that ceramic frog in the front flower bed."

Once Nadia had finally agreed, Charlotte depressed the switch-hook, then immediately called Judith.

"What's up, Auntie?"

"Do you remember the nightmares Davy's been having? The ones where he claims that his daddy— Ricco, that is—comes to see him?"

"Hmm . . . yeah—vaguely, I guess. What about them?"

"I just got off the phone with Nadia. Davy had another one last night. Only thing—now get this—this time he claims his daddy was hurt and bleeding."

"Bleeding!"

"Yes, bleeding."

There was a long pause over the phone line. "Surely you don't think—" Several seconds passed, and even over the phone Charlotte could hear Judith drumming her fingers against a tabletop.

"You know, Auntie," she finally said, "it *could* be possible now that I think about it. We still haven't received the DNA report back from the state boys on the bones yet." There was another long pause. "It's a bit far-fetched, that's for sure, but stranger things have happened."

"I told Nadia to get Davy and come over here until you had a chance to check out his room. There might still be some blood there."

"Good thinking. I'm on my way. I'll let you know if I find anything. Call you later."

Charlotte slowly hung up the receiver, her mind racing. Now that she thought about it, the possibility had always been there. But because Ricco's billfold had been found in the urn with the bones and because Will Richeaux had been handling the case, no one had pushed to get the DNA results.

Charlotte glanced around, her insides churning. She glanced at the cuckoo. It was time to leave for work. Marian Hebert would be expecting her. But at the moment, work was the last thing Charlotte wanted to think about.

Charlotte sighed. From experience, she knew that the best thing she could do was to stay occupied. Besides, if she canceled the job and stayed home, all she'd do was fret and worry.

With another frustrated sigh, Charlotte took her empty coffee cup back to the kitchen, then headed for the bathroom to shower and dress.

That day Charlotte worked like a demon and had Marian's house cleaned in record time. But not even the rigorous physical labor was enough to squelch all of the questions swirling in her head.

As she packed up her cleaning supplies to head home, she wondered for at least the hundredth time if Judith had found any traces of blood in Davy's room. For at least the thousandth time, she asked herself if it could be possible that Ricco Martinez was alive. And if it was possible, then who on earth did the bones in the urn belong to? Even more puzzling, if the bones didn't belong to Ricco, then why was his billfold in the urn?

By the time Charlotte turned down Milan Street that afternoon, she was beside herself wondering if Judith had found out anything yet.

Charlotte pulled into her driveway, but out of the corner of her eye, Louis's mailbox near the front door of his side of the double caught her attention. The mailbox wasn't that large to begin with, but even from the driveway she could tell that it was stuffed to overflowing.

As Charlotte switched off the engine, she shook her head. She couldn't believe that she'd forgotten she was supposed to collect his mail while he was gone.

While he was gone . . . "And just what does that say about you," she muttered as she climbed out of the van. "One minute you're thinking you might have a future with the man, and the next—" Her voice trailed away as she slowly climbed the steps to the porch. *And the next minute, you completely forget that he's even left town,* she finished silently.

Charlotte wanted to make excuses for herself. After all, a lot had happened since Friday night, including the big blowup she'd had with Louis and Judith. But the problem was, they were just that: excuses. Almost five days had passed since Louis had left, and not once in

those five days had she even thought about him or wondered how or what he was doing. And the overstuffed
mailbox was the proof.

Of course, she hadn't heard from him, either. He
hadn't called to check on her or even just to talk.

Just more excuses. Maybe the old adage, out of sight,
out of mind, was true after all.

Not if you truly cared for him, a tiny voice insisted.
More years than she wanted to count had passed since
Hank Senior had left for Vietnam, never to return, and
hardly a day passed without her thinking about *him* in
some way.

Charlotte dug the mail out of Louis's mailbox. Sorting
through the envelopes, she placed the larger ones on the
bottom of the stack and the smaller ones on top.
Tucking the mail beneath her arm, she stepped over to
her own front door, unlocked it, and let herself inside.

Maybe it was time she faced the truth, she decided.

Sweety Boy squawked and began his normal routine
to get her attention. "I know, I know, Sweety. I've been
neglecting you lately." She glanced toward the desk and
eyed the answering machine.

To her disappointment, the light glowed steady as a
rock. No messages. She placed the mail on the small
table near the door, then slipped out of her shoes and
stepped into her moccasins. "Give me just a second,
Boy, and I'll let you out for a while."

Truth . . . Louis . . . Charlotte slowly walked over to
Sweety Boy's cage and opened the door. The little bird
immediately sidled up to the opening, hopped out, and
took flight. But Charlotte, tormented by confusing emo-

tions, simply stood there staring at the cage.

Truth. She really cared for Louis, maybe even loved him, but she didn't love him with the kind of all-encompassing love she'd had for Hank Senior. Still, she knew that there were different kinds of love, different degrees. Even so, she wasn't sure that what she felt would ever be the kind that would overlook and excuse the tiny flaws that otherwise drove a couple apart.

Truth. She was lonely. Yes, she had family and friends, but at times there was a huge gap in her life where she yearned for that man-woman, one-on-one relationship that family and friends couldn't fill.

Truth. No matter how much she wished for a relationship like the one she'd had with her son's father, she'd never find it with Louis Thibodeaux.

Louis just flat-out wasn't interested in her, not in that way, and not for lack of opportunity. He'd had ample opportunities to carry a relationship with her to a deeper level and hadn't made a move to do so.

When all was said and done, Charlotte had to deduce that once again she'd let her imagination get the best of her, and the only logical conclusion was that the whole supposed relationship was totally one-sided. Her side. And the pity of it all was that poor Louis didn't have a clue.

Charlotte felt her cheeks grow hot. "Enough already," she grumbled. "You're being totally ridiculous about the whole thing anyway."

It was almost eight o'clock that evening when Judith finally called Charlotte.

"Sorry it's taken me so long to get back to you, Aunt Charley," she said. "But I haven't stopped since you called this morning."

"Did you find traces of blood in Davy's room?"

"Yes ma'am. You called it right. And we also found Ricco. Unfortunately, he's dead."

"Dead?"

"Oh, he was alive when we found him, but just barely. He was in the Quarter. At first no one paid attention to him—just another homeless drunk, passed out on the sidewalk—but a tourist spotted blood on his shirt and flagged down a patrolman.

"An ambulance was called," Judith continued, "and he was rushed to Charity. By then, though, the infection in his wound had spread into his bloodstream. If he'd been in better health, he might have had a fighting chance. But he wasn't, and the infection was too far gone. He didn't make it, but before he died, he did ask for a priest, and he did make a confession that pretty much explains everything."

Chapter Twenty-five

"I told them this would be just the thing that they needed to put all of that ugly stuff behind them," Madeline told Charlotte as she carefully wrapped the last punch cup in newspaper.

A month had passed since Ricco had been found half-dead in front of a dirty alley on Bourbon Street, and, with Madeline's enthusiastic encouragement, Daniel and Nadia had finally agreed to go ahead with their wedding reception celebration.

"I also insisted that they should use Mother's punch set—you know, something old." Madeline placed the cup she'd wrapped in tissue paper inside the punch bowl along with the others she'd wrapped and packed in the sturdy cardboard box.

Charlotte smiled. "I think the 'something old, something new' thing applies to the actual ceremony, Maddie."

Madeline waved her hand. "Whatever."

"Anyway," Charlotte continued, "I'm glad they're using the punch set. Our mother would have loved Nadia and Davy."

"Well, of course," Madeline said. "What's not to love? Why, that little boy is just too precious for words. And Nadia—well, I know we got off on the wrong foot, but she's a real sweetheart. I don't think I've ever seen Daniel happier. And just think, Charlotte, in only a few months we're going to have a brand new baby in the family. A precious little girl, according to the ultrasound."

Madeline had come a long way and had changed her tune, big-time, in the weeks since Daniel's release from jail. Though Charlotte had her own ideas about the reasons for her sister's about-face, the reasons really didn't matter anymore. What mattered was that for once in her life, Madeline had finally been able to reach deep within and put her son's happiness above her own selfish desires.

Madeline glanced at her watch. "Oh my goodness. Just look at the time. I've got to get going." She closed the box. "I'm supposed to meet the caterers at five, but I told Nadia that I would pick Davy up from day-care on the way."

"Need me to help you tote this?" Charlotte patted the cardboard box.

Madeline shook her head. "No, I don't think so." She dug her keys out of her purse and handed them to Charlotte. "But I do need you to get the front door, then open the trunk of the car for me."

She hooked her purse strap over her shoulder, wrapped her arms around the box, and lifted it off the table. "It's not really that heavy."

They had just loaded the box in the car and closed the trunk when Louis pulled into the driveway on his side of the double. "I didn't know Louis was back," Maddie said in an aside to Charlotte as she waved at him.

"That's because he just got back this very minute," Charlotte murmured, her eyes on Louis's car while a crush of mixed feelings and confused emotions surged through her.

"Well, I've got to run, but be sure and tell him about the reception, and bring him along tonight. I sent him an invitation, but judging from that stack of mail you've been collecting for him, it might be tomorrow before he gets to it."

Charlotte nodded and swallowed the sudden lump in her throat. Louis's two-week trip had turned into almost four weeks, and the only word she'd received from him were a couple of brief postcards that simply stated that the job was taking longer than expected and he would be delayed coming home.

As Madeline backed out of the driveway, Louis walked toward Charlotte, a briefcase in one hand and a suitcase in the other.

Charlotte nodded. "Welcome home, stranger."

By unspoken mutual consent, they both walked toward the steps.

"It's good to be home," he responded, following her up the steps onto the porch. "So what's been happening? Any breaks yet on the Ricco Martinez murder?"

Charlotte froze, then turned to stare at him, a puzzled frown on her face.

"Have they found the real murderer yet?" he asked.

"Oh, my dear Lord, you don't know, do you?"

"Know what?"

"It's a long story." Charlotte motioned toward his luggage. "Go put your stuff away, then come over to my place, and I'll catch you up. I'll make a fresh pot of coffee."

By the time Louis entered her kitchen, the coffee had brewed. "I take it that huge stack of stuff on the front table is my mail."

Charlotte nodded. "I meant to bag it up for you, but—" she shrugged, then handed him a cup of coffee.

"I really appreciate you collecting it for me." He settled at the kitchen table, and after he'd taken a sip of his coffee, his expression grew serious. "Okay, now tell me, what's happened?"

Charlotte sat opposite him at the table. "First of all, the bones didn't belong to Ricco Martinez after all."

"No kidding!"

"Nope."

"So—is Martinez alive or dead, and who the heck did the bones belong to?"

Charlotte sighed. "Like I said, it's a long, convoluted story. If you remember, Ricco was arrested way back when as part of that gang that was stealing cemetery artifacts."

Louis nodded.

"Well, guess who hired him to steal the stuff?" When Louis shrugged, Charlotte told him, "Patsy Dufour."

His eyebrows shot up in surprise. "Why on earth would someone like Patsy Dufour dirty her hands with that type of thing?"

"Revenge. Pure and simple. Patsy was out for revenge against Lowell Webster."

Louis frowned. "What the devil was her beef with Lowell Webster?"

Charlotte rolled her eyes. "You're not going to believe this."

By the time that Charlotte finished the story about Patsy's past relationship with Lowell and her botched abortion, Louis was shaking his head. "My, my, my. Who would have figured? Guess the old saying's true after all. 'Hell hath no fury like a—' "

Charlotte shot him a don't-even-go-there look, and Louis abruptly bit off the rest of the saying. "Okay, so Patsy's out for revenge. But why go to all that trouble? Why not just call in the press?"

"Good point," Charlotte said. "My guess is that if she'd called in the press, her name and reputation would be involved. Guess she didn't want that kind of attention. But, then, who knows?"

"Yeah, I guess that makes sense." He waved a hand for her to continue.

"Anyway, Patsy found out that Ricco and Mark Webster were friends and that they'd had a falling out."

"The argument Nadia told you about," he clarified.

Charlotte nodded. "That's the one."

"So how did Patsy know about it?"

"Because of Nadia," Charlotte answered. "When Mark wouldn't pay up, Ricco took out his frustration on Nadia. Patsy spotted Nadia's bruises. One thing led to another—anyway, that's how Patsy learned about his association with the Websters.

"So once she found out about the disagreement," Charlotte continued, "she tried to persuade Ricco to get his revenge against Mark—which was really her revenge against Lowell—by having Ricco implicate Mark and Lowell in the cemetery thefts. She even offered to pay Ricco. At first he went along with it, and he did make sure some of the artifacts were moved into Lowell's warehouse. But about that time was when he was arrested.

"Once Daniel got him out of jail, Ricco turned the tables and tried blackmailing Patsy. When that didn't work, he went to Lowell and told all, hoping to garner Lowell's favor."

Louis shook his head. "Big mistake."

"Yes—yes, it was," Charlotte agreed. "For years Patsy had been a thorn in Lowell's side, and evidently this wasn't the first stunt she'd pulled. Anyway, after what Ricco told him, Lowell decided that something had to be done about Patsy. Apparently, he decided that Ricco was a liability as well. He came up with a scheme to kill two birds with one stone, so to speak. He instructed Will Richeaux to—"

Louis threw up his hand. "Whoa, hold up. How did Will Richeaux get involved?"

"It seems that Will Richeaux has been moonlighting for years, doing a lot of dirty work for Lowell."

Louis closed his hand into a fist and thumped the tabletop with his knuckles. "I knew it! I knew he was dirty. I just couldn't prove it."

"Yes, well, he's not dirty anymore. He's not anything anymore but dead."

Louis raised both eyebrows. "Dead, huh? Humph! Good riddance to bad rubbish."

Charlotte swallowed hard and felt like squirming. "That's another story," she murmured.

When Louis gave her an expectant look, she shook her head. "Another day. I'll tell you about that another day."

She could tell Louis didn't want to leave it at that, but to give him credit, he didn't push it. "So . . . you said something about Lowell giving Will instructions. What kind of instructions?"

"Actually, two sets of instructions. First of all, Lowell put out a hit on Ricco, and gave specific instructions for Ricco to be stuffed in the urn that was in his warehouse. And, second, since he knew about Patsy's penchant for old statues and things, he told Will to pretend to be a dealer and make sure that she ended up with the urn. Either he figured that the bones would be discovered eventually, or he paid the workers to make sure the urn cracked. Whichever, he meant it to be a warning for Patsy to leave him alone or else.

"Only problem with his scheme was that somehow Ricco found out about the hit. Ricco knew the hit was going down when Mark called and wanted to set up a meeting at the warehouse to supposedly pay back the money he owed Ricco."

Charlotte sighed. "I guess Ricco wasn't as dumb as I thought he was, after all. He went out and found a homeless man who was about his size and had the same color hair and so forth. Then he paid the homeless man to wear his clothes and go to the meeting, promising him more money later. Sure enough, the hit man was waiting in the warehouse, and, thinking the homeless man was Ricco, he killed him."

Louis whistled long and low. "And of course Ricco had left his billfold inside the jacket pocket for proof."

Charlotte nodded. "Yep, and then Ricco hightailed it out of town. But not for good." Charlotte went on and told Louis about Davy's dreams. Even now, a whole month later, it made her shiver to think about Ricco sneaking into Nadia's home to see Davy without Nadia ever being the wiser.

"But he sneaked back into town one too many times," she said. "The last time was when the urn and the bones were discovered, and Daniel and Nadia were accused of the murder."

"Now it all makes sense," Louis said. "No wonder Daniel was railroaded. Wasn't Jonas Tipton the judge who denied Daniel bail?"

When Charlotte nodded, Louis nodded too. "It figures," he said. "That old geezer is one of the uppity-ups who's been pushing for Webster to run for mayor." He waved a hand. "So?"

"So about that time was when Ricco grew a conscience. Guess nobody's ever all good or all bad. Anyway, with him supposedly dead and Nadia accused of his murder, that would leave Davy an orphan, so he attempted to make a deal with the police to try and clear Nadia and to stop Lowell for good. Only problem was that he tried to make a deal with the wrong policeman."

"Let me guess. Will Richeaux."

Charlotte nodded. "Richeaux told Lowell, who then instructed him to kill Ricco himself. Evidently, he tried and missed, because even after Richeaux got killed, Ricco still went after Lowell. He figured that Lowell would just keep sending someone after him and the only way he'd survive would be to kill Lowell."

"And he did kill him, but not before Lowell stabbed him with a letter opener." As Charlotte filled Louis in on the rest of the story, it was hard to gauge his reaction to the part about Davy's last visit from Ricco.

Finally, all that he said was, "Poor little guy. It's a good thing he's got Daniel. One of these days, when he's older, he's going to need a strong man to help him understand it all." He shook his head. "What I want to know is who in hell pieced it all together? Judith?"

Charlotte gave him a level look. "Part of it. But most of it came from Ricco making a deathbed confession."

For the time being, Charlotte didn't see any use in telling Louis about her part in it. "Like I said," she continued, "somewhere along the way he grew a conscience, so he asked for a priest before he died. But he also gave permission for Judith to hear it."

Charlotte figured that eventually Louis would find out all the details about her involvement. But for now, she really didn't want to hear any lectures from him about it. She'd heard enough from Judith and Hank to last her a lifetime.

Besides, she thought, as she lowered her gaze to her empty coffee cup, all the guilty parties had been dealt with, one way or another. Even Patsy, who would end up serving time in jail not only for assault but also for her part in instigating the cemetery thefts.

What goes around comes around, and people get paid back for what they do. Charlotte sighed. Once again, the old adage had proved to be true . . . thank goodness.

"So much for good intentions," Charlotte murmured that evening as she glanced at her watch.

She was later getting to Daniel and Nadia's reception than she'd planned. She had hoped to get there early enough to help out wherever needed. But by the time she entered the hotel ballroom, most of the guests had already arrived, and from the looks of the place, everything seemed to be running smoothly.

Music from a string quartet provided a gentle background for the buzz of the chattering guests, and Charlotte noted that the wedding planners Nadia had hired had done a superb job of decorating the ballroom.

The whole room resembled a spring garden, complete with several trellises and gorgeous baskets filled with spring flowers. Each of the small round tables along the sides of the ballroom was covered with a pristine white tablecloth and decorated with even more flowers.

There was a wedding-cake table, a punch table, and several other tables that were filled with all kinds of food. The overall effect was simple yet elegant.

Had Louis come? she wondered as she glanced around the room. She'd told him about the reception and made sure he knew that he was invited when he'd left her house earlier. On his way out, though, all he'd said was that he was tired and had a lot to take care of after being gone for a month.

And just why does it matter so much whether he did or didn't come? Charlotte ignored the nagging question and continued to search the room, this time looking for her family. Then she spied Hank striding toward her. Dressed in a tuxedo, he was the spitting image of his father. As always, the sight of him filled her with love and pride, yet at the same time caused an ache of regret deep in her heart for what might have been if his father had lived.

"Hey, Mom," he said and leaned down to kiss her on the forehead. "I was beginning to get worried about you. Why so late?"

"Sorry you worried, hon. I was ready to walk out the door when I remembered that I'd let Sweety out of his cage earlier. Then I couldn't find the little rascal. And after his mishap in the shower that time, I don't dare leave him out of his cage when I'm not around."

Hank chuckled. "I swear, you and that bird are some-thing else." He shook his head. "So—where was he?"

Charlotte rolled her eyes. "Would you believe he was under my bed? He's never gone under the bed before. And get this. I found him perched on top of a sock—Davy's sock—the one I couldn't find when I packed his bag to give to Judith."

"Strange," Hank commented. "Who would have thought that a parakeet could get that attached to someone?"

Charlotte smiled. "Davy was easy to get attached to. Makes me wish I had a grandchild." She cleared her throat. "But to have a grandchild, my son would need to get a wife."

"Aw, come on, Mom. Don't start. Okay?"

Charlotte gave him a saucy grin. "Just want to make sure you know how I feel about such things. So, where is everyone?"

"Nadia, Daniel, and Aunt Madeline are in the receiving line over there." He motioned across the room.

Charlotte had noticed the line of people on the far side of the ballroom, but she'd thought they were there because the caterers had already begun serving food. "And what about the rest?" she asked.

"Carol took Davy to the bathroom, and Judith is getting grilled by Louis about that Ricco Martinez mess."

"Uh oh," Charlotte murmured. Evidently Louis had showed up after all. And if he was grilling Judith, Charlotte figured it was a sure bet that he was getting the lowdown on her part in the whole affair as well.

Hank narrowed his eyes and peered down at her. "Why the 'uh oh,' Mom?"

Charlotte shrugged and gave her son a tight little smile. "No reason, hon. Just muttering to myself. Maybe I should go rescue Judith. See you later, hon." Without waiting for him to comment, Charlotte turned and headed toward the front of the ballroom in search of her niece and Louis. She figured that there might be a remote chance that Judith hadn't spilled the beans on her yet.

Louis would find out eventually. Of that she had no doubt. But she had hoped to have time to adjust to everything that had happened herself before having to contend with him.

It took Charlotte a few minutes to locate Judith and Louis. One look at Louis's angry face and Charlotte knew she was too late. Judith had already blabbed.

Neither Judith or Louis had seen her yet, and for a moment Charlotte was tempted to walk away. But only for a moment. There was no way she could avoid Louis all evening. Besides, what she did or didn't do was really none of Louis Thibodeaux's business.

Isn't that a contradiction? One minute you're worried about what he's going to say, and the next minute you've decided that what you do is none of his business. Ignoring the aggravating voice in her head, Charlotte straightened her shoulders and lifted her chin. She didn't like confrontations, but she'd never made a habit of running from them, either.

Plastering a smile on her face, she marched over to join Louis and her niece. When they first saw her, it was almost amusing to see their reactions. Almost, but not quite.

Judith immediately began to fidget, and after the briefest smile of greeting she lowered her gaze and couldn't seem to look Charlotte in the eyes.

Guilty.

Louis simply nodded his greeting, but the look he gave her made her want to cringe.

Guilty.

It didn't take a rocket scientist to figure out that they had indeed been discussing her.

"I see you made it after all," she told Louis. When he didn't offer a response, she turned to Judith. "You look lovely, hon. That color of blue is perfect for you."

"Thanks," Judith murmured.

"So where's Billy?" Charlotte glanced around as if searching for him. "I haven't seen him yet. Didn't he come?"

"Ah . . . no ma'am," Judith answered, still unable to look Charlotte straight in the eyes. "He had to work." Judith visibly swallowed. "Guess I need to go check on Davy and give Carol a break." With one last tight smile, she said, "See y'all later." Then she turned and hurried away.

After a moment, Charlotte took a deep breath and faced Louis. "Okay, let's get it over with."

Louis gave her a pitying look and shook his head. "Charlotte, Charlotte, what am I going to do about you?"

Charlotte crossed her arms and sighed. "I'm still waiting, so let's have it."

Louis rolled his eyes. "Could we at least sit down

somewhere first. I've been on my feet all day, and these new shoes are killing me."

Her automatic reaction was one of sympathy, but Charlotte squashed the emotion and headed toward the nearest table. Once she was seated, Louis seated himself in the chair beside her.

"Oh yeah," he drawled. "That's much better." He turned sideways to face Charlotte. "As you already suspect, Judith filled me in on the part that you purposely neglected to tell me.

"How you get yourself in these predicaments never ceases to amaze me. And I'd really like to yell at you right now, but not for the reasons you think. I think it's about time for me to get something straight with you. If I yell and stomp and snort, it's purely because it scares the sh—it scares me to think of you getting hurt. And it has nothing to do with whether I think you're intelligent, capable, or any of that stuff."

Louis suddenly looked really uncomfortable, and Charlotte wasn't sure what to say or even if she should say anything.

He finally cleared his throat and continued. "Knowing you," he said, "I figure you're still blaming yourself for Will Richeaux's death. I just wanted you to know that the first time something like that happened to me, I felt the same way . . . for a while, anyway. And, no, you don't ever get completely over it, but with time you come to grips with it.

"What you have to keep remembering is that Richeaux had a choice, and he made the wrong choice. As sure as I'm sitting here, he would have killed you without a second thought if you hadn't been so quick to react."

Charlotte's throat grew tight, and something deep inside broke loose. Once again Louis had surprised her, which, in turn, only served to confuse her more. If she lived to be a hundred, she would never figure him out.

All she knew to do at the moment was to say, "Thank you, Louis. I appreciate your concern, and I'll try to keep what you've told me in mind."

Louis nodded. "Good. And another thing. You know . . . whether you want to admit it or not, we're a lot alike."

It was the last thing she'd expected him to say, and though his statement left her speechless, she was also intrigued.

"Both of us have lived single lives and are pretty set in our ways," he continued. "We've both raised sons without the benefit of a spouse's help. Neither of us likes having to depend on anyone else for anything. What's more, I aggravate the stuffing out of you, and you—you . . . well, let's just say there's never a dull moment." He threw up his forefinger. "Whoa, now. Don't go getting all huffy on me—at least not yet, not until you hear me out."

Louis took a deep breath and sighed. "All I'm trying to say is that I'm glad we can be friends, and though I would like for us to be more than just friends, I won't push it. Mainly because I wouldn't want someone pushing me when it comes to something like that."

Once again Charlotte wasn't quite sure how to

respond, and couldn't have responded if her life had depended on it. She'd wondered about his feelings, and now she knew. But until she had time to really think about what he'd just said, she wasn't about to say anything herself, except, "Thanks."

Feeling a real need to lighten things up, she made an attempt to change the subject. "So . . . how was New York and your new job?"

Louis laughed. "Changing the subject, huh?" He held up his hand. "Now don't get huffy. I'm just teasing. New York was crowded and loud, and my new job was not exactly what I'd pictured myself doing. I was told I'd be serving as a bodyguard; the last four weeks were a trial run to see if our company is suitable for the job. But baby-sitting is what I'd call it. And baby-sitting some spoiled, self-proclaimed diva is not my idea of fun."

"So, who is this spoiled diva? Anyone I've ever heard of?"

"Oh yeah," he drawled. "Unless you're comatose, I'm sure you've heard of her. Most of the country has."

"Well?"

" 'Well' what?" He feigned innocence.

"Well nothing, if you're going to be like that."

Louis laughed. "The diva is Angel James."

"Nooo—no way," Charlotte scoffed.

Louis held up his hand, palm out. "I swear. If I'm lying I'm dying."

There weren't that many modern-day singers who impressed Charlotte, but Angel James was one of them. Everyone, but everyone, had heard of Angel James, the teenage wonder who had taken the music scene by storm and had every person from eight to eighty humming her songs.

"And did your company get the job?"

Louis grinned. "Yeah, we did."

"Does that mean you'll be leaving again?"

He shook his head. "Not right away. She's planning on taking a hiatus, here in New Orleans, before her fall tour."

Charlotte frowned. "Don't I remember something about her buying a house here?"

"Yep, she owns one over on First Street. That's where she'll be staying for a couple of months."

Charlotte grinned. "Well, if she needs a maid, you will be sure and recommend Maid-for-a-Day, won't you?"

A Cleaning Tip from Charlotte

To have a fresh-smelling room, use the following procedure when cleaning ceiling fans: Dust the blades and base of the fan well. Then saturate a cloth in a mixture of approximately one part pine or lemon-scented cleaner to five parts water. Ring out the wet cloth well and wipe each fan blade, top and bottom. Rinse the cloth in clear water, squeeze out excess moisture then wipe down each blade again.

Now turn on the fan, and the pine or lemon scent will waft through the room, leaving it smelling clean and fresh.

Center Point Publishing
600 Brooks Road ● PO Box 1
Thorndike ME 04986-0001 USA

(207) 568-3717

US & Canada:
1 800 929-9108